Lisa Tuttle is a Texas-born writer w
working in Britain for the past t
journalist, she is the author of se
Gabriel and *Lost Futures*, and of
collections.

By the same author

Gabriel
A Spaceship Made of Stone
Lost Futures

Non-fiction

Encyclopedia of Feminism

LISA TUTTLE

Memories of the Body

Tales of Desire and Transformation

Grafton
An Imprint of HarperCollins*Publishers*

To the Muse

Grafton
An Imprint of HarperCollins*Publishers*
77–85 Fulham Palace Road
Hammersmith, London W6 8JB

A Grafton Original 1992
9 8 7 6 5 4 3 2 1

A catalogue record for this book
is available from the British Library

ISBN 0 586 21362 7

Set in Times

Printed in Great Britain by
HarperCollinsManufacturing Glasgow

Contents

Acknowledgements

'Heart's Desire' was first published in *Other Edens III* edited by Christopher Evans and Robert Holdstock (Unwin). Copyright © 1989 Lisa Tuttle

'The Wound' was first published in *Other Edens* edited by Christopher Evans and Robert Holdstock (Unwin). Copyright © 1987 Lisa Tuttle

'Husbands' was first published in *Alien Sex* edited by Ellen Datlow (Dutton). Copyright © 1990 Lisa Tuttle. Reprinted by permission

'Riding the Nightmare' was first published in *Night Visions 3* edited by George R. R. Martin (Dark Harvest). Copyright © 1986 Lisa Tuttle

'Jamie's Grave' was first published in *Shadows 10* edited by Charles Grant (Doubleday). Copyright © 1987 Lisa Tuttle

'The Spirit Cabinet' was first published in *Women of Darkness* edited by Kathryn Ptacek (Tor). Copyright © 1988 Lisa Tuttle

'The Colonization of Edwin Beal' was first published in *The Magazine of Fantasy and Science Fiction* October 1987. Copyright © 1987 The Mercury Press

'Lizard Lust' was first published in *Interzone 39*, September 1990. Copyright © 1990 Lisa Tuttle

'Skin Deep' was first published in *Dark Fantasies* edited by Chris Morgan (Legend). Copyright © 1989 Lisa Tuttle

'A Birthday' was first published in *Tales from the Forbidden Planet* edited by Roz Kaveney (Titan). Copyright © 1987 Lisa Tuttle

'A Mother's Heart: A True Bear Story' was first published in *Isaac Asimov's Science Fiction Magazine* January-February 1978. Copyright © 1977 Davis Publications

'The Other Room' was first published in *Whispers*, Vol. 5, No. 1-2. Copyright © 1982 Stuart David Schiff

'Dead Television' was first published in *Zenith 2* edited by David S. Garnett (Orbit). Copyright © 1990 Lisa Tuttle.

'Bits and Pieces' was first published in *Pulphouse* No. 9, November 1990. Copyright © 1990 Lisa Tuttle

'Memories of the Body' was first published in *Interzone 22*, Winter 1987-88. Copyright © 1987 Lisa Tuttle

Heart's Desire

I don't know how it happened, or even what. I try to remember, and when I can't remember, I tell myself stories, to try to understand.

There was a yellow plastic cup. I couldn't have been more than two years old; I may have been less. I have forgotten so much from that time, but I remember this. I remember the cup. It was mine. Now it was somewhere I had not put it, on the seat of a ladder-backed chair, one of a set my mother had rescued from some junk-shop, stripped, and painted a glossy white. Paintbrush in her hand, she was decorating the chair, painting a circle of tiny red roses in the centre of the top slat. She was close enough to touch, but she wasn't looking at me. I reached for the cup and drank.

I don't remember the taste. I remember the yellow plastic cup. I remember how my hand closed on it, and then the feel of the ridged rim against my lower lip as I poured the liquid into my mouth and swallowed automatically. Then: the gasping noise my mother made, sucking in hard, as she stared, as if seeing me for the first time. Then a barely controlled flurry of activity. She was holding me tight, talking desperately into the telephone. She was giving me something to drink, horrible yuck. She was holding me over the sink, pushing my head down, telling me to throw up. She was pleading with me, and coaxing, and calming me – although I don't remember feeling alarmed – and asking me, again and again, the question I could not answer, then or ever: 'Why? Why did you drink? What made you swallow?'

Jill went, one warm, wet summer's evening, with her friend Harriet on the Northern Line from Clapham to Leicester Square, and from there on the Piccadilly Line to Finsbury

Park. Simon lived there; Simon, whom Harriet had loved. Jill had not met him, although she'd had an affair with him, vicariously, through Harriet.

'Why, why, why are they all like that? He's the same age I am – a year older – and he's never been married. Why doesn't that bother him? Why doesn't he want to settle down? How can men and women be so different? It doesn't make sense. They're like children. Short attention span. Constantly wanting to be amused. Unwilling to give, terrified of commitment . . . He actually talked about *himself* in those terms. "Afraid of love," he said, "unable to commit" – God, it was like one of those books: *Women Who Love Men Who Won't* or whatever. I mean, who *isn't* afraid, and so what? Is he going to stay a lonely, single coward all his life?'

'Probably,' said Jill.

Harriet slumped a little in her seat. 'You're supposed to be providing moral support.'

'I am. You know you're doing the right thing. Simon's not going to change. You're better off without him.'

'I know.' She sounded unconvinced. 'But maybe, this evening, when we see each other . . .'

'Same song, second verse?'

They looked at each other and both sighed. 'I know it's not enough, but when he looks at me, when he touches me . . .'

'Then I won't leave you alone with him. Unless you really, really want me to.'

It was both relief and disappointment to discover that Simon was not at home. He'd left a note taped to the door saying that if he hadn't returned by the time Harriet was ready to leave, would she please push the keys back in through the letter-slot.

'Coward,' said Harriet wistfully.

'Let's not hang about,' said Jill. 'Need a hand with the packing? Tell me what to do.'

'I didn't leave much here. A few clothes. I'll get them. You can, well, why don't you just have a look around?' She vanished into the bedroom. Licensed to prowl, Jill wandered into the sitting room. It was decorated in shades of brown and beige and sparsely furnished, but each piece was a good one. Jill was attracted particularly to a many-drawered apothecary's chest. She touched the smooth, reddish wood, feeling the tug of material desire, and pulled out one of the drawers. It was empty. She pushed it shut and tried another. Empty, too. Then a third. In its depths, something rattled.

Reaching inside, her fingers closed on something small and round. A wooden box, no more than an inch in diameter. As she admired it, the top came off in her hand. Inside was lined with black satin, and within that dark nest something gleamed. A jewel? With forefinger and thumb she plucked it out and held it aloft. It glowed dark red in the light, like a ruby or a garnet, but it was warm and soft, lacking the hardness of stone.

Without thinking, Jill popped it into her mouth, and it had slipped down her throat before she could decide otherwise.

Harriet was coming down the hall, saying something. Hot and confused, heart pounding hard enough to choke her, Jill dropped the little box into the drawer and closed it.

In the pub on the corner, Simon suddenly lost all appetite for his pint. He felt quite queasy, in fact. Inexplicably nervous. He wondered if Harriet had come and gone yet. Maybe he should have acted on his first impulse, to stay in and talk to her, to try to rescue their relationship. When he had thought, a few days ago, that he would never see Harriet again he had felt so miserable that he'd known it was love. This morning, though, the thought of what he would have to do to win her back – the apologies, the explanations, the evasions, the effort – had filled him with such paralyzing, suffocating boredom that he simply had to escape. He reminded himself that just because the sex was good, and she was smart and pretty, that didn't mean he had to tie himself down to her for the rest of his life. Which was what she wanted. Of course he wanted to settle down eventually, but meanwhile what he wanted was . . . freedom. Freedom to take chances, to follow his heart, to act on his desires instead of hers. Freedom to go out when he chose, where he chose, with whom he chose. Freedom to sit right here and finish his drink, instead of rushing back to her. He picked up the drink he no longer wanted, and raised it to his lips.

That night Jill dreamed. This was no ordinary dream; it felt more like waking. And she was not alone. There was someone very close to her, so close she could feel the breath moving his lungs, could feel the rhythm of his heart and blood, different and somehow more real than her own. He was closer than if he was in her bed; closer than any lover had ever been. It was as if she was inside him, her own body miraculously slimmed and stretched to mere filaments of being, around which his bone and flesh and blood and skin wrapped like layers of clothing. She was still conscious, still herself, but not separate from him. When he breathed, so did she; what she felt, he did. Perfect harmony; perfect happiness.

Then she woke to the electronic beeping of her alarm, to the grey light and emptiness of morning, and she was alone. And aware of her solitary state – although she had lived by herself fairly contentedly for almost eight years – in a new and painful way. It was a bereavement, and a fiercely physical one. Going out into the crowded street was worse; there, her senses were constantly assaulted by the world, abraded by the incomprehensible otherness of other people. Everything was at the same time remote and unbearably close. She would go mad or die, she thought, but of course she did not. As the unbearable day wore on, she learned to bear it; gradually she built up defences until sensation dulled to the level she recognized as 'normal'. The pain she felt ceased to be agony. It was merely discomfort; merely life.

But she had lost something, and she knew it, even if it was only her innocence. She knew now what she had never fully realized before, that she was alone. The knowledge had made her lonely. But life didn't have to be like this. She knew, from her dream, that something else was possible.

Jill was travelling on the Piccadilly Line to Finsbury Park again. She hadn't thought about why. Even when she found herself outside Simon's door, pressing the buzzer, she didn't know what she would say. Maybe she wouldn't have to say anything, she thought. Maybe he would simply look at her, and he would know, and they would be together.

But he wasn't in. At least, he didn't answer his bell. She tried pressing the other two in turn, but there was no response. She had to go on standing on the doorstep, exposed to what was turning into a chilly drizzle. It couldn't be long; surely it wouldn't be long before he came home. She wondered what he looked like, and tried without success to imagine his face. She couldn't even remember what colour Harriet had said his eyes were.

Finally – it was really raining now – she retreated to the pub on the corner. If she stood near the door and kept an eye on the street, she would be sure to see him when he passed. That she had never seen Simon before did not worry her. She would know him.

There was a drunken woman on his doorstep.

'Simon? Simon, I'm Jill. A friend of Harriet's? She must have mentioned me . . . Anyway, I came with her yesterday. When you weren't here. Look, could I come inside? I could explain it to you. I'm not drunk, not actually, I just had a few drinks while I was waiting – you were ever such a long time coming! – Well, maybe I am a bit pissed. Coffee would . . . Would you make me a cup of coffee? And then we can talk.'

He didn't want to let her in. Harriet's friend! Harriet wasn't the sort to send her friends around to plead her case . . . besides, he had never sent Harriet away; it had been her decision to leave him.

'What do you want?'

'I can explain, if you'll let me in.'

She was so close that, short of physically pushing her away, he would hardly be able to keep her out once he opened the door. He did not want to let her in, but could see no real alternative.

Under the bright kitchen light she was not unattractive. She might, under other circumstances, have been someone he fancied – but the way she stared at him! As if she would eat him up with her eyes. He felt uneasy turning his back on her to plug in the kettle, and was glad the knives were in the drawer he blocked with his body. 'It'll have to be instant, I'm afraid. And I don't mean to be inhospitable, but I am quite tired, and it is quite late . . .' Looking up, he caught her hungry gaze straight on, like a blow. 'What *is* this?'

She had seemed about to smile, but now her expression flickered uncertainly. 'I'm sorry . . . I . . . don't quite know how to explain . . . I had hoped you would know.'

'Know? Know what? I never even heard of you until a few minutes ago.'

'I thought . . . Harriet might have said something.'

'Harriet and I are finished. If you're her friend, you should know that.'

'Yes, I was here, with her, yesterday. That's when I . . . lost something. At least, I think I did.'

'What sort of something?' She was lying, he was sure of it. But why? What was she hiding?

'A little . . . a ring. My grandmother's ring. I mean it's mine, she gave it to me, but I've lost it. I thought I might have dropped it . . . I might have left it here.'

'I haven't seen anything like that.' He remembered coming home from the pub, how empty his flat had felt. As if something vital had been taken away. Harriet, of course. Not her things – they'd been few enough – but her presence, even her anticipated presence, and even, somehow, the memories of her presence in the past. Simon wasn't one for irrational feelings or metaphysical speculation, but there was a quality to his solitude he'd never felt before. It was almost as if by going, Harriet had taken away something more than herself – something he couldn't name, but could ill afford to lose. He almost phoned her, to call her back, but he had stopped with his hand on the telephone, knowing that she wouldn't be home yet. She was out there somewhere, crossing London, unreachable. And then the moment had passed.

'I didn't see a ring, nothing new. Things were missing, that's all,' he said.

'Missing?' She looked at him. It made his skin crawl, the way she looked at him. He didn't lack self-confidence; strangers had found him attractive before now – but why her? Why like this? Her interest seemed a threat.

'Here's your coffee,' he said. 'We'll take it through to the sitting room, and you can look for your ring.'

Still she stared at him. 'What did you mean when you said things were missing?'

'Harriet's things were gone. Nothing of mine.' Briefly, he wondered if she had lifted something, maybe a record or a videotape, something he wouldn't notice right away. He wasn't going to ask. He didn't want her confession. If she was a kleptomaniac, he didn't want to know. Let her keep it, whatever it was. 'The sitting room is just through here.'

'And there's the chest,' she said. 'It's a beautiful piece. I was admiring it, and . . . I'm afraid I took the liberty of opening a few drawers . . . I didn't mean to pry, you know, I wasn't thinking what I was doing, just pulling out a few drawers . . .' She gave him a look heavy with meaning.

'That's all right,' he said. 'I don't keep anything in it, as I'm sure you found out.'

'Yes, you did.'

She spoke so certainly he could hardly contradict her. Besides, he wasn't sure. Maybe he had dropped something in there once, a spare set of keys or something small, unimportant, quickly forgotten. 'Well, nothing valuable.'

'You don't mind if I . . .'

'Have another look? No, by all means. Go ahead. Pull out every drawer. See what you can find.' A yawn racked him, and he sank down on the couch.

She was clumsy, fumbling with the tiny knobs, first too rough and then too gentle, plunging a hand into each empty drawer in turn, as if she couldn't believe the evidence of her eyes. And when she had been through them all and found nothing, she turned on him, looking so despairing that, even though he neither knew nor trusted her, he pitied her.

'There was something,' she said. 'There was something in one of the drawers . . . where is it? What was it?'

'I don't know. You tell me.'

'It was a little, round, wooden box, very carefully made and lined with black satin. And there was something in it. I never saw it very well. It looked like a ruby – it gleamed red – but when I felt it, it was more rubbery, something like a wine-gum or a cough-sweet.'

He laughed.

'You know what I'm talking about! It was yours!'

He swore. 'You're drunk. Or crazy. I don't know what you're talking about.'

'You *do*. You must.'

He struggled for calm, but that was no longer possible. She made him angry. 'So what if I do? That chest is mine, and whatever's in it is mine, and it has nothing to do with you. If

I want to keep cough-sweets in my apothecary's chest, I don't have to tell you. It's not your business.'

'But it is. It is now. Because I swallowed it, you see. I didn't mean to. I don't know why – I was just going to feel it with my lips, it looked so smooth, and then it was in my mouth and I was swallowing before I'd had time to think. If I'd thought about it, I wouldn't have. But I couldn't help myself.'

There were tears in her eyes, and he felt sorry for her again. 'It's all right,' he said wearily. He traced a cross in the air. 'I forgive you, God forgives you. Bless you, my child. Now, go, and steal no more wine-gums.'

'It wasn't a wine-gum!'

'Cough-sweets, then. Look –'

'No, you look! I've told you the truth. I don't know what it means, but it's real, it's important. I dreamed about you last night. I'd never met you before, but I knew you, as soon as you came near. You know what I'm talking about. You must feel it too. I didn't ask for it any more than you did. All right, I know it was my fault, but . . . I didn't mean it; I didn't know what I was doing. And now it's done. You can't deny it. It affects both of us.'

How easy it would be, he thought, to let it happen. To let go, and let her entangle him in her madness. All he had to do was open his arms. All he had to do was take her to bed. That was what she wanted . . . why shouldn't he want what she wanted, just for once? Except that it wouldn't be for once. It would go on and on, and she'd want more and more. He remembered the way she had looked at him in the kitchen. She wanted to consume him utterly; she wouldn't be satisfied with anything less.

Fear turned to anger, and he held it like a shield. 'What do you want from me?' His tone said that whatever it was, he would not give it to her.

The slump of her shoulders said she understood. 'Please . . . let me stay.'

'No.'

'Please. Just for tonight . . . it's late; the tube's closed now.'

'I'll call a minicab for you.' He got up and went to the phone. He felt, as he moved and spoke, that he was playing a part, echoing something done by an earlier self. He remembered a quarrel with Harriet.

16

'Hello. Could you send a car . . .'

Behind him, motion, displacement of air. He heard his door open and shut, and then the muffled slam of the street door.

'Oh, never mind, cancel that order. I'm sorry to have troubled you.' His heart raced. As he hung up, his body tensed, ready to run. Not to run away, he realized, but to run after her. But why? He'd made his decision. He knew what he wanted – or, at least, he knew what he didn't want.

Only, the flat seemed so empty now. He looked at the apothecary's chest. He had grown up with it. His grandmother had made hats, and had used the little drawers to hold her trimmings. The chest was so familiar, he'd almost stopped seeing it. His mother had made him a gift of it when he bought this flat and, although he was very fond of it, he'd never actually found a use for it. And yet, from time to time, hadn't he deposited odds and ends in the little drawers? The image of something red and gleaming like a gem teased his memory. Had he hidden something away for safekeeping only to forget all about it?

He stopped himself, hand outstretched. No. There was nothing. She hadn't stolen anything from him. He hadn't lost anything. How could he lose something he'd never had? She was crazy, that woman, but it was nothing to do with him. Nothing at all.

He sat down again, feeling hollow and so light the merest breeze could have blown him away.

Once I thought desire had an object; thought that I wanted someone or something that was missing from my life, whether it was a pair of lapis lazuli earrings or my own baby; I thought I wanted back something that had been lost, whether my yellow plastic cup or a man who had left me. But desire is not so simple as a wish. Desire *is*. It possesses you, or it does not. It's a feeling, a force, a natural disaster like an earthquake or gravity, and there's no denying it. There's no satisfying it, either. *I want* is a sentence which can never be finished.

Jill was in despair. She'd blown it. She had frightened him, and ruined everything. Her best chance. But she must have another. She could try again. After much thought, and agonizing over

17

the choice of both words and picture (Gwen John's 'The Convalescent' was surely sufficiently cool and unthreatening?) she sent him a postcard apologizing for her behaviour while 'under the influence', and suggesting he could show his forgiveness by letting her take him to dinner. But, although she gave him her address and her work as well as home telephone number, Simon did not get in touch with her.

She couldn't understand it. Why didn't he feel as drawn to her as she was to him? She had his heart, after all: she could feel it beating slowly and steadily between the beats of her own. For most of the time she was not consciously aware of it, any more than she had ever been aware of her own, but late at night, lying awake in the quiet dark of her lonely bed, she felt the two hearts beating together, and the tears ran down her face as the pain of his absence became almost more than she could bear. She wanted to go to him, to cast herself, body and soul, at his feet. But she didn't dare. She remembered too well how he had looked at her, and drawn back. If he looked at her like that again, she thought, she would die. Better that he should not see her at all. But she had to see him.

She could hardly think of anything else. Work, and even the most ordinary business of day-to-day existence, became steadily more difficult. She found herself going to Finsbury Park at all hours – she would start off intending to go to work, or to lunch, or to do some shopping, and she would find herself, once again, on the Piccadilly Line going north. With no idea of whether or not he was in it, she would watch his house like a faithful hound, bargaining with herself each time for the right to stay just a little longer . . . until, finally, one day she was rewarded by the sight of him coming out of the house.

He didn't notice her, and she did not draw attention to herself. She kept a safe distance as she followed him down the street to the underground station, and she was careful to enter a different carriage. She went with him all the way to Leicester Square, and watched him go into a pub. She waited on the street for a few minutes, plotting a 'chance' meeting. He would be wary at first, of course, not pleased to meet her again, but she would be as light and charming as she knew how to be, and he would gradually relax, suggest they continue this enjoyable conversation over dinner . . .

But when she entered the pub she saw him at once, and knew her plan was doomed. For he was sitting at a table near the far wall, already in conversation – light and charming – with an attractive young woman.

Her heart thudded so hard she thought he should feel it, and she ran out into the street, cursing her, cursing him, cursing the passion that had driven her mad.

She knew it was madness, but the next evening found her again in front of his house.

Following him became her routine. It was more than just a habit: it was her life. She found out where he worked, and she saw him shopping. She knew what he ate and where he drank. She saw the women he met from time to time, and they meant no more, or less, to her than they did to him; no less, or more, than anything else that impinged upon his life, the life she longed to share. She memorized the way he moved, his own particular walk, his small gestures when talking, the width of his back and the way his hair grew. In her dreams she was with him, so close no one could see her, and in her waking hours she got as close to him as she dared.

Until, one day, she went too close, and he turned at the sound of her breath at his back, and she saw him see her, saw him see the unspeakable, unacceptable hunger in her eyes.

And, in his eyes, that look that she had never wanted to see again; the fear she had never meant to inspire. In that moment of mutual shock and recognition she saw herself through his eyes: saw herself and was repelled.

Jill turned and ran as if she could outrun her own madness.

How did desire ever come to be confused with love? It has nothing to do with the human connections and needs and emotions that lead to marriages, families, children . . . Desire is an affliction. Madness. No, not madness. Because whatever else it is and does, it is *real*.

Jill went to stay with relatives in Yorkshire. Things had gone too far, and she understood that if she did not make some radical change in her life things would go farther still. Where the end might be she could not, would not let herself, imagine. Staying in London was obviously not on, when from one day to the next she couldn't control her own movements. Maybe, if she took herself far enough away from him, she would no longer feel the pull. At any rate, situating herself miles from the nearest railway station would at the very least slow her down. She no longer had a job to quit, so there was no problem about that. All her relatives needed or wanted to know was that she'd been disappointed in love; a man had let her down. When she was with them, she talked and thought as they did, about normal, ordinary things: dinner, the weather, and the people and the world as seen on television. She ate large meals, slept long hours, watched television, helped about the house, went for walks. This was her convalescence, and also her cure.

Always, of course, her thoughts were drawn to Simon: distance made no difference. But, just as she would not allow herself to see him, so she tried to forbid the very thought of him. She cut off all fantasies and reminiscences sharply, as soon as they began. She used relaxation techniques and methods of behaviour modification learned from books. She had decided to treat her feelings about Simon as she would any addiction. Habits can be changed, even habits of thought.

But she could not control the dreams she had while sleeping. And awake, while thinking of something utterly removed from Simon – advising a friend of her aunt's on a new wallpaper pattern, or playing bridge – she would suddenly realize that she had, quite unconsciously, made one of Simon's gestures, or feel his slightly lopsided smile on her lips. Walking to the shops she sometimes stopped dead, sensing that her stride was absurdly masculine for someone wearing a skirt but unable to remember how she usually walked. She heard his laugh coming from her mouth, and when she swore, it was with his scowl and tightened shoulders. And regardless of whether she allowed herself to think about it, his heart went on beating inside her breast.

Desire must eventually wither away for lack of nourishment, Jill thought. She concentrated on other things: becoming a better cook, sewing, building her physical endurance with long, hard walks, and reading a great many books. As the days and the weeks passed she felt better and stronger, and she knew she was healing. Perhaps she dreamed of Simon, but she woke from her dreams without anguish. She had not forgotten him – she knew now that she never would – but she no longer felt that horrible empty aching loneliness that meant she needed him. She didn't need him to make her whole; she *was* whole. It was time to go back to London and take up her life again.

Simon shrank back against the doors of the train. Christ! There she was, that woman, Harriet's friend!

Months without a sight of her, and now – was it starting up again?

Then he realized that she couldn't have been following him. She was already in the carriage, already seated, when he got on. So it had to be coincidence.

He eyed her cautiously. Absorbed in her book, she didn't seem to have noticed him. Even so, he thought he'd better get off at the next stop, move to another car. He was afraid of attracting her attention, but he could not stop staring at her with hungry, curious eyes.

Since she had run away from him, Jill's absence had haunted Simon far more than her unsuspected presence ever had. That last time, when he had seen her on the street, he knew at once that this was no coincidence; that she must have been trailing him for days. But it had taken a very long time for him to believe that his discovery of her had really frightened her off for good. For weeks he had been on edge, sleeping badly, checking the locks on his door obsessively – he even had them changed, just in case – jumping at unexpected sounds, glimpsing her in every crowd. Finally, he had decided to confront her. He was glad, then, that he had never thrown away the postcard she had sent him (in fact, he had tucked it away in one of the drawers of the apothecary's chest). But when he called her office they told him she had left the company, and no matter when or how often he tried her home number there was never a reply. He had been forced to accept that she had left his life just as abruptly and inexplicably as she had entered it. He had thought about her from time to time, wondering if he would ever see her again. And now, here she was. He could confront her, if he wanted to.

He had looked away from her for a moment, to collect his thoughts, not wanting to be caught staring until he knew what he meant to do – whether or not to show he recognized her.

Now, looking back, he thought he was ready for anything. But he was not ready for what he saw.

She was gone, and in her place – in the same seat, reading the same book – was a man. Except that she *hadn't* gone; she was still there, somehow within the man – it could have been done on film, a simple overlay of images, a double-exposure – inside the man like his living soul. And the man was himself.

Simon's hands were like ice, and his muscles had seized up. He couldn't move, not even his eyes. He had to go on looking at this impossible sight, terrified that he/she would look up and see him, and yet wanting it. Whether or not he'd ever heard the legend that to meet your double is to meet your death, he sensed danger. Surely, once their eyes met, something would end? How could they both continue to exist?

The train was pulling into a station. Passengers were standing up and moving towards the doors. The figure that was Jill/Simon shimmered. Boundaries flowed and lost definition, then the body redefined itself, closing the book it held, and standing up. When Jill got off the train she was herself again.

The Wound

Once, the seasons had been more distinct, but not in living memory. Now, mild winter merged gently into mild summer, and Olin knew it was spring only by the calendar and by his own restlessness.

That morning, Olin's bus took a different route, road repairs forcing a detour through the old city. As he stared out the window at the huge, derelict buildings crumbling into ruin and colonized by weeds, he caught sight of figures through gaps in the walls. No one lived in the old city, but there were always people here. Olin had been one of them once, when he was young, coming here with his lover. He remembered that time as the best of his life.

Recalling the past made him feel sad and prematurely old. His lover had become his wife, and after ten years of marriage they had separated. He had lived alone for the past two years.

Olin reached into his breast pocket for diary and pen, turned to the blank page of that day, and wrote 'phone Dove' in his small, precise hand. About once a month he phoned her, and they would arrange to meet for a meal. Always he went to her in hope, with fond memories and some vague thoughts of reconciliation which would fade over the course of the evening.

As he left the bus, two other teachers, senior to Olin, also got off. They did not speak as they crossed the street together and passed through the heavy iron gates onto the school grounds. Olin caught sight of another colleague, a little ahead of them: Seth Tarrant, the new music master. Tarrant was young, handsome, and admired by the students. His cream-coloured coat flared like a cape from his shoulders, and he seemed to be singing as he strode across the bright green lawn. He carried an expensive leather case in one hand, and a bunch of blue and yellow flowers in the other. Olin felt a brief flare of envy, and he touched his breast pocket. He would phone Dove, he thought. She would be glad to hear from him.

During his lunch-break, Olin went into the telephone alcove by the cafeteria, and was startled to see Seth Tarrant there, his long body slumped in an attitude of defeat, his head pressed against one of the telephones. Before Olin, embarrassed, could retreat, the other man looked around.

He straightened up, brushing a strand of fair hair out of his eyes. 'Mr Mercato,' he said.

'Olin,' said Olin, embarrassed still more by the formality. 'Please.'

'Olin. I'm Seth.'

'Yes, I know. Ah, are you all right?'

'I'm fine. Do you like opera?'

'Opera? Yes. Yes, I do, actually. Not that I know anything about it – maths is my subject, really – but I do like to listen. On the radio, and I have a few recordings . . .'

'You don't think it's tedious, pretentious and antiquated?'

Olin wondered who the music master was quoting. He shook his head.

'You might even think it worth your while to attend a live performance?'

'If it weren't so expensive –'

With a conjuror's flourish, Seth produced two cards from his pocket. 'I happen to have two tickets to tonight's performance of *The Insufficient Answer*, and one is going begging. Would you care to be my guest?'

'I'd love to. But, are you sure?'

'Do I seem uncertain to you?'

Olin shook his head.

'That's settled, then. We'll meet on the steps of the opera house at seven o'clock, which will give us time for a drink in the bar before it begins.'

'Thank you. It's very kind –'

'Not at all. You are the kind one, agreeing at such short notice. Please don't be late. I hate to be kept waiting.'

The opera house was on the river, in an area of the city far older than that part known as the old city. Olin had been there once before, in the early days of his marriage, to attend a performance of *Butterfly*. Dove had been pregnant then, and she had fallen asleep during the second act. It was probably the quarrel they'd had afterwards, and not the price of tickets, which was the real reason Olin had never been to the opera since.

The steps were crowded with people meeting friends, but Seth's tall, elegant figure was immediately noticeable. When he reached his side, Olin began to apologize for his lateness, although it was barely five past the hour. He felt awkward, worried about the evening, certain that Seth had regretted his spur-of-the-moment invitation by now. Seth brushed aside both apologies and thanks with a flick of one long-fingered hand.

'Let's get a drink,' he said.

He seemed distracted and brooding in the bar, but Olin contrived a conversation by asking him questions about opera: after all, music was the man's subject. Olin felt like a student taken on a cultural outing by a master; an odd reversal, since he was at least ten years Seth's senior. It was a relief when the bell rang and they could find their seats and stop talking.

The Insufficient Answer was a love tragedy, a popular story which Olin already knew in outline. He had seen some of the most famous scenes enacted on television, but never with the technical brilliance displayed in this production. By ingenious use of lights and projections, the physical miracle of love appeared to be actually taking place on stage during the opening love-duet. After that breathtaking scene, the familiar tragedy was set in motion as the lovers, Gaijan and Sunshine, discovered they were not cross-fertile. Because there could be no children, marriage was out of the question. Social as well as biological forces drove Gaijan to take other lovers while Sunshine watched, and wept, and waited. For Gaijan still swore that he loved her the best of all, and he returned to her after every coupling. He told her he considered her his true wife and would never marry. His other lovers, led by the young and beautiful Flower, discovered Sunshine's existence and reproached her in the choral, 'We are all his wives.' When Sunshine protested that she could not live without his love, Flower responded with the thrilling 'Then you must die.' The duet between Sunshine and Flower which followed echoed the earlier duet between Gaijan and Sunshine only, instead of a transformation, it was concluded by a suicide. In the final act, Gaijan threatened to follow Sunshine into death until Flower wooed him away from the cliff-edge. As Gaijan and Flower exchanged vows of marriage, Flower promised to be to him all that Sunshine had been, and all that Sunshine could not be. The stage had been growing darker all the while, and Olin expected the curtain to fall on the final, throbbing notes of Flower's promise and the lovers' embrace. Instead, Flower turned to face the audience, and opened her robe. Olin caught his breath at the sight of an embryo, seen as if through Flower's flesh, growing within her body. It grew, as he watched, and even without opera glasses Olin could see that the unborn baby wore Sunshine's face.

There was a moment of awed silence as the curtain fell, and then an explosion of applause. Olin clapped, too, full of emotion he was unable to express in any other way. He glanced at Seth and then hastily looked away again at the sight of tears on the younger man's face.

The murmuring, satisfied crowd bore them away, and there was no need, or chance, to speak. On the steps again, Olin began to say his thanks, but was stopped by a gesture.

'Don't rush off,' said Seth. 'I'd really like to discuss what we've just seen. That's why I don't like going to these things alone – it's never complete for me until I've been able to talk about it. Won't you walk with me by the river? I need to stretch my legs, and somehow I think better when I'm moving.'

Olin felt flattered that Seth had not tired of his company after the strained effort of their earlier conversation in the bar, but he glanced at his watch saying, 'I'm afraid the last bus is –'

'Oh, don't worry about that. I have a car. I can run you home.'

'Your own car? On a teacher's salary?'

Seth smiled faintly. 'No. Not on a teacher's salary. Nor this coat, nor a subscription to the opera. It won't last long at the rate I'm going, but I have a little money. From my wife's family.'

Olin remembered the despairing way Seth had leaned against the telephone, and the flowers that morning, and he was surprised. 'You're married?'

'Separated. It lasted less than a year. A youthful mistake.'

The night was dry and not cold, the river path paved and lighted, but they were alone.

'My wife and I separated two years ago,' Olin offered.

'How long were you married?'

'Ten years.'

'Children?'

'Two. At school now.'

'Not a youthful mistake, then,' said Seth. 'Why didn't you stay together? Why – I'm sorry. Please forgive me. It's none of my business, of course.'

It would have been a rude question even from someone less a stranger than Seth, and Olin knew he should have taken offence. But suddenly he wanted to talk about his marriage with someone, anyone, who was not Dove. He had never had the chance before.

'I suppose we separated because we ran out of reasons for staying together. We'd stopped loving each other long since, the children were at school and didn't need us, and there was no reason for two people who didn't like each other very much to go on sharing the same house. We'd never had much in common except the physical.'

'That's supposed to be enough,' said Seth. 'It is in all the operas, in literature, in ballads. The miracle of love is physical love – a biological affinity. Which would be fine, only it never lasts. And nobody will admit that. Everybody expects it to last, and when it doesn't we think there's something wrong with *us*. We're failures. Why can't we be taught to see love in perspective, to see it as a physical pleasure which belongs to one part of life but doesn't ever, can't by its very nature, ever last. We outgrow it, and we're *meant* to outgrow it. So why do we ruin our lives, wasting so much time and energy on love, dreaming about it, waiting for it, hoping for it against all odds?'

Although they were walking side by side, not looking at one another, Olin was vividly aware of Seth's anguish.

'You're too young to be talking like that,' Olin said, trying for a cheerful, bracing tone. 'It's all very well for me to resign myself to a solitary life, but you're still young and you should have hope. You can marry again – you *will* marry again. As you say, the first was a youthful mistake. You'll meet someone else . . .'

'Oh, yes, I'll meet someone else, and start the whole messy process all over again. I won't be able to help myself. But what's the point? To come to this again. Honey's pregnant. Already. I found out today. I suppose I should feel grateful. At least relieved that I didn't ruin her life. It would be so awful for her to find out she couldn't have kids ever, with anyone. It's not so terrible for a man to be infertile, but to be a woman . . .'

'There's no reason to assume you're infertile,' said Olin. 'Lots of people aren't cross-fertile with each other, but that doesn't mean they're infertile. Like in the opera we just saw – it's a question of finding the right partner.'

'So why should it be so complicated? It's just biology. Biological compatability. Why all this stuff about love? It has nothing to do with physical attraction, or being a nice person, or having common interests, or the meeting of souls. It's not spiritual destiny. It's blind chance. It could have been worked out better, don't you think? So that we couldn't fall in love with someone unless we were cross-fertile.'

'But then it wouldn't be love,' Olin said. 'Then it *would* just be biology – we'd just be animals attracted to each other in the mating season.'

'I think we are, and we just don't know it. In our ignorance, we've screwed it up. We try to make it something noble, try to pretend that sex and reproduction are the by-products of love, instead of the other way around. Why should sex get this special treatment? Why can't we see it clearly, as a need like hunger? Why mystify it? Why can't we just admit that we're just animals who need to reproduce, and *do* it?'

Olin was conscious that their argument was operating on two levels. However abstract and intellectual it might become, Seth was speaking out of his own hurt. He was looking for comfort, and Olin responded with the wish to help. But what wisdom could he offer? He was older than Seth, but no wiser. He hadn't found the answer in marriage or out of it. He had told himself that love was for the young, and safely in his own past, but something in him still responded to romance.

After a little silence Olin said, 'We're animals, but not only animals. Yes, we need to reproduce – but we have other needs, too. Emotional, social needs. We have a need for love, however you define it. Maybe it's misguided to connect love with sex, but everyone does, so there must be some sense in it, there must be some hope –' he stopped talking as they both stopped walking, having come to the end of the paved, lighted river-path. The river wound on, out of sight behind the embankment to their left, but ahead of them was a dark, rough wasteland.

Staring into the night Seth said, 'There's a need, but is it natural? Is it something basic in us, or was it constructed? Does it have to be that way, or can we change it? Should we?'

Disturbed, Olin turned away. 'We'd better start back. There's no way through here. It's odd – you'd think the path would go somewhere, wouldn't you? I mean, to pave it, and put up lights – you'd think it would go somewhere. At least to the next bridge, or up to the main road. Just to end like this. Are you coming?'

As they walked back, Olin turned the conversation to architecture, a subject about which he knew little but had many opinions. He soon provoked Seth into disagreement, and by the time they reached the opera house they were arguing as merrily as old friends, all restraint between them gone. Seth's bitter mood had passed, and Olin was glad to agree when he suggested they stop for a snack in a late-night cafe on the way home. Even knowing he would have to get up in the morning to teach, Olin was not ready for the evening to end. He was enjoying himself with Seth, but he didn't trust their friendship to survive even the shortest separation. In the morning, he thought, they would be strangers again.

But he was wrong. The next day at school, passing each other on the stairs, Seth suggested they meet for a drink after work. He spoke as casually and easily as if they were friends and, suddenly, they were.

Drinks led to dinner and to another walk; to more drinks, dinners and walks. Despite, or perhaps because of, having a car, Seth loved to walk. It was his only exercise – like Olin, he had developed a hatred of sports at school – and after days cooped up indoors, he longed for the chance to move in the open air. He said that it not only relaxed him, but it helped him to think. Olin, always lazy, enjoyed their walks because the talk that accompanied them allowed him to forget he was exerting himself. Some of their best – and most disturbing – conversations took place while they walked. There were things which could not be said in a restaurant or a bar, looking at each other. But striding along, talking into the open air as if thinking aloud, unable to see each other's expression, anything might be voiced. Anything at all. And one day, Olin thought, Seth would say something . . . Seth would go too far. The thought gave him a strange feeling at the pit of his stomach. It was a pleasurable excitement he remembered from long ago, from the last time he'd had such a close friendship. The feeling was fear, but it was also desire.

Women had friendships among themselves, but women had nothing to lose. Older men sometimes managed it, becoming as if boys again in their age, but for everyone else friendship was a risk. Olin was well aware of this, and thought Seth must be, too. They never spoke of the danger they might be courting, although they came close. For love – or sex, or biology, or marriage – was the topic they continued to be drawn to, again and again, in their night-time, walking conversations. The subject was like a sore Seth could not stop probing, or a cliff-edge he had to lean over. It was during those conversations that Olin became aware of what a dangerous edge it was on which they balanced. If one of them fell . . .

But if one of them fell, it would be Seth, he was certain. Seth, with his youth, his passion, his sorrow, his 'mistaken' marriage, would fall in love with his older friend, and not the other way around. Olin could imagine Seth in love with him, and the idea of making love to a transformed, newly receptive Seth aroused him. But Olin did not let himself dwell on such thoughts. He didn't really want it to happen. He liked this not-sexual friendship; he wanted to believe that it could last. He wanted to go on balancing. He didn't want Seth to change.

One morning, about six weeks after the performance of *The Insufficient Answer*, Olin's telephone rang before he left for school.

It was Dove. 'I've been trying to phone you for days, and you're never in,' she said.

He remembered his long-ago, never-kept resolution to phone her, and felt guilty. 'I've been busy – I'm sorry I haven't been in touch –'

'It doesn't matter. But I thought you might have forgotten that it's parents' day this weekend. I thought the 8:45 would be the best train to catch. Could you meet me at the station by 8:30 on Saturday morning? Tristan wants a new football, I know – do you think you could manage to buy one? And some books for both of them – you know the sort of thing they'd like better than I would.'

Olin winced and closed his eyes as his wife's voice poured into his ear. He had forgotten. Worse than that, he didn't want to go. There had been a time when he welcomed the ritual visits to his children at their school. Then, his life had been so dull that any events were treasured as a break from routine. But his life was different now. A day spent with Dove and the boys meant a day without Seth. They had made tentative plans for Saturday already: a drive in the country, a visit to some site of historic interest, some place from the old times. Olin knew what he wanted to do, but he also knew his duty. He told Dove that he would meet her at the station.

They embraced as they always did on meeting – former desire transformed to awkward ritual – and then stood back to examine each other for signs of change.

Her hair was too short, Olin thought, the style too severe. It made her look older than she was, harsher and no longer pretty. But she looked fit, and still dressed well.

'You've put on weight,' Dove said.

He was surprised, and a little indignant, for since spending time with Seth he was not only getting more exercise, but also eating less. He tucked a thumb into the waistband of his trousers to show Dove how loose they were.

In answer, she touched his chest. 'Look how tight. That button's ready to pop.'

He flinched away from her hand. 'Maybe the shirt shrunk.'

'Shirts that old don't shrink. *I* bought you that shirt. You're bigger in the chest, and it isn't muscle. Your face is fuller, too. It doesn't look bad – you look younger, actually. Softer.'

Olin shrugged, annoyed and not wanting to think about why. 'Let's get on the train before it goes without us.' He was dreading the two-hour journey. Usually he told Dove about his life and she listened. But he didn't want to tell her about Seth, and he could think of nothing else that had happened to him in the last two months – nothing that would take more than two or three minutes to tell. He had brought along a book to read, but he was so aware of Dove watching him that he found it difficult to concentrate. The familiar train journey had never seemed longer.

Their children, Tristan and Timon, acted pleased to see them, but they clearly had lives of their own in which parents played no very large role. Olin knew this was normal – he remembered his own school-days. And it was only fair that they be uninterested in him, considering how seldom he thought of them, but, confronted with them in the flesh, with their inescapable separateness, Olin felt his own estrangement the more. Once they had been at the centre of his life, he thought. When he hugged them, and could feel and smell their familiar bodies, he loved them, but when they moved out of reach he was left with only memories. He loved his babies, but his babies had grown into strangers. He wondered if Dove felt the same way. Perhaps it was worse for her. Or perhaps she had come to terms with it long before. It had to be different for a mother, who had brought forth children from her own body. He had *always* been separate from his children. Suddenly, confusingly, Olin wanted to cry. To cover his feelings, he began to rough-house with the boys until he realized he was embarrassing them. He wasn't acting like the other fathers. Desperately, Olin watched the other fathers for clues, and tried to act like them. He tried to remember what he had done six months ago, during his last visit to the school. What had he felt then, who had he been? Surely it hadn't always been this difficult, this painful?

Fortunately the day was structured to make life easy for everyone. Olin and Dove were taken around by their children, reintroduced to their children's friends and teachers, observed various competitions, sporting and dramatic events, and then took Tristan and Timon out for the traditional feast. Presents were given out, and then the farewell kisses and goodbyes.

Back on the train, Olin was too exhausted even to pretend to read his book. He didn't think Dove would have let him, anyway. It was obvious she had something to say, even if she was taking her time about saying it.

'So,' she said at last. 'You going to tell me about him?'

'Who?'

'Your friend.'

'What makes you think I have a friend?'

'You always thought I was stupid,' she said. 'But there are some things you don't get to know out of books. You're different than you were the last time I saw you. You're always out, too busy to call me, instead of lonely and bored like you were before. And instead of telling me in detail about your boring life, you got on the train and stuck your nose in a book. Because your life isn't boring anymore. Because there's somebody in your life. Somebody new. Maybe it's early days yet, maybe you're not really sure, and you don't want to jinx it by saying anything too soon in case it doesn't happen, but – I don't think it's that. I think something's happening that you didn't expect –'

'What are you babbling about?'

'The main thing is, the reason I'm so sure, is that you remind me –' again, she stopped short. It was almost like a dare to him to tell her what she already knew.

He gave in. Maybe, after all, he did want to talk about it; maybe he wanted confirmation from someone else. 'What do I remind you of?' he asked gently. 'Do I remind you of how I used to be, when you and I were first in love? Do I remind you of how I was then?'

She shook her head. 'No. You remind me of how *I* was.'

Dove was right, and he was in hell. He had denied it to her, and had tried to deny it to himself, but Sunday morning Olin woke and saw the blood in his bed and could no longer hide the truth from himself. He had fallen in love with Seth.

It wasn't much blood – a dried brownish spot no larger than his thumbnail. He stripped off the sheet and saw that it had soaked through to the mattress. As he scrubbed at the stain with a wet, soapy towel, Olin blinked back tears and struggled to think logically.

He was changing. No doubt about that, but the change was far from complete. Dove had seen the signs, but Dove had been through it herself. It might not be too late to stop what was happening to him. His only hope was to get away from Seth before it was too late. Parents did sometimes save their sons from shame by sending them away when they recognized the threat of a developing romance. Olin couldn't actually go away – he couldn't afford to leave his job – but he might be able to contrive something to keep him safely out of Seth's company.

Olin sat back and surveyed his work. There was a large wet spot on the mattress, but that would soon dry. The bloodstain was gone.

The telephone rang, making Olin jump. He stared at the thing, knowing already who it would be. Maybe he should start now, ignore it. But he couldn't resist the summons.

'Took you long enough,' said Seth's voice in his ear. 'I thought you said you lived in one room?'

'I do. I was in bed – I'm not feeling well.'

'Oh, what's wrong?'

'I'm not sure. I'm probably just tired out from the day with Dove and the boys.'

'Why don't I come over and cheer you up?'

'No!' The leap his heart had given – of pure desire – made him shout.

There was a short silence on the other end. Olin tried not to think about what Seth was thinking, not to worry whether he was hurt or angry.

Seth said, 'What's wrong?'

'I told you. I'm tired. I don't feel well. I'm fed up with people – I just need to be alone.'

'You're the doctor. I'll leave you alone, then. You'd just better be over this by Wednesday.'

'Wednesday?'

'You hadn't forgotten that we've got opera tickets?'

'No, of course not. I'll be better before Wednesday – I have to be well enough to go to school tomorrow. I can't afford to pay a substitute.'

Olin knew Seth's schedule like his own. It was easy enough to avoid him at school, just as, a week earlier, it had been easy to engineer brief, 'accidental' encounters. At the end of the day, Olin crept out by a side-entrance and went to a movie and then had dinner in a cafe of the sort Seth would never enter. He felt like a hunted animal, following a similar routine on Tuesday. But on Wednesday one of the boys brought him a note:

Opera steps, 7 sharp, yes? Don't be late! S.

Olin folded the note and tucked it into his pocket, aware that his students were staring at him and giggling.

'Is that a love-note, Sir?' asked one of the boys.

Another, in a loud whisper, corrected him, 'Is that a love-note, *Miss!*'

The whole class exploded into mocking laughter.

Olin pounded on his desk, painfully aware that he was blushing. He regained control of the class, but he knew how weak was his hold on them. Boys that age were sensitive to hints of sex even where they did not exist, and once they knew the truth about him he would lose their respect forever. He tried to take comfort from the fact that they couldn't really know – and nothing, after all, had happened – and then, with a chill, he wondered if Seth also suspected. If Seth, perhaps, knew.

Against the rules, Olin dismissed his final class ten minutes early. He didn't go to a film or a cafe. He had decided to do something positive, and he caught the bus which would take him to the north-eastern suburb where Dove lived.

She seemed surprised and, he thought, not pleased when she opened the door to him. Entering at her reluctant invitation, he saw that she already had a visitor, a woman dressed, like Dove, in dark-blue overalls. Olin had not seen Dove in her work clothes since the days when they lived together: she always dressed up for him when he came to call. She looked taller and stronger to him now, more of a stranger.

'Is something wrong?' she asked. She did not offer to introduce him to the woman.

'No, no, I just thought I'd like to take you out to dinner.'

'Why didn't you phone?'

He shrugged uneasily. 'It was a spur of the moment thing. I thought you'd be pleased.'

There was a silence, and then the other woman set down her tea-cup and rose from her chair. 'I'd better be getting along,' she said to Dove. 'I'll see you tomorrow at work.'

'I'll phone you later,' Dove said.

The two women exchanged a look which made Olin feel

even more uncomfortable, and then the other woman smiled, becoming almost beautiful. 'Take care, Leo,' she said.

'Leo?' said Olin when Dove had closed the door behind her departing guest. 'Why did she call you that?'

'It's my name.'

'It *was*. Dove –'

'Dove is *your* name for me. I still have my own. I prefer my friends to use it.'

He wondered what she meant by the word friend, and what that woman was to her, and he did not want to know. 'I didn't know you didn't like it. I could have chosen another name if you'd ever said –'

'I didn't say I didn't like it. It's all right *you* calling me Dove. Let's not argue. Come into the kitchen and have a cup of tea. Or would you rather have a beer? I've got some.'

'Tea.' He followed her into the kitchen. 'I'm sorry I didn't phone first. I really didn't think about it until I was on the bus coming out here, and then it seemed too late. If you really want me to leave –'

'No, now you're here, stay.'

'I can wait while you change,' he said as she put the kettle on.

She shook her head. 'I don't want to change; I don't feel like going out.' She turned around to face him, leaned against the counter and crossed her arms over her chest. 'Why don't you just say what you have to say?'

He didn't want to talk to her in such a self-possessed, almost aggressive mood. He had hoped to make her pliable with drink and good food, to lead up to it gently, but she wasn't giving him the chance and he couldn't afford to wait for a better time. He drew a deep breath.

'I want to try again,' he said.

'Try what?'

'Us. I'd like us to try again. I'd like to move back in here with you.'

She simply stared. He couldn't tell what she was thinking. The kettle was boiling. She turned away and poured the water into the teapot.

'He's really got you scared,' she said.

'Who?'

'It won't work,' she said. 'You can't get away from him that easily. You can't just pretend you've got a wife –'

'Why should it be a pretence? We loved each other once – why can't we go back to that?'

'Because we've changed.'

'*I* haven't,' he said furiously. 'I haven't changed! It's started, yes, but *he* doesn't know – we haven't done anything – it's not too late – if I stay away from him – I don't have to be his woman –'

'And I don't have to be yours.'

Olin stared at her. 'But you can't – you can't change back. You can't ever be a man again. Becoming a woman – that change is forever. I changed you.'

She smiled. 'What makes you think I *want* to be a man again? There are other kinds of change. There's such a thing as growing.'

'Have you met someone else? Who is he? Do you want to marry someone else?'

'No.'

But there was something . . . Olin felt sick. 'Not her – that woman who was here? Is *she* your lover? Do women do that?'

He saw her tense, and it occurred to him that she wanted to hit him. But she was very controlled as she said, 'We're friends. We'll probably make love some day. But not in the way *you* mean. It's not that kind of thing. There aren't any men and women among us.'

'I wouldn't try to stop you,' Olin said. 'If that was what you wanted, if you wanted her as well . . . You could do as you liked. Let me move back in here.'

'No.'

'Why won't you help me? Do you hate me that much, for what I did to you?'

She sighed. 'Olin . . . I don't hate you at all. If I can help you, I will. But I'm not going to live a lie for you.'

'Why should it be a lie? We were happy together once, weren't we?'

'We were, but that's over. Olin, you know it is. You spend an evening with me, and by the end of it you can't wait to get away. The Dove you've got in your mind isn't me. You'd know that if you weren't so afraid right now. Why are you so afraid?

Memories of the Body

It's natural; it happens to people all the time. Why can't you just accept what's happening to you?'

'I'm too old,' he said, anguished.

She almost laughed. 'The fact that it's happening means you're not too old. All right, maybe too old for babies, but that can be a blessing. Since you've done your bit for the species already, with Timon and Tristan, you don't even have to feel guilty. Let yourself enjoy it. There *is* pleasure in it, you know. Pain, too, but you might find that the pleasure makes up for it. I remember the pleasure, Olin. You don't have to feel guilty about what you did to me. Oh, I know you feel guilty. Otherwise you wouldn't be so afraid of it happening to you. Don't be. It isn't *so* terrible to be a woman.'

Of course it was terrible to be a woman. Olin had feared it all his life. Everyone feared becoming a woman. Parents feared it for their sons. And friends, in their intimacy, battled grimly not to lose. To lose was to become a woman. Olin had been through that in his youth, and he had won. He thought he could relax, then, he thought he was safe. He had not realized, until it was too late, that the battle to retain manhood never ended. He had not truly understood that one victory was not the end. He had not realized until now that he might yet lose.

After leaving Dove, Olin rode around the city on buses, unable to think what to do next, unable even to decide upon a restaurant. But eventually he became restless and decided that, like Seth, he would be able to think better if he could walk. He left the bus at a stop near the old city, so that was where he went to walk.

Darkness had fallen, and the broken pavement was treacherous underfoot. Here and there among the looming vastness of ancient buildings tiny lights glowed and flickered: candles lit by lovers in the abandoned rooms which were their trysting places. They were all around him – he heard the indistinct murmur of their voices and, occasionally, a cry of pain.

He broke out in a sweat. Once these surroundings would have induced nostalgic memories of his time with Dove. Now they brought only fear. Why had he come here? Why had he chosen these streets, of all there were in the city to walk? He had to get away.

38

Olin turned around and there, in the darkness, unmistakable, was Seth.

'I knew you'd come here,' said Seth. 'I knew I only had to wait.'

'It was a mistake,' said Olin. 'I'm leaving.'

'You'll come with me first.'

'No.'

As he tried to go past, Seth caught him by the arm. It was the first time he had ever touched Olin, and now Olin knew that it really was too late. They could fight: although Seth was taller, Olin was heavier and better coordinated and under other circumstances he could have taken Seth. But as he stood very still, feeling Seth's fingers like a chain around his arm, feeling the unwanted, unmistakable trickle of wetness between his legs as his wound began to bleed, Olin knew that Seth had already won this fight. He shuddered, as his fear was transformed into desire.

'Where will we go?' he asked.

'I know a room. Come on.' Now Seth, seeming kind, released his bruising hold and laid his arm gently across Olin's shoulders. 'Don't be frightened,' he said, leading Olin away. 'I'll be very gentle; it won't hurt so much.'

It was only the first of his lies.

Husbands

1 Buffaloed

My first husband was a dog, all snuffling, clumsy, ardent devotion. At first (to be fair to him) we were a couple of puppies, gambolling and frisking in our love for each other and collapsing in a panting heap on the bed every night. But time and puppyhood passed, as it tends to do, and as he grew into a devoted, sad-eyed, rather smelly hound, I found myself becoming a cat. It is not the dog's fault that cats and dogs fight like cats and dogs, and probably (to be fair to myself) it is not the cat's fault, either. It is simply in their nature to find everything that is most typical in the other to be the most difficult to live with. I became more and more irritable, until everything he did displeased me. Finally, even the sound of his throat-clearing sigh when I had rebuffed him once again would make my fur stand on end. I couldn't help what I was, any more than he could. It was in our nature, and there was nothing for it but to part.

My second husband was a horse. Well-bred, highly-strung, with flaring nostrils and rolling eyes. He was a beauty. I watched him for a long time from a distance before I dared approach. When I touched him (open-palmed, gently but firmly on his flank, as I had been taught), a quiver rippled through the muscles beneath the smooth skin. I thought this response was fear, and I vowed I would teach him to trust and love me. We had a few years together – not all of them bad – before I understood that nervous ripple had been an involuntary expression not of fear but of distaste. Almost, before he left me, I learned to perceive myself as a slow, squat, fleshy creature he suffered to cling to his back. We both tried to change me, but it was a hopeless task. I could not become what he was; I did not even, deep down, want to be. It was not until we both realized that such a profound difference could not be resolved that he left me for one of his own kind.

I didn't intend to have a third husband; I don't believe the phrase 'third time lucky' reflects a natural law. With two honourable, doomed tries behind me, and having observed the lives of my contemporaries, I concluded that the happy marriage was the oddity; in most cases, a fantasy. It was a fantasy I wanted to do without. I still liked men, but marrying one of them was not the best way to express that liking. Better to admit my allegiance to the tribe of single women. My women friends were more important to me than any man. They were my family and my emotional support. Most of them had not given up the dream of a husband, but I understood their reasons, and sympathized. Jennifer, bringing up her daughter alone, longed for a partner; Annie, single and childless and relentlessly ageing, wanted a father for her child. Janice, who worked hard and lived with her invalid mother, dreamed of a handsome millionaire. Cathy was quite explicit about her sexual needs, and Doreen about her emotional ones. I had no child and didn't want one, earned a good living, seldom felt lonely, had friends for emotional sustenance, and as for sex – well, sometimes there was a lover, and when there wasn't, I tried not to think about it. Sex wasn't really what I missed, although I could interpret it that way. I yearned for something else, something more; it was an old addiction I couldn't quite conquer, a longing it seemed I had been born with.

There was a man. Now the story begins. It can't have a happy ending, but still we keep hoping. At least it's a story. There was a man where I worked. I didn't know his name, and I didn't want to ask, because to ask would reveal my interest. My interest was purely physical. How could it be anything else, when I'd never even spoken to him? What else did I know about him but how he looked? I watched how he moved through the corridors, head down, leading with his shoulders. He had broad shoulders, a short neck, a barrel chest. Such a powerful upper torso that I suspected he had built it by lifting weights. Curling black hair. An impassive face. On bad days, I thought it was noble. On good days, he looked irritatingly stupid. I did not seek him out. I tried to avoid him. But chance brought us together, even though we didn't speak. I wondered if he had noticed me. I wondered how what I felt could not be mutual, could not be real, could be, simply, a one-sided fantasy; an obsession.

Pasiphaë fell in love, they say, with a snow-white bull.

One day I went to the zoo with Jennifer and her daughter. Little Lindsay was thrilled, running from one enclosure to another, demanding to know the animals' names, herself naming the ones she recognized from her picture-books.

'Tiger.'

'Tiger! Lion!'

'Ocelot.'

'Ocelot!'

'Leopard.'

'Leopard!'

'Panther.'

'Panther!'

I wondered what *his* name was. And what about his soul. What was his sign, his clan, his totem? What animal was he? The bull? The ox. The water buffalo. I considered the Chinese horoscope. A man born in the year of the ox was steady and trustworthy, a patient and tireless worker. Undemonstrative, traditional, dedicated. Boring, I reminded myself. And a determined materialist. He wouldn't even know what I meant if I talked about the union of souls. He was certainly married already, a husband devoted to his wife and children, never dreaming of any alternatives.

I watched Jennifer watching her daughter. I looked at the fine lines which had begun to craze the delicate fair skin of her face, and at the springy black hair compressed into an untidy bun on top of her head. The red scarf (which I had given her) swathing her neck. The set of her shoulders. Her fragile wrists. She felt me watching, and caught my hand with her thin, strong fingers; squeezed. We knew each other so well. We felt the same about so many things; we understood and trusted each other. Sometimes I knew what she was going to say before she said it. We loved each other. The love of two equals, with nothing excessive, romantic or inexplicable about it.

'Zebra.'

'Zebra!'

'Okapi.'

'Okapi!'

'Giraffe.'

'Giraffe!'

'Buffalo.'

Buffalo. The American Bison. Order: Artiodactyla; Family: Bovidae. A powerful, migratory, gregarious, horned grazing animal of the North American plains.

Thick, curly, dark-brown hair grew luxuriously on head, neck and shoulders; a shorter, lighter-brown growth covered the rest of the body. The bull stood there, solid and motionless as a mountain-side, and yet it was a warm, living mountain; there was nothing cold or hard about it. I remembered how, as a child, travelling in the back of the car on family holidays, I had gazed out at the changing landscapes and dreamed that I could stroke the distant, furry hills. Something about this creature – wild, yet tame; strange, but familiar – stirred the same, childish response. If I could touch it, I thought, if only I could touch it, something would change. I would know something, and everything would be different.

The set of his shoulders. The curve of his horns. The springy curl of his luxuriant hair. A wild, musty, grassy smell hung on the air, filled my nostrils, and I could feel a sun that wasn't there, beating down on my naked back.

'Buffalo.'

Pasiphaë fell in love, they say, with a snow-white bull.

To have her desire, Pasiphaë hid inside a hollow wooden cow, and so the fearsome Minotaur was conceived.

Was that her desire? To be impregnated by a bull? I understand her passion, but not the logic of her actions. It is not Pasiphaë's story that we have been told. What we hear is the greed of Minos, the anger of Poseidon, the cunning of Daedalus.

She was a tool, the conduit through which the Minotaur came to be. When her passion died, did she understand what she had done, or why? Did she think, suddenly, too late, as the bull mounted her: But this isn't what I meant! This isn't what I wanted! Or was she triumphant, fulfilled? Afterwards, was she satisfied? Did the desire she had felt vanish once Poseidon's will had been served, or was it waiting, nameless, incapable of fulfilment, waiting to erupt again?

We are told that Pasiphaë's love for the bull was an unnatural desire. But what is natural about any desire, for anything not necessary to sustain life? What does it mean to want a man? To want a husband?

Staring at the buffalo that cloudy day in the zoo, separated from it by distance, by time, by species, by everything that can distance one creature from another, I felt a wordless, naked desire. It was a desire that could not be named, and certainly could not be fulfilled. It was the purest lust I had ever known, unmuddied, for once, by any of the usual misinterpretations. If that had been a man staring back at me across emptiness with his round, brown, uncomprehending eye, I would have invited him home with me. I would have thought my feelings were sexual – sexual desire, at least, allows satisfaction – and if they persisted beyond that, I would have used the word love. I might have convinced myself that marriage was possible; I certainly would have tried to convince him. To have him. Forgetting that it was impossible; forgetting that desire, by its nature, can never be satisfied.

Remember, I told myself. And then, forgetting, I wondered what his name was.

'Buffalo?'
'Husband.'

2 This Longing

'Sometimes I think we made them up,' I said to Rufinella. 'Mythical creatures for the mythical time before Now.'

We had just been to see an old movie about the relations between men and women – husbands, single women and wives – a horrible story which stirred up emotions unfelt for more than thirty years. At least in me. I don't know what Rufinella felt: she had seemed to enjoy it. Although, given the number of times she had had to lean over and ask me, in a loud whisper, which ones were the men and which the women, I wondered what it was she had enjoyed, and just how much she had understood.

Rufinella gave me a disbelieving look. 'What's this? You've joined the revisionists? You're about to confess you were a part of the conspiracy all along? That you've been lying to your students all these years, pretending that myth is history?'

'No conspiracy,' I said. 'I've always taught the truth as I've understood it, but sometimes I wonder – what did I ever understand? How much of what I remember was true? Did they really exist, this other . . . gender? Like us, yet so unalike? Face it, the details are so unlikely!'

'But you said you had one.'

'You can't say "had one" like they were property –'

'People talk about them like that in the movies. And I've heard you say it – you've always said you had a husband. What are you telling me now – that it didn't exist?'

'He,' I corrected automatically, teacher that I am. 'Oh, yes, I had a husband . . . and a father, and a brother, and lovers, and male colleagues . . . At least, I think I did. When I remember them, they don't seem so terribly different from the women I knew that long ago. They don't seem like strange, extinct creatures . . . they were just individuals, whom I knew. Other people, you know? I was twenty-eight years old when the men went away. That's – well, more than thirty years ago now. I've lived longer without men than I lived with them. What I remember might almost be a dream.'

'If it was a dream, everybody else had it, too,' said Rufinella. 'And there's the evidence: there they are – or at least their shadows – on film, on video, in the newspapers, in books, in the news . . . They were real; if you're going to judge by the evidence they left behind, they were more real than the women.'

'Then maybe they woke up to reality one day, and found that the women were gone.'

'Nobody dreamed *me*,' said the daughter of my best friend, very firmly. Rufinella was two months old when the men disappeared. Therefore, unlike her own daughter, she had a father, but she cannot possibly remember him, or any man. Although she has tried, through hypnotic regression. According to her, she succeeded in going back before her birth, to her time in the womb. She said she could remember her mother's body. But she could not remember her father. She couldn't remember a male presence, any more than imagine how creatures called men might have differed so dramatically from creatures called women, as all history, all art, tells us they did.

Art is metaphor, and history is an art. It was *like* this. It was not like *that*. We are language-using, story-telling creatures. Trying to explain reality, we transform it. We can't travel in time and know the past that way, but only, endlessly, try to recreate it. As a teacher (I'm semi-retired, now), I tried to make my students understand something they could never know for themselves. Imaginative reconstruction of a place which no longer exists. They can't go there, but neither can I. My own memories are stories I tell myself.

Maybe women did make up men, invented them the way earlier civilizations created gods, to fill a need. A group of revisionist historians – psycho-historians, they call themselves – would like us all to believe that there was never any 'second sex', never any 'other' kind of human being except ourselves. According to them, men were a cultural invention. After all, if they were truly other than us, necessary in the same way as are male animals, how is it that we women have managed to continue to reproduce ourselves, managed to conceive and bear children, without any of the equipment or the contortions depicted in illustrated texts on human sexuality, and in a certain class of film?

I've heard many clever and convincing arguments for the revisionist view of human history, and there are times when I feel that only a native stubbornness keeps me clinging to what I 'know'. Yet the argument they think is the clincher for their point of view does not convince me.

Like all sane and sensible people, they still, thirty-four years after the fact, cannot come to terms with, can hardly believe, the way that men disappeared. Overnight; all at once; in the twinkling of an eye. They simply were no longer. Reality doesn't work like that; dreams do. So it makes a certain comforting sense to conclude that the whole class or gender of *men* was a dream. Nothing vanished except an illusion. There was no sudden, world-wide disappearance, but only an equally sudden change in perception. Men no longer existed because we no longer needed to pretend that they did.

Things that exist do not suddenly cease to be. They change, possibly out of all recognition, but something doesn't become nothing except through a process of transformation. This is true not only of objects, but also of needs. What happened to that need which made women invent the story of men in such convincing detail, and cling to it for so many thousands of years? Why should it be any easier to erase such a need than half the human race? How could it vanish in the blink of an eye, between one breath and the next?

I said something of this sort to Rufinella. She looked tired and sad. 'Oh, yes,' she said. 'You're right. The need is still there, and we still don't understand it. That's why I think men are coming back.'

'The same way they left?' I loved my husband very much, and grieved for him and other male friends and family when they disappeared; I had mourned for years, wanting them back. And yet, now, the thought that they might all return, be found back in place tomorrow morning, was strangely horrible.

'Oh, no. I don't think so. I don't think you're going to roll over in bed one night and find you're not alone. I think they're coming back in a different way . . . more slowly, but more surely. We've had this time, all these years, to learn to understand ourselves and to change, and we haven't done it. We've missed our chance. We've blown it, as your generation says. We still need them, and we don't know why. So men are coming back. And I think it's going to be worse for us this time; a lot worse.'

Rufinella is bright and observant and cautious, not given to making rash, unprovable statements.

'Why?'

'You don't spend much time around children, do you?'

'Not much,' I said. 'In fact, hardly any. I suppose your Leni's birthday party was the last time.'

'I spend two afternoons a week in the community nursery,'

Rufinella said. 'And of course I live with Leni, and there's her friends, and Alice has an eight-year-old . . . since I've noticed, I've been talking to more mothers, and teachers, and nursery workers and . . . it's consistent. It's not isolated incidents; there's a pattern to it, and it's –'

'What?'

'I didn't mean to tell you yet – I didn't mean to tell anyone, until I was certain. Until I had more evidence. I could be wrong, I could be over-reacting, imagining things . . . I thought it was just a fad, at first. Most people who've noticed it probably think that. Because you only see a part of it, you only see what the kids in your house, or your school, or your neighbourhood are doing, and you don't realize that they are all doing the same thing, all across the city; all across the country . . . all over the world, I suspect, although of course I don't *know* . . . yet. At first I thought . . . you know how children are; I remember what it was like, myself. Making up codes, secret languages, little rituals . . . It's part of childhood. A children's culture. And that's what this is. They have their own culture.'

I felt the way I always feel before a medical examination. I wanted to leap ahead of her; tell her before she could tell me. 'And you recognize it – this culture – from the old movies.'

'Not the details. The details are different. I guess they'd have to be. But, yes, I do recognize it . . . at least, I recognize one thing about it. You would, too, I think.'

'Tell me.'

'They have their own language, their own rituals . . . those might differ from group to group, but the worst of it is, there are always two. Two separate classes, if you like. They've created certain differences . . . certain, consistent, differences. Two types of language, two types of ritual. One group of children uses one, and one is for the other. No cross-over allowed. You can't change the group you belong to, once you've picked it . . . or once it's picked *you*. I can't quite work out how the division is determined, or how early it is established . . . but somehow they all seem to know. A two-year-old going to nursery for the first time – it's settled before a word is spoken. They all know which group she belongs to, and there's no mistake possible, no appeal allowed. Almost as if they can see signs we can't . . . as if it were established at birth, the way sex used to be.'

Rufinella looked at me steadily, yet somehow desperately. She was pleading, I realized; hoping that I would have some advice, some wisdom from the age before hers.

'You think they're reinventing gender.'

She nodded.

'What do they say about it? Have you asked them?'

'They can't explain it. They say that's just how things are. They invent new languages, they create differences, but they talk about it as if they can't help it. As if these are discoveries, not inventions.'

'Maybe –'

'Don't say it! You mean that we've been blind for thirty-four years and now our children can see?'

I felt such longing, and such hope. I wished I were younger. I wanted another chance; I had always wanted another chance. I didn't understand the despair on Rufinella's face unless it was because she, too, knew she wouldn't be a part of the coming age. I said, 'Maybe they'll get it right this time.'

3 The Modern Prometheus

'It was on a dreary night of November that I beheld the accomplishment of my toils.'

Yes, I have been successful! I have dared to try, and managed to bring life to what to others has ever been only a dream: another race of beings, a partner-species, to end our long loneliness by being our planetary companions. Enough like us that we can communicate; yet different, so that each will have something worth communicating, bringing different visions, different experiences, to enrich the relationship of true equals.

Perhaps I shall have cause to regret my deed, but I do not think so. I think my name will go down in history as a positive example of how science can make the world a better place. I have not acted out of pride or ignorance; not for personal gain nor ambition. Nor do I believe that anything that can be done should be; that scientific achievement is a valuable end in itself. No, I have thought long and hard about what I meant to do. I have considered the dangers carefully and established certain limits. And all along I have felt myself to be not an individual pursuing personal goals, but rather the representative of all womankind, acting for the greater good.

Not, of course, that everyone agrees with what I have done. Many do not see the necessity. Why create a new species? Why bring another life-form into existence? Isn't that playing God? Yes, I say, and why not? Don't we do that already, every day, as we struggle to change the world for the better? Why should we suffer the lack of something we can create? But, of course, some do not believe there *was* any such lack. Some do not even believe in the yearning which has driven me to this. Because they have never felt it, they say it is imaginary. Solid materialists, they refuse to accept the possibility that one might desire something that does not exist. Something – I hasten to qualify – that does not *yet* exist. For I believe that these unnamed longings are expressions of memory . . . a racial memory, if you will; whether of past or future hardly matters. Desire is timeless, but it does not deal in the imaginary. If it seems that what we want does not exist, that is true only of this time. You may be certain that you had what you desire in the past, or you may have it in the future.

I have been driven by the desire to know someone else, another being, who is not like me. Not my lover, not my child, not my mother, not any friend or stranger on this earth. And so I have created it.

What is this new creation? I thought of calling it 'man' for the obvious, mytho-historical reasons. But the emotions connected to that word are mixed; and there are aspects of history better buried . . . not forgotten, but certainly not recreated. I have been careful to ensure that my 'man' should not be like any man who lived before, not like any previous companion women have known. To signal this, I have given him a name that represents what many women want; I have named this, our hearts' desire, 'husband'.

So, now, on this not-so-dreary November night, I look through the glass side of the tank at my creation. He looks back at me, interested, intelligent and kind, his body sleek and beautiful, his mind and spirit equal to my own. Equal, but different. I'm sure I've got it right. There will be no misunderstandings, no doomed attempts at domestication, and no struggles for power, for although we are enough alike to love each other, we will always live apart: women on dry land, husbands in the sea. Their beautiful faces and their complicated minds are like ours, but their bodies are very different. We will always live in different worlds. They must swim, having no legs to walk with, and although they breathe the same air we do, their skin needs the constant, enveloping caress of the water. We each will have our own domain, each be happy among our own kind, and yet they will find us as attractive as we find them, and so we shall seek each other out from time to time, and come together not for gain or of necessity, but from pure desire.

I look at him, the first of the new race, and when I smile, so does he. He waves a flipper; I wave a hand. I feel love bubbling up inside me, washing away the pain of the past, and I know, as he does a back-flip for my admiration, that my husband feels the same. This time, it will work out for the best.

Riding the Nightmare

Twilight, *l'heure bleue*: Tess O'Neal sat on the balcony of her sixth-floor apartment and looked out at the soft, suburban sprawl of New Orleans, a blur of green trees and multicoloured houses, with the jewels of lights just winking on. It was a time of day which made her nostalgic and gently melancholy, feelings she usually enjoyed. But not now. For once she wished she were not alone with the evening.

Gordon had cancelled their date. No great disaster – he'd said they could have all day Sunday together – but the change of plans struck Tess as ominous, and she questioned him.

'Is something wrong?'

He hesitated. Maybe he was only reacting to the sharp note in her voice. 'Of course not. Jude . . . made some plans, and it would spoil things if I went out. She sends her apologies.'

There was nothing odd in that. Jude was Gordon's wife and also Tess's friend, a situation they were all comfortable with. But Jude was slightly scatter-brained, and when she confused dates, it was Tess who had to take second place. Usually, Tess did not mind. Now she did.

'We'll talk on Sunday,' Gordon said.

Tess didn't want to talk. She didn't want explanations. She wanted Gordon's body on hers, making her believe that nothing had changed, nothing would ever change between them.

They're in it together. Him and his wife. And I'm left out in the cold.

She looked up at the darkening sky. As blue as the nightmare's eye, she thought, and shivered. She got up and went inside, suddenly feeling too vulnerable in the open air.

She had never told Gordon about the nightmare. He admired her as a competent, sophisticated, independent woman. How could she talk to him about childhood fears? Worse, how could she tell him that this was one childhood fear which hadn't stayed in childhood but had come after her?

As she turned to lock the sliding glass door behind her, Tess froze.

The mare's long head was there, resting on the balcony rail as if on a stable door, the long mane waving slightly in the breeze, the blueish eye fixed commandingly on her.

Tess stumbled backward, and the vision, broken, vanished.

There was nothing outside that should not be, nothing but sky and city and her own dark reflection in the glass.

'Snap out of it, O'Neal,' she said aloud. Bad enough to dream the nightmare, but if she was going to start seeing it with her eyes open, she really needed help.

For a moment she thought of phoning Gordon. But what could she say? Not only would it go against the rules to phone him after he'd said they could not meet, but it would go against everything he knew and expected of her if she began babbling about a nightmare. She simply wanted his presence, the way, as a child, she had wanted her father to put his arms around her and tell her not to cry. But she was a grown woman now. She didn't need anyone else to tell her what was real and what was not; she knew that the best way to banish fears and depression was by working, not brooding.

She poured herself a Coke and settled at her desk with a stack of transcripts. She was a doctoral candidate in linguistics, working on a thesis examining the differences in language use between men and women. It was a subject of which, by now, she was thoroughly sick. She wondered sometimes if she would ever be able to speak unselfconsciously again, without monitoring her own speech patterns to edit out the stray, feminine modifiers and apologies.

The window was open. Through it, she could see the black and windy sky and there, running on the wind, was the creamy white mare with tumbling mane and rolling blue eye. Around her neck hung a shining crescent moon, the golden *lunula* strung on a white and scarlet cord. And Tess was on her feet, walking toward the window as if hypnotized. It was then that she became aware of herself, and knew she was dreaming, and that she must break the dream. With a great effort of will, she flung herself backwards, towards the place where she knew her bed would be, tossing her head as she strained to open her eyes.

And woke with a start to find herself still at her desk. She must have put her head down for a moment. Her watch showed it was past midnight. Tess got up, her heart beating unpleasantly fast, and glanced toward the sliding glass door. That it was not the window of her dream made no difference. The window in her dream was always the bedroom window of her childhood, the scene always the same as the first time the nightmare had come for her. There was no horse outside on the balcony, or in the sky beyond. There was no horse except in her mind.

Tess went to bed, knowing the nightmare would not come again. Never twice in one night, and she had succeeded in refusing the first visit. Nevertheless, she slept badly, with confused dreams of quarrelling with Gordon as she never quarrelled with him in life, dreams in which Gordon became her father and announced his intended marriage to Jude, and Tess wept and argued and wept and woke in the morning feeling exhausted.

Gordon arrived on Sunday with champagne, flowers, and a shopping bag full of gourmet treats for an indoor picnic. He gave off a glow of happiness and well-being which at once put Tess on the defensive, for his happiness had nothing to do with her.

He kissed her and looked at her tenderly – so tenderly that her stomach turned over with dread. He was looking at her with affection and pity, she thought – not with desire.

'What is it?' she asked sharply, pulling away from him. 'What's happened?'

He was surprised. 'Nothing,' he said. Then: 'Nothing bad, I promise. But I'll tell you all about it. Why don't we have something to eat first? I've brought –'

'I couldn't eat with something hanging over me, wondering . . .'

'I told you, it's nothing bad, nothing to worry about.' He frowned. 'Are you getting your period?'

'I'm *not* getting my period; I'm *not* being irrational –' she stopped and swallowed and sighed, forcing herself to relax. 'All right, I am being irrational. I've been sleeping badly. And there's this nightmare – the same nightmare I had as a kid, just before my mother died.'

'Poor baby,' he said, holding her close. He sounded protective but also amused. 'Nightmares. That doesn't sound like my Tess.'

'It's not that I'm superstitious –'

'Of course not.'

'But I've been feeling all week that something bad was about to happen, something to change my whole life. And with the nightmare – I hadn't seen it since just before my mother died. To have it come now, and then when you said we'd talk –'

'It isn't bad, I promise you. But I won't keep you in suspense. Let's just have a drink first, all right?'

'Sure.'

He turned away from her to open the champagne, and she stared at him, drinking in the details as if she might not see him again for a very long time: the curls at the back of his neck, the crisp, black beard, his gentle, rather small hands, skilled at so many things. She felt what it would be to lose him, to lose the right to touch him, never again to have him turn and smile at her.

But why think that? Why should she lose him? How could she, when he had never been 'hers' in any traditional sense, nor did she want him to be. She liked her freedom, both physical and emotional. She liked living alone, yet she wanted a lover, someone she could count on who would not make too many demands of her. In Gordon she had found precisely the mixture of distance and intimacy which she needed. It had worked well for nearly three years, so why did she imagine losing him? She trusted Gordon, believed in his honesty and his love for her. She didn't think there was another woman, and she knew he hadn't grown tired of her. She didn't believe he had changed. But Jude might.

Gordon handed her a long-stemmed glass full of champagne, and after they had toasted one another, and sipped, he said, 'Jude's pregnant. She found out for sure last week.'

Tess stared at him, feeling nothing at all.

He said quickly, 'It wasn't planned. I wasn't keeping anything from you. Jude and I, we haven't even – hadn't even – discussed having children. It just never came up. But now that it's happened . . . Jude really likes the idea of having a baby and . . .'

'Who's the father?'

She felt him withdraw. 'That's not worthy of you, Tess.'

'Why? It seems like a reasonable question, considering –'

'Considering that Jude hasn't been involved with anyone since Morty went back to New York? I thought you and Jude were friends. What do you two talk about over your lunches?'

The brief, mean triumph she had felt was gone, replaced by anguish. 'Not our sex lives,' she said. 'Look, you've got an open marriage, you tell me it was an accident. I'm sorry, I didn't know you'd take it that way. I was just trying to find out what – forget I asked.'

'I will.' He turned away and began to set out the food he had brought onto plates. The champagne was harsh in her mouth as Tess watched his so-familiar, economical movements, and wanted to touch his back where the blue cloth of his shirt stretched a little too tightly.

She drew a deep breath and said, 'Congratulations. I should have said that first of all. How does it feel, knowing you're going to be a father?'

He looked around, still cautious, and then smiled. 'I'm not sure. It doesn't seem real yet. I guess I'll get used to it.'

'I guess it'll change things,' she said. 'For you and me.'

He went to her and took her in his arms. 'I don't want it to.'

'But it's bound to.'

'In practical ways, maybe. We might have less time together, but we'll manage somehow. Jude and I were never a traditional couple, and we aren't going to be traditional parents, either. I'll still need you – I'm not going to stop loving you.' He said it so fiercely that she smiled, and pressed her face against his chest to hide it. 'Do you believe me? Nothing can change the way I feel about you. I love you. That's not going to change. Do you believe me?'

She didn't say anything. He forced her head up off his chest and made her look at him. 'Do you believe me?' He kissed her when she wouldn't reply, then kissed her again, more deeply, and then they were kissing passionately, and she was pulling him onto the floor, and they made love, their bodies making the promises they both wanted.

After Gordon had left that night, the nightmare came again.

Tess found herself standing beside the high, narrow bed she'd slept in as a child, facing the open window. The pale curtains billowed like sails. Outside, galloping in place like a rocking horse, moving and yet stationary, was the blue-eyed, cream-coloured mare.

With part of her mind Tess knew that she could refuse this visit. She could turn her head, and wrench her eyes open, and find herself, heart pounding, safe in her bed.

Instead, she let herself go into the dream. She took a step forward. She felt alert and hypersensitive, as if this were the true state of waking. She was aware of her own body as she usually never was in life or in a dream, conscious of her nakedness as the breeze from the open window caressed it, and feeling the slight bounce of her breasts and the rough weave of the carpet beneath her feet as she walked towards the window.

She clambered onto the window-sill and, with total confidence, leaped out, knowing that the horse would catch her.

She landed easily and securely on the mare's back, feeling the scratch and prickle of the horsehair on her inner thighs. Her arms went around the high, arched neck and she pressed her face against it, breathing in the rough, salty, smoky scent of horseflesh. She felt the pull and play of muscle and bone beneath her and in her legs as the mare began to gallop. Tess looked down at the horse's legs, seeing how they braced and pounded against the air. She felt a slight shock, then, for where there should have been a hoof, she saw instead five toes. Tess frowned, and leaned further as she stared through the darkness, trying to see.

But they were her own hooves divided into five toes – they had always been so since the night of her creation. The thinly-beaten gold of the *lunula* on its silken chain bounced against the solid muscle of her chest as she loped through the sky.

Some unquestioned instinct took her to the right house. Above it, she caught a crosswind and, tucking her forelegs in close to her chest, glided spirally down until all four feet could be firmly planted on the earth. This was a single-storey house she visited tonight. She turned her head and, at a glance, the window swung open, the screen which had covered it a moment earlier now vanished. The mare took one delicate step closer and put her head through the window into the bedroom.

The bed, with a man and woman sleeping in it, was directly beneath the window. She breathed gently upon the woman's sleeping face and then drew back her head and waited.

The woman opened her eyes and looked into the mare's

blue gaze. She seemed confused but not frightened, and after a moment she sat up slowly, moving cautiously as if for fear of alarming the horse. The horse was not alarmed. She suffered the woman to stroke her nose and pat her face before she backed away, pulling her head out of the house. She had timed it perfectly. The woman came after her as if drawn on a rope, leaning out the window and making soft, affectionate noises. The mare moved as if uneasy, still backing, and then, abruptly flirtatious, offered her back, an invitation to the woman to mount.

The woman understood at once and did not hesitate. From the window ledge she slipped onto the mare's back in a smooth, fluid movement, as if she had done this every night of her life.

Feeling her rider in place, legs clasped firmly on her sides, the mare leaped skyward with more speed than grace. She felt the woman gasp as she was flung forward, and felt the woman's hands knot in her mane. She was obviously an experienced rider, not one it would be easy to throw. But the mare did not wish to throw her, merely to give her a very rough ride.

High over the sleeping city galloped the nightmare, rising at impossibly steep angles, shying at invisible barriers, and now and then tucking her legs beneath her to drop like a stone. The gasps and cries from her rider soon ceased. The woman, concentrating on clinging for her life, could have had no energy to spare for fear.

Not until dawn did the nightmare return the woman, leaping through the bedroom window in defiance of logic and throwing her onto the motionless safety of her bed, beside her still-sleeping husband.

When Tess woke a few hours later she was stiff and sore, as if she had been dancing, or running, all night. She got up slowly, wincing, and aware of a much worse emotional pain waiting for her, like the anticipation of bad news. The nightmare had come for her, and this time she had gone with it – she was certain of that much. But where had it taken her? What had she done?

In the bathroom, as she waited for the shower to heat up, racking her sleepy brain for some memory of the night before, Tess caught a glimpse in the mirror of something on her back, at waist level. She turned, presenting her back to the glass, and then craned her neck around, slowly against the stiffness, to look at her reflection.

She stared at the bloodstains. Stared and stared at the saddle of blood across her back.

She washed it off, of course, with plenty of hot water and soap, and tried not to think about it too hard. That was exactly what she had done the last time this had happened: when she was nine years old, on the morning after the night her mother had miscarried; on the morning of the day her mother had died.

All day Tess fought against the urge to phone Gordon. All day she was like a sleep-walker as she taught a class, supervised studies, stared at meaningless words in the library, and avoided telephones.

She thought, as she had thought before, that she should see a psychiatrist. But how could a psychiatrist help her? She *knew* she could not, by all the rules of reason and logic, have caused her mother's death. She knew she felt guilty because she had not wanted the little sister or brother her parents had planned, and on some level she believed that her desire, expressed in the nightmare, had been responsible for the miscarriage and thus – although indirectly and unintentionally – for her mother's death. She didn't need a psychiatrist to tell her all that. She had figured it out for herself, some time in her teens. And yet, figuring it out hadn't ended the feeling of guilt. That was why the very thought of the nightmare was so frightening to her.

If Jude is all right, she thought, if nothing has happened to her, then I'll know it was just a crazy dream and I'll see a psychiatrist.

Gordon telephoned the next day, finally. Jude was all right, he said, although Tess had not asked. Jude was just fine. Only – she'd lost the child. But miscarriage at this early stage was apparently relatively common. The doctors said she was physically healthy and strong and would have no problem carrying another child to term. Only – although she was physically all right, Jude was pretty upset. She had taken the whole thing badly, and in a way he'd never expected. She was saying some pretty strange things –

'What sort of things?' She clutched the phone as if it were his arm, trying to force him to speak.

'I need to see you, Tess. I need to talk to you. Could we meet for lunch?'

'Tomorrow?'

'Better make it Friday.'

'Just lunch?' She was pressing him as she never did, unable to hide her desperation.

'I can't leave Jude for long. She needs me now. It'll have to be just lunch. The Italian place?'

Tess felt a wave of pure hatred for Jude. She wanted to tell Gordon that she needed him just as much, or more than, his wife did; that she was in far more trouble than Jude with her mere, commonplace miscarriage.

'That's fine,' she said, and made her voice throb with sympathy as she told Gordon how sorry she was to hear about Jude. 'Let me know if there's anything at all I can do – tell her that.'

'I'll see you on Friday,' he said.

Gordon didn't waste any time on Friday. As soon as they had ordered, he came right to the point.

'This has affected Jude much more than I could have dreamed. I'd hardly come to terms with the idea that she was pregnant, and she's responding as if she'd lost an actual baby instead of only . . . I've told her we'll start another just as soon as we can, but she seems to think she's doomed to lose that one, too.' He had been looking into her eyes as he spoke, but now he dropped his gaze to the white tablecloth. 'Maybe Jude has always been a little unstable, I don't know. Probably it's something hormonal, and she'll get back to normal soon. But whatever . . . it seems to have affected her mind. And she's got this crazy idea that the miscarriage is somehow *your* fault.' He looked up with a grimace, to see how she responded.

Tess said quietly, 'I'm sorry.'

'Maybe she's always been jealous of you on some level – no, I can't believe that. It's the shock and the grief, and she's fixed on you . . . I don't know why. I'm sure she'll get over it. But right now there's no reasoning with her. She won't even consider the idea of seeing you. Don't try to call her, and –' he sighed deeply. 'She doesn't want me to see you, either. She wanted me to tell you, today, that it's all over.'

'Just like that.'

'Oh, Tess.' He looked at her across the table, obviously pained. She noticed for the first time the small lines that had appeared around his eyes. 'Tess, you know I love you. It's not that I love Jude any more than I love you. I'd never agree to choose between you.'

'That's exactly what you're doing.'

'I'm not. It's not forever. But Jude is my wife. I have a responsibility to her. You've always known that. She can't cope right now, that's all. I've got to go along with her. But this isn't the real Jude – she's not acting like herself at all.'

'Of course she is,' said Tess. 'She's always been erratic and illogical and acted on emotion.'

'If you saw her, if you tried to talk to her, you'd realize. She just won't – or can't – listen to reason. But once she's had time to recover, I know she'll see how ridiculous she was. And once she's pregnant again, she'll be back to normal, I'm certain.'

Tess realized she wasn't going to be able to eat her lunch. Her stomach was as tight as a fist.

Gordon said, 'This won't last forever, I promise. But for now, we're just going to have to stop seeing each other.'

No apologies, no softening of the blow. He was speaking to her man to man, Tess thought. She wondered what he would do if she burst into tears or began shouting at him.

'Why are you smiling?' he asked.

'I didn't know I was. Do we have to stop all contact with each other? Do I pretend you've dropped off the face of the earth, or what?'

'I'll phone you. I'll keep in touch. And I'll let you know if anything changes – when something changes.'

Tess looked at her watch. 'I have to get back and supervise some tests.'

'I'll walk you –'

'No, stay, finish your food,' she said. 'Don't get up.' She had suddenly imagined herself clinging to him on a street corner, begging him not to leave her. She didn't want to risk that, yet she could not kiss him casually, as if she would be seeing him again in a few hours or days. As she came around the table, she put her hand on his face for just a moment, then left without looking back.

* * *

61

As a child, Tess had been mad about horses, going through the traditional girlish phase of reading, talking, drawing and dreaming of them, begging for the impossible, a horse of her own. For her ninth birthday her parents had enrolled her for riding lessons. For half a year she had been learning to ride, but after her mother's death Tess had refused to have anything more to do with horses, even had a kind of horror of them. She had only one memento from that phase of her life: the blue-glazed, ceramic head of a horse. In her youth she'd kept it hidden away, but now she took pleasure in it again, in its beauty, the sweeping arch of the sculpted neck and the deep, mottled colour. It was a beautiful object, nothing like the nightmare.

Tess sat alone in her apartment sipping bourbon and Coke and gazing at the horse head, now and again lifting it to touch its coolness to her flushed cheek.

You didn't kill your mother, she told herself. Wishing the baby would not be born is not the same thing as *making* it not be born. You weren't – aren't – responsible for your dreams. And dreams don't kill.

Outside, the day blued towards night and Tess went on drinking. She felt more helpless and alone than she had ever before felt as an adult, as if the power to rule her own life had been taken from her. She was controlled, she thought, by the emotions of others: by Jude's fear, by Gordon's sense of responsibility, by her own childish guilt.

But Tess did not allow herself to sink into despair. The next morning, although hungover and sad, she knew that life must go on. She was accustomed, after all, to being alone and to taking care of herself. She knew how to shut out other thoughts while she worked, and she made an effort to schedule activities for her non-working hours so that dinner out, or a film, or drinks with friends carried her safely through the dangerous, melancholy hour of blue.

Over the next six weeks, Gordon spoke to her briefly three times. Jude seemed to be getting better, he said, but she was still adamant in her feelings towards Tess. Tess could never think of anything to say to this, and the silence stretched between them, and then Gordon stopped calling. After three months, Tess began to believe that it was truly over between them. And then Gordon came to see her.

He looked thin and unhappy. At the sight of him, Tess forgot her own misery and only wanted to comfort him. She poured him a drink and hovered over him, touching his hair shyly. He caught her hand and pulled her down beside him on the couch, and began to kiss and caress her rather clumsily. She was helping him undress her when she realized he was crying.

'Gordon! Darling, what's wrong?' She was shocked by his tears. She tried to hold him, to let him cry, but understood he didn't want that. After a minute he blew his nose and shook his head hard, repudiating the tears.

'Jude and I,' he began. Then, after a pause, 'Jude's left me.'

Tess felt a shocking sense of triumph, which she repressed at once. She waited, saying nothing.

'It's been hell,' he said. 'Ever since the miscarriage. That crazy idea she had, that you were somehow responsible for it. She said it was because you didn't mind sharing me with her, but that a baby would have changed things – you would have been left out of the cosy family group. I told her that you weren't like that, you weren't jealous, but she just laughed at me, and said men didn't understand.'

She must go carefully here, Tess thought. She had to admit her responsibility, and not let Gordon blame Jude too much, but she didn't want Gordon thinking she was mad.

'Gordon,' she said. 'I *was* jealous – and I was very afraid that once you were a father things would change and I'd be left out in the cold.'

He dismissed her confession with a grimace and a wave of his hand. 'So what? That doesn't make any difference. Even if you'd wanted her to have a miscarriage you didn't make it happen. You couldn't. Jude seems to think that you wished it on her, like you were some kind of a witch. She's crazy, that's what it comes down to.'

'She might come back.'

'No. It's over. We'd talked about a trial separation, and we started seeing a marriage counsellor. It made it worse. All sorts of things came up, things I hadn't thought were problems. And then she found somebody else, she's gone off with somebody else. She won't be with him for long, but she won't come back.'

* * *

63

Tess had thought for a long time that the break-up of Gordon and Jude would inevitably lead to the break-up between Gordon and herself, and so for the next few months she was tense, full of an unexamined anxiety, waiting for this to happen. Gordon, too, was uneasy, unanchored without his wife. Unlike Tess, he did not enjoy living alone, but he made a great effort to ration his time with Tess, not to impose upon her. They tried to go on as they always had, ignoring the fact that Jude was no longer there to limit the time they spent together. But when Tess finished her doctorate, they had to admit to the inevitability of some major, permanent change in their relationship. Tess could stay on in New Orleans, teaching English as a foreign language and scraping a living somehow, but that wasn't what she wanted. It wasn't what she had worked and studied for, and so she tried to ignore the feeling of dread that lodged in her stomach as she sent out her CV and searched in earnest for a university which might hire her. She had always known this time would come. She didn't talk about it to Gordon. Why should she? It was her life, her career, her responsibility. She would make her plans, and then she would tell him.

An offer came from a university in upstate New York. It wasn't brilliant, but it was better than she'd expected: a heavy teaching schedule, but with a chance of continuing her own research.

She told Gordon about it over dinner in a Mexican restaurant.

'It sounds good, just right for you,' he said, nodding.

'It's not perfect. And it probably won't last. I can't count on more than a year.'

'You're good,' he said. 'They'll see that. You'll get tenure.'

'Maybe I won't want it. I might hate it there.'

'Don't be silly.' He looked so calm and unmoved that Tess felt herself begin to panic. Didn't he care? Could he really let her go so easily? She crunched down hard on a tortilla chip and almost missed his next words. '. . . scout around,' he was saying. 'If I can't find anything in Watertown, there must be other cities close enough that we could at least have weekends together.'

She stared, disbelieving. 'You'd quit your job? You'd move across the country just because I'm . . .'

'Why not?'

'Your job . . .'

'I'm not in love with my job,' he said.

Tess looked into his eyes and felt herself falling. She said, 'Upstate New York is not the most exciting place –'

'They need accountants there just like everywhere else,' he said. 'I'll find a job. I'm good. Don't you believe me?' He grinned at her with that easy arrogance she'd always found paradoxically both irritating and attractive.

'Are you sure?' she asked.

'I'm sure about this: I'm not letting you go without a fight. If you're not sure about me, better say so now, and we can start fighting.' He grinned again, and, beneath the table, gripped her knees between his. 'But I'm going to win.'

Six months later they were living together in a small, rented house in Watertown, New York. But although living together, they saw less of each other than they had in New Orleans. Unable to find a job actually in Watertown, Gordon spent at least three hours on the road every day, travelling to and from work. He left in the mornings while Tess still slept, and returned, exhausted, in time for a late dinner and then bed. It was a very different life they led from the one they'd known in New Orleans. They had left behind all those restaurant meals, the easy socializing in French Quarter bars, the flirtations with other people, the long, sultry evenings of doing very little in the open air. The days this far north were short, the nights long and cold. Because Tess didn't like to cook, and Gordon had time for it only on the weekends, they ate a lot of frozen convenience foods, omelettes, and sandwiches. They watched a lot of television, complaining about it and apologizing to each other. They planned to take up hobbies, learn sports, join local organizations, but when the weekends came almost always they spent the two days at home, in bed, together.

Her own happiness surprised Tess. She had always believed that she would feel suffocated if she lived with a man, but now whenever Gordon was out of the house she missed him. Being with him, whether talking, making love, or simply staring like twin zombies at the flickering screen, was all she wanted when she wasn't working. She couldn't believe that she had imagined herself content with so little for so long – to have shared Gordon with another woman without jealousy. She knew she would be jealous, now, if Gordon had another lover, but she also knew she had nothing to worry about. She had changed, and so had he. When he asked her to marry him she didn't even hesitate. She knew what she wanted.

Within four months of the marriage Tess was pregnant.

It wasn't planned – and yet it wasn't an accident, either. She had been careful for too many years to make such a simple mistake, and in Gordon's silence was his part of the responsibility. Without a word spoken, in one shared moment, they had decided. At least, they had decided not to decide, to leave it to fate for once. And afterwards Tess was terrified, waking in the middle of the night to brood on the mistake she was making, wondering, almost until the very last month, if she couldn't manage to have an abortion, after all.

Gordon did everything he could to make things easier for her. Since he couldn't actually have the baby for her, he devoted himself to her comfort. And except for the physical unpleasantness of being pregnant, and the middle of the night terrors, Tess sometimes thought, as she basked in the steady glow of Gordon's attentive love, that this might be the happiest time of her life.

In the months before the baby was born they decided that Gordon's continuing to commute to work wouldn't be possible. Instead, he would set up on his own as an accountant, and work from home. It might be difficult for the first few years, but Gordon had a few investments here and there, and at a pinch they could scrape by on Tess's salary. Gordon said, with his usual self-confidence, that he could make far more money self-employed than anyone ever did as an employee, and Tess believed him. Things would work out.

Her labour was long and difficult. When at last the baby was placed in her arms Tess looked down at it, feeling exhausted and detached, wondering what this little creature had to do with her. She was glad when Gordon took it away from her. Lying back against the pillows she watched her husband.

His face changed, became softer. Tess recognized that rapturous, melting expression because she had seen it occasionally, during sex. She had never seen him look at anyone else like that. She burst into tears.

Gordon was beside her immediately, pushing the baby at

her. But she didn't want the baby. She only wanted Gordon, although she couldn't stop crying long enough to tell him. He held her as she held the baby, and gradually his presence calmed her. After all, the baby was *theirs*. She and Gordon belonged to each other more certainly now than ever before. No longer merely a couple, they were now a family. She knew she should be happy.

She tried to be happy, and sometimes she was, but this baby girl, called Lexi (short for Alexandra), made her feel not only love, but also fear and frustration and pain. Motherhood was not as instinctive as she had believed it would be, for Gordon was clearly better at it than she was, despite her physical equipment. Breast-feeding, which Tess had confidently expected to enjoy, was a disaster. No one had told her, and she had never dreamed, that it would *hurt*. And her suffering was in vain. Lexi didn't thrive until they put her on the bottle. Watching Gordon giving Lexi her late-night feed while she was meant to be sleeping, Tess tried not to feel left out.

It was a relief, in a way, to be able to go back to work after six weeks: back to her own interests, to her students and colleagues, doing the things she knew she was good at. But it wasn't quite the same, for she missed Lexi when she wasn't around. Always, now, she felt a worrying tug of absence. For all the problems, she couldn't wish Lexi away. She only wished that loving Lexi could be as simple and straightforward as loving Gordon. If only she could explain herself to Lexi, she thought, and Lexi explain herself to Tess – if only they shared a language.

When she said this to Gordon one evening after Lexi had been put to bed, he laughed.

'She'll be talking soon enough, and then it'll be why? why? why? all the time, and demanding toys and candy and clothes. Right now, life is simple. She cries when she wants to have her diaper changed, or she wants to be fed, or she wants to be burped or cuddled. Then she's happy.'

'But you have to figure out what she wants,' Tess said. 'She can't tell you – that's my point. And if you do the wrong thing, she just goes on crying and getting more and more unhappy. I'm no more complex than Lexi, really. I have the same sorts of needs. But I can tell you what I want. If I started crying now, you'd probably think I wanted my dinner. But what I really want is a cuddle.'

He looked at her tenderly, and left his chair to join her on the couch. He kissed her affectionately.

She kissed him more demandingly, but he didn't respond.

'You'll have to do better than that,' she said. 'Or I'll start crying.'

'I was thinking about dinner.'

'Forget about dinner. Why don't you check to see if my diapers need changing?'

He laughed. Maybe he laughed too loudly, because a moment later, like a response, came Lexi's wail.

'Leave her,' said Tess. 'She'll fall back to sleep.'

They sat tensely, holding each other, waiting for this to happen. Lexi's cries became louder and more urgent.

Tess sighed. The moment had passed, anyway. 'I'll go,' she said. 'You fix dinner.'

Time alone with Gordon was what Tess missed most. Their desires, and the opportunity to make love, seldom meshed. As Lexi approached her first birthday she seemed to spend even more time awake and demanding attention. This affected not only her parents' relationship, but also Gordon's fledgling business. He was floundering, distracted by the demands of fatherhood, unable to put the time and energy he needed into building up a list of clients. Time was all he needed, Tess thought, and he must have that time. She thought it all through before approaching him about it, but she was certain that he would agree with her. He would be reasonable, as he always was. She didn't expect an argument.

'Day-care!' he repeated, pronouncing it like an obscenity. 'Leave Lexi in some crummy nursery? Are you kidding?'

'Why are you so sure it would be crummy? I'm not proposing we look for the cheapest place we can find. Of course we'll look around and see what's available, and choose the best we can afford.'

'But why?'

'Because there's no way we can afford a full-time babysitter, you know that.'

'We don't need a full-time babysitter. We've got me.'

'That's what I mean. You're not being paid to look after

Lexi, but while you're taking care of her you can't make a living.'

He stared at her. She couldn't read his expression; he was miles away from her. 'I see. I've had my chance, and I've failed, so now I have to get a real job.'

'No!' She clutched his hand, then lowered her voice. 'For heaven's sake, Gordon, I'm not criticizing you. And I'm not saying you should go to work for some company . . . I believe in you. Everything you said about being able to make a lot of money in a few years, I'm sure that's true. I know you'll make a success of it. Only . . . you need time. You can't be out meeting people, or writing letters, or balancing books if you have to keep breaking off to get Lexi her rattle. Your work needs attention just as much as she does . . . you have to be able to really commit yourself to it.'

'You're right,' he said in his usual, reasonable tone. He sighed, and Tess's heart lifted as he said, 'I've been thinking about it a lot, and coming to the same conclusion. Well, not quite the same conclusion. You're right that I can't get much work done while I'm looking after Lexi. Weekends aren't enough. But why do we have to pay someone else to look after Lexi? We can manage ourselves – we just need to be a little more flexible. We could divide up the week between us. You don't have classes on Tuesdays and Thursdays. If you stayed home then, and took responsibility for the weekends, too – why are you shaking your head?'

'Just because I don't have classes on Tuesdays and Thursdays doesn't mean I don't have work to do. I have to be around to supervise, and advise, and there's my research. When am I ever going to get my book written if I don't have some time to myself? We can't manage by ourselves. There's no shame in that. It's why day-care centres exist. We both have to make a living, and for that we need –'

'What about what Lexi needs?'

'Gordon, she'll get plenty of attention, we're not going to deprive her of anything –'

'We're going to deprive ourselves, though.' He was almost vibrating with intensity. 'Look, one of the greatest experiences in the world is bringing up a child. Teaching her, watching her change and grow every day. I don't want to miss out on that.

Maybe in a couple of years, but not now. We can manage. So what if we're not rich? There are things more important than money and careers. If you spent more time with her yourself you'd know what I mean.'

'You think I don't spend enough time with her?' Tess said quietly.

'I didn't say that.'

'But it's what you think. You think I'm selfish, or that my job is more important to me. It's not that. I love Lexi very much. I love her as much as you do. But I won't – I can't – let her absorb me. I miss her whenever I'm away from her, but I know I can't let my whole life revolve around her. You can't hold on to her forever. Eventually she'll have to grow up and leave us.'

'For God's sake, she's not even a year old! You're talking like I'm trying to stop her from going to college or something.'

'She may be a baby, but she's still a person. She has a life apart from you and me – she has to. And so do we. Not just individually, but as a couple. Or aren't we a couple anymore? Are we only Lexi's parents? I *miss* you, Gordon; I feel like –' She stopped, because if she said anything more she knew she would be crying.

'Let's go to bed,' Gordon said, not looking at her. 'Let's not argue. We'll talk about it later.'

They went to bed and made love and, for a little while, Tess felt they had reached an understanding, had confirmed the love they still had for each other.

But then the nightmare came.

Lying in bed, drowsily aware of Gordon's close, sleeping warmth, Tess heard the window fly open. When she opened her eyes she saw, as she had known she would, the familiar, bone-white head of the mare staring in at her, waiting for her.

Her heart sank. I won't move, she thought. I won't go. I will wake myself. But she struggled in vain to open her eyes, or to close them, or even to turn her head so that the creature would be out of her sight. She felt the bitter chill of the winter night flooding the bedroom, and she began to shiver. I must close the window, she thought, and as she thought that, she realized she was getting up, and walking toward the creature who had come for her.

Tess stared at the horse, recognizing the invitation in the toss of the pale head. She tried to refuse it. I don't wish anyone any harm, she thought. I love my daughter. I love my husband. I don't want you. Go away.

But she could not wake, or speak, or do anything but walk in slow, somnambulist fashion towards the window, outside of which the nightmare ran in place on the wind.

I don't want to hurt anyone – I won't! Oh, please, let me wake!

But it was her own body which carried her, despite her mental protests, to the window and onto the sill. And as she struggled against the dream, almost crying with frustration, she flung herself through the open window, into the cold night, upon the nightmare's back.

And then she was clinging desperately to the creature's neck, feeling herself slipping on its icy back, as it mounted the sky. This ride was nothing like the last one. She was terrified, and she knew she was in imminent danger of falling, if not of being thrown. Whatever she had once known of riding had vanished. The muscles in her thighs ached, and the cold had numbed her fingers. She didn't think she would be able to hang on for very long, particularly not if the mare continued to leap and swerve and climb so madly. Closing her eyes, Tess tried to relax, to let instinct take over. She pressed her cheek against the mare's neck and breathed in the smell of blood. Choking back her revulsion, she struggled to sit upright, despite the pressure of the wind. Neck muscles knotted and moved within her embrace, and the mare's long head turned back, one wild eye rolling to look at her.

Tess felt herself slipping, sliding inexorably down. Unless the mare slowed her pace she would fall, she thought. She struggled to keep her grip on the creature's twisting neck, and because she still could not speak, sent one final, pleading look at the mare to ask for mercy. And just before the nightmare threw her, their eyes met, and Tess understood. Within the nightmare's eye she saw her daughter's cold, blue gaze: judgemental, selfish, pitiless.

Jamie's Grave

Mary sat at the kitchen table, a cup of tea gone cold by her left hand, and listened to the purring of the electric clock on the wall.

The house was clean and the larder well-stocked. She had done the laundry and read her library books and it was too wet for gardening. She had baked a cake yesterday and this wasn't her day for making bread. She had already phoned Clive twice this week and could think of no excuse to phone again. Once she might have popped across the road to visit Jen, but she had been getting the feeling that her visits were no longer so welcome. There had been a time when Jen was grateful for Mary's company, a time when she had been lonely, too, but now Jen had her own baby to care for, and whenever Mary went over there – no matter what Jen said – Mary couldn't help feeling that she was intruding.

She looked at the clock again. In twenty minutes she could start her walk to the school.

Clive said she should get a job. He was right, and not just for the money. Mary knew she would be happier doing something useful. But what sort of job could she get? She had no experience, and in this Wiltshire village there was not much scope for employment. Other mothers already held the school jobs of crossing-guard and dinner-lady, and what other employer would allow her to fit her working hours to those when Jamie was in school? She wouldn't let someone else look after Jamie – no job was worth that. Her son was all she had in the world, all she cared about. If she could have kept him home with her and taught him herself, instead of having to send him to school, Mary knew she would have been perfectly content. She had been so happy when she had her baby, she hadn't even minded losing Clive. But babies

72

grew up, and grew away. Jen was going to find that out in a few years.

Mary rose and walked to the sink, poured away the tea, rinsed and set the cup on the draining-board. She took her jacket from the hook beside the door and put it on, straightening her collar and fluffing her hair without a mirror. The clock gave a dim, clicking buzz, and it was time to leave.

The house where Mary lived with her son was one of six bungalows on the edge of a Wiltshire village, close enough to London, as well as to Reading, to be attractive to commuters. After the grimy, cramped house in Islington, the modern bungalow with its large garden and fresh country air had seemed the perfect place to settle down and raise a family. But while Mary had dreamed of being pregnant again, Clive had been dreaming of escape. The house for him was not a cosy nest, but a gift to Mary and a sop to his conscience as he left.

Five minutes leisurely walk brought the village school in sight. Mary saw the children tumbling out the door like so many brightly-coloured toys, and she reached the gate at the same moment as Jamie from the other side.

Jamie was involved with his friends, laughing and leaping around. His eyes flickered over her, taking in her presence but not acknowledging it, and when she hugged him she could feel his reluctance to return to her and leave the exciting, still-new world of school.

He pulled away quickly, and wouldn't let her hold his hand as they walked. But he talked to her, needing to share his day's experiences, giving them to her in excited, disconnected bursts of speech. She tried to make sense of what he said, but she couldn't always. He used strange words – sometimes in a different accent – picked up from the other children, and the events he described might have been imaginary, or related to schoolyard games rather than to reality. Once they had spent all their time together, in the same world. She had understood him better then, had understood him perfectly before he could even talk.

She looked at the little stranger walking beside her, and caught a sudden resemblance to Clive in one of his gestures. It struck her, unpleasantly, that he was well on his way to becoming a man.

'Would you like to help me make some biscuits this afternoon?' she asked.

He shook his head emphatically. 'I got to dig,' he said.

'Dig? In the garden? Oh, darling, it's so wet!'

He frowned and tilted back his head. 'Isn't.'

'I know it's stopped raining, but the ground . . .' Mary sighed, imagining the mess. 'Why not wait until tomorrow? It might be nicer then, the sun might come out, it might be much nicer to dig in the garden tomorrow.'

'I dig tomorrow, too,' Jamie said. He began to chant, swinging his arms stiffly as he marched, 'Dig! Dig! Dig!'

During the summer they had taken a trip to the seashore and Mary had bought him a plastic shovel. He had enjoyed digging in the soft sand, then, but had not mentioned it since. Mary wondered what had brought it back to mind – was it a chance word from his teacher, or an enthusiasm caught from one of the other children? – and realized she would probably never know.

He found his shovel in the toy chest, flinging other toys impatiently across the room. Not even the offer of a piece of cake could distract him. He suffered himself to be changed into other clothes, twitching impatiently all the while. When he had rushed out into the garden, Mary stood by the window and watched.

The plastic shovel, so useful for digging at the beach, was less efficient in the dense soil of the garden. As Jamie busily applied himself, the handle suddenly broke off in his hands. He looked for a moment almost comically shocked; then he began to howl.

Mary rushed out to comfort him, but he would not be distracted by her promises of other pleasures. All he wanted was to dig, and he would only be happy if she gave him a new shovel. Finally, she gave him one of her gardening spades, and left him to it.

She felt rejected, going into the house and closing the door, staying away from the windows. He didn't want her to hover, and she had no reason to fear for his safety in their own garden. Had she waited all day just for this?

The next day, Saturday, was worse. Mary looked forward to Saturdays now more fervently than she ever had as a child. On

Jamie's Grave

Saturdays she had Jamie to herself all day. They played games, she read him stories, they went for walks and had adventures. But that Saturday all Jamie wanted to do was dig.

She stood in the garden with him, staring at the vulnerable white bumps of his knees, and then at his stubborn, impatient face. 'Why, darling? Why do you want to dig?'

He shrugged and looked at the ground, clutching the spade as if she might take it away from him.

'Jamie, please answer me. I asked you a question. Why are you digging?'

'I might find something,' he said, after a reluctant pause. Then he looked at her, a slightly shifty, sideways look. 'If I find something . . . can I keep it?'

'May I,' she corrected automatically. Her spirits lifted as she imagined a treasure hunt, a game she might play with him. Already, her thoughts were going to her old costume jewellery, and coins . . . 'Probably,' she said. 'Almost certainly, anything you find in our garden would be yours to keep. But there are exceptions. If it is something *very* valuable, like gold, it belongs to the Queen by right, so you would have to get her permission.'

'Not gold,' he said scornfully.

'No?'

'No. Not treasure.' He shook his head and then he smiled and looked with obvious pride at his small excavation. 'I'm digging a grave,' he said. 'You know what they do with graves? They put dead people inside. I might find one. I might find a skellington!'

'Skeleton,' she said without thinking.

'Skeleton, yeah! Wicked, man! Skellyton!' He flopped down and resumed his digging.

Feeling stunned, Mary went inside.

'And that's what you phoned me about?' said Clive.

'He's your son, too, you know.'

'I know he's my son. And I like to hear what he's doing. But you know I like to sleep in. You could have picked a better time than early on a Saturday morning to fill me in on his latest game.'

'It's not a game.'

'Well, what is it, then? A real grave? A real skeleton?'

'It's morbid!'

'It's natural. Look, he probably saw something on television, or heard something at school . . .'

'When I was little, I was afraid of dead things,' Mary said.

'You think that's healthier? What do you want me to say, Mary? It'll pass, this craze. He'll forget about it and go on to something else. If you make a big deal about it, he'll keep on, to get a reaction. Don't make him think it's wrong. Want me to come over tomorrow and take him out somewhere? That's the quickest way to get his mind on to other things.'

Mary thought of how empty the house was when her son was gone. At least now, although he was preoccupied, she was aware of his presence nearby. And, as usual, she reacted against her ex-husband. She was shaking her head before he had even finished speaking.

'No, not tomorrow. I had plans for tomorrow. I –'

'Next weekend. He could come here, spend the night –'

'Oh, Clive, he's so young!'

'Mary, you can't have it both ways. He's my son, too. You can't complain that I take no interest and leave it all to you, and then refuse to let me see him. I do miss him, you know.'

'All right, next weekend. But just one day, not overnight. Please. He's all I have. When he's not here I miss him dreadfully.'

Mary stood by the window watching Jamie dig his grave, and she missed him. She could see him, and she knew that if she rapped on the glass he would look up and see her, but that wasn't enough; it would never be enough. Once, she had been the whole world to him. Now, every day took him farther from her.

She thought of Heather, Jen's little baby. She thought of the solid weight of her in her arms, and that delicious, warm, milky smell of new babies. She remembered how it had felt to hold her, and how she had felt when she had to give her back. She remembered watching Jen nurse her child. The envy which had pierced her. The longing. It wasn't Jen's feelings which made Mary reluctant now to visit her but her own jealousy. She wanted a baby.

She went on standing by the window for nearly an hour,

holding herself and grieving for the child she didn't have, while Jamie dug a grave.

For lunch Mary made cauliflower soup and toasted cheese sandwiches. Ignoring his protests that he could wash his own hands, she marched Jamie to the bathroom and scrubbed and scrubbed until all the soil beneath his fingernails was gone.

Twenty minutes later, a soup moustache above his upper lip, Jamie said, 'I got to go back to my digging.'

Inside, she cried a protest, but she remembered Clive's words. Maybe he did want a reaction from her. Maybe he would be less inclined to dig a grave if his mother seemed to favour it. So, with a false, bright smile she cheered him on, helped him back into his filthy pullover and wellies, and waved vigorously from the back door, as if seeing him off on an expedition.

'Come back in when you get cold,' she said. 'Or if you get hungry . . .'

She turned on Radio Four, got out her knitting and worked on the sweater which was to be a Christmas present for her sister in Scotland. She worked steadily for about an hour. Then the panic took her.

A falling-elevator sensation in her stomach, and then the cold. It was a purely visceral, wordless, objectless fear. Her shaking fingers dropped stitches and then dropped the knitting, and she lurched clumsily to her feet.

If anything happened to Jamie she would never forgive herself. If she was too late, if anything had happened to him –

She knew he was safe in the back garden, where there was nothing to hurt him. She knew she'd had this experience before, and there had never been anything threatening her son. Logic made no impact on the fear.

He was so fragile, he was so young, and the world was so dangerous. How could she have let him out of her sight for even a moment?

She ran to the back door and out, cursing herself.

She saw his bright yellow boots first. He was lying flat on the ground, on his stomach, and she couldn't see his head. It must have been hanging over the edge, into the hole he had dug.

'Jamie!' She didn't want to alarm him, but his name came out as a shriek of terror.

He didn't move.

Mary fell on the ground beside him and caught his body up in her arms. She was so frightened she couldn't breathe. But he was breathing; he was warm.

Jamie gave a little grunt and his eyelids fluttered. Then he was gazing up at her, dazed and sleepy-looking.

'Are you all right?' she demanded, although it was clear to her, now the panic had subsided, that he was fine.

'What?' he said groggily.

'Oh, you silly child! What do you mean by lying down out here, when the ground's so cold and wet . . . you'll catch your death . . . if you were tired, you should have come in. What a silly, to work so hard you had to lie down and take a nap!' She hugged him to her, and for once he seemed content to be held so, rubbing his dirty face against her sweater and clinging.

They rocked together in the moist grey air and country silence for a time, until Jamie gave a deep, shuddering sigh.

'What is it?'

'Hungry,' he said. His voice was puzzled.

'Of course you are, poor darling, after so much hard work. It's not time for tea yet, but come inside and I'll give you a glass of milk and a biscuit. Would you like that?'

He seemed utterly exhausted, and she carried him inside. Although he had claimed to be hungry, he drank only a little milk and seemed without the energy even to nibble a biscuit. Mary settled him on the couch in front of the television, and when she came back a few minutes later she found him asleep.

After she had put Jamie to bed, Mary went back to the garden to look at his excavation.

It was a hole more round than square, no more than a foot across and probably not more than two foot deep. As Mary crouched down to look into it she saw another, smaller hole, within. She didn't think Jamie had made it; it seemed something quite different. She thought it looked like a tunnel, or the entrance to some small animal's burrow. She thought of blind, limbless creatures tunnelling through the soft earth, driven by needs and guided by senses she couldn't know, and she shuddered. She thought of worms, but this tunnel was much too large. She had not been aware of moles in the garden, but possibly Jamie had accidentally uncovered evidence of one.

She picked up the spade which Jamie had abandoned, and used it to scoop earth back into the hole. Although she began casually, she soon began to work with a purpose, and her heart pounded as she pushed and shovelled furiously, under a pressure she could not explain, to fill it in, cover up the evidence, make her garden whole again.

Finally she stood and tamped the earth down beneath her feet. With the grass gone, the marks of digging were obvious. She had done the best she could, but it wasn't good enough. It wasn't the same; it couldn't be.

As she walked back into the house, Mary heard a brief, faint scream, and immediately ran through to Jamie's room.

He was sitting up in bed, staring at her with wide-open yet unseeing eyes.

'Darling, what's wrong?'

She went to him, meaning to hug him, but her hands were covered with dirt from the hole; she couldn't touch him.

'What's that?' he asked, voice blurred with sleep, turning towards the window.

Mary looked and saw with a shock that the window was open, if only by a few inches. She didn't remember opening it, and she was sure it was too heavy for Jamie to lift by himself.

'I'll close it,' she said, and went to do so. Her hands looked black against the white-painted sash, and she saw bits of earth crumble and fall away. She felt as disturbed by that as if it really had been grave-dirt, and felt she had to sweep it up immediately.

When she returned to the bed Jamie was lying down, apparently asleep. Careful not to touch him with her dirty hands, she bent down and kissed him, hovering close for a time to feel the warmth of his peaceful breathing against her face. She loved him so much she could not move or speak.

In the morning Jamie was subdued, so quiet that Mary worried he might be getting ill, and kept feeling his face for some evidence of a fever. His skin was cool, though, and he showed no other signs of disease. He said nothing more about wanting to dig, nothing about graves or skeletons – that craze appeared to have vanished as suddenly and inexplicably as it had arrived.

It was a wet and windy day, and Mary was glad Jamie didn't want to play in the garden. He seemed worried about something, though, following her around the house and demanding her attention. Mary didn't mind. In fact, she cherished this evidence that she was still needed.

When she asked what he wanted for his tea, the answer came promptly. 'Two beefburgers. Please.'

'Two!'

'Yes. Two, please.'

'I think one will be enough, really, Jamie. You never have two. If you are very hungry, I could make extra chips.'

He had that stubborn look on his face, the look that reminded her of his father. 'Extra chips, too. But please may I have two beefburgers.'

She was certain he wouldn't be able to eat them both. 'Very well,' she said. 'After you've eaten your first beefburger, if you still want another one, I'll make it then.'

'I want two. I know I want two! I want two now!'

'Calm down, Jamie,' she said quietly. 'You shall have two. But one at a time. That's the way we'll do it.'

He sulked, and he played with his food when she served it, but he did manage to eat all the beefburger, and then immediately demanded a second, forgetting, this time, to say 'please'.

'You haven't eaten all your chips,' she pointed out.

He glared. 'You didn't *say* I had to eat all my chips first. You *said* if I ate one burger I could have another – you *said*.'

'I know I said it, lovey, but the chips are part of your dinner, too, and if you're really hungry –'

'You *said!*'

His lower lip trembled, and there were tears in his eyes. How could she deny him? She couldn't bear his unhappiness, even though she was quite certain that he wasn't hungry and wouldn't be able to eat any more meat.

'All right, my darling,' she said, and left her own unfinished meal to grow cold while she went back to the cooker. Clive would have been firm with him, she thought, and wondered if she had been wrong to give in. Maybe Jamie had wanted her to say no. The thought wearied her. It was too complicated. He had asked for food, and she would give it to him.

Jamie fidgeted in his chair when she put the food before him, and would not meet her eyes. He asked if he could watch TV while he ate. Curious, she agreed. 'Just bring your plate in to me when you've finished.'

A suspiciously few minutes later, Jamie returned with his plate. The second beefburger had vanished without a trace. There were only a few smashed peas and stray chips on the plate. Jamie went back to watch television while Mary did the washing-up. Almost immediately, above the noise of the television, she heard the back door open and close quietly. When she rejoined Jamie he seemed happier than he had all day, freed of some burden. They played together happily – if a little more rowdily than Mary liked – until his bedtime.

But after she had tucked him into bed, Mary went out into the dark garden. In the gloom the whiteness of a handkerchief gave off an almost phosphorescent glow, drawing her across the lawn to the site of Jamie's excavation.

Like some sort of offering, the beefburger had been placed on a clean white handkerchief and laid on the ground, on the bare patch. Mary stared at it for a moment, and then went back inside.

Mary usually woke to the sounds of Jamie moving about, but on Monday morning for once she had to wake him. He was pale and groggy, with greenish shadows beneath his eyes. But when she suggested he could stay home and spend the day resting in bed, he rallied and became almost frantic in his determination to go to school. He did seem better, out in the fresh air and away from the house, but she continued to worry about him after she had left him at school. Her thoughts led her to the doctor's. She didn't mind waiting until all the scheduled patients had been seen; she paged through old magazines, with nothing better to do.

Dr Abden was a brisk, no-nonsense woman who had raised two children to safe and successful adulthood; Mary was able to trust her maternal wisdom enough to tell her the whole story of Jamie's grave.

'Perhaps he found his skeleton and didn't like it so much,' said Dr Abden. 'There, don't look so alarmed, my dear! I didn't mean a human skeleton, of course. You mentioned seeing something like a tunnel . . . isn't it possible that your son came across a mole – a dead one? That first encounter with death can be a disturbing one. Perhaps he thought he killed it with his little shovel and so is guiltily trying to revive it . . . Perhaps he doesn't realize it is dead, and imagines he can make a pet of it. If you can get him to confide in you, I'm sure you'll be able to set his mind at rest. Of course, he may have forgotten the whole thing after a day at school.'

Mary hoped that would be the case, but it was obvious as soon as she saw him that afternoon that his secret still worried him. He rejected all her coaxing offers of help, pushing her away, hugging his fear to himself, uneasy in her presence. So Mary waited, kept the distance he seemed to want, and watched.

He was sneaking food outside. Biscuits, bits of chocolate, an apple . . . she meant to let him continue, but at the thought of the mess eggs and baked beans would make in his pockets, she caught his hand before he could transfer food from his plate to his lap.

'Darling, you don't have to do that,' she said. 'I'll give you a plate, and you can put the food on that and take it out to your little friend. Just eat your own meal first.'

His pale face went paler. 'You know?'

Mary hesitated. 'I know . . . you're upset about something. And I know you've been leaving food outside. Now, why don't you tell Mummy what's going on, and I'll help you.'

Emotions battled on his face; then, surrender.

'He's hungry,' Jamie said plaintively. 'He's so hungry, so, so hungry. I keep giving him food, but it's not right . . . he won't eat it. I don't know what he . . . I don't want . . . I can't . . . I'm giving him everything and he won't eat. What does he eat, Mummy? What *else* does he eat?'

Mary imagined a mole's tiny corpse, Jamie thrusting food beneath its motionless snout. 'Maybe he doesn't eat anything,' she said.

'No, he has to! If you're alive, you have to eat.'

'Well, Jamie, maybe he's dead.'

She half-expected some outburst, an excited protest against that idea, but Jamie shook his head, an oddly mature and thoughtful expression on his face. He had obviously considered this possibility before. 'No, he's not dead. I thought, I thought when I found him in my grave, I thought he was dead, but then he wasn't. He isn't dead.'

'Who isn't dead? What is this you're talking about, Jamie? Is it an animal?'

He looked puzzled. 'You don't know?'

She shook her head. 'Will you show him to me, darling?'

Jamie looked alarmed. He shook his head and began to tremble. Mary knelt beside his chair and put her arms around him, holding him close, safe and tight.

'It's all right,' she said. 'Mummy's here. It's all right.'

When he had calmed, she thought to distract him, but he returned to the subject of feeding this unknown creature.

'Well,' said Mary, 'if he's not eating the food you give him, maybe he doesn't need to be fed. He might find his own food – animals usually do, you know, except for pets and babies.'

'He's like a baby.'

'How is he like a baby? What does he look like?'

'I don't know. I don't remember now. I can't. He doesn't look like anything – not like anything except himself.'

It was only then that it occurred to Mary that there might be no animal at all, not even a dead mole. This creature Jamie had found was probably completely imaginary. That was why he couldn't show it to her.

'He can probably find his own food,' Mary said.

But this idea obviously bothered Jamie, who began to fidget. 'He needs me.'

'How do you know that? Did he tell you? Can't he tell you what sort of food he wants, then?'

Jamie shrugged, nodded, then shook his head. 'I have to get something for him.'

'But he must have managed on his own before you found him –'

'He was all right before,' Jamie agreed. 'But he needs me now. I found him, so now I have to take care of him. But . . . he won't eat. I keep trying and trying, but he won't take the food. And he's hungry. What can I give him, Mummy? What can I give him to eat?'

Mary stopped trying to be reasonable, then, and let herself enter his fantasy.

'Don't worry, darling,' she said. 'We'll find something for

your little friend – we'll try everything in the kitchen if we have to!'

With Jamie's help, Mary prepared a whole trayful of food: a saucer of milk and one of sweetened tea; water-biscuits spread with peanut butter; celery tops and chopped carrots; lettuce leaves; raisins; plain bread, buttered bread, and bread spread with honey. As she carried the tray outside, Mary wondered what sort of pests this would attract, then dismissed it as unimportant. She pretended to catch sight of Jamie's imaginary friend.

'Oh, we've got something he likes here,' she said. 'Just look at him smacking his lips!'

Jamie gave her a disapproving look. 'You don't see him.'

'How do you know? Isn't that him over there by the hedge?'

'If you saw him, you'd probably scream. And, anyway, he hasn't *got* lips.'

'What does he look like? Is he so frightening?'

'It doesn't matter,' Jamie said.

'Shall I put the tray down here?'

He nodded. The playfulness and interest he had shown in the kitchen had vanished, and he was worried again. He sighed. 'If he doesn't eat this . . .'

'If he doesn't, there's plenty more in the kitchen we can try,' said Mary.

'He's so hungry,' Jamie murmured sadly.

He was concerned, when they went back inside, about locking the house. This was not a subject which had ever interested him before, but now he followed Mary around, and she demonstrated that both front and back doors were secure, and all the windows – particularly the window in his room – were shut and locked.

'There are other ways for things to get in, though,' he said.

'No, of course not, darling.'

'How do my dreams get in, then?'

'Your dreams?' She crouched beside him on the bedroom floor and stroked his hair. 'Dreams don't come in from the outside, darling. Dreams are inside, in your head.'

'They're already inside?'

'They aren't real, darling. They're imaginary. They aren't real and solid like I am, or like you are, they're just . . . like thoughts. Like make-believe. And they go away when you're awake.'

'Oh,' he said. She couldn't tell what he thought, or if her words had comforted him. She hugged him close until he wriggled to be free, and then she put him to bed.

She checked on him twice during the night, and both times he appeared to be sleeping soundly. Yet in the morning, again, he had the darkened eyes and grogginess of one who'd had a disturbed night.

She thought about taking him to the doctor instead of to school, but the memory of her conversation with Dr Abden stopped her. This was something she had to cope with herself. There was nothing physically wrong with Jamie. His sleeplessness was obviously the result of worry, and the doctor had already reminded her that it was her duty, as his mother, to set his mind at rest. If only he would tell her what was wrong!

That afternoon Jamie was again subdued, quiet and good. Mary actually preferred him like this, but because such behaviour wasn't normal for him, she worried even while she appreciated his nearness. They sat together playing games and looking through his books, taking turns reading to each other. Later, she left the dishes to soak in the sink and watched her son as he sat with his crayons and his colouring book, wondering what went on in his mind.

'Has your little friend gone away, to find food somewhere else?' she asked.

Jamie shook his head.

'We could put some more food out for him, you know. I don't mind. Anything you like.'

Jamie was silent for a while, and then he said, 'He doesn't need food.'

'Doesn't he? That's very unusual. What does he live on?'

Jamie stopped colouring, the crayon frozen in his hand. Then he drew a deep, shuddering breath. 'Love,' he said, and began colouring again.

He was no longer worried about the doors and windows, and it was Mary, not Jamie, who prolonged the bedside chat and goodnight kisses, reluctant to leave him alone. He didn't seem afraid, but she was afraid for him, without knowing why.

'Goodnight, my darling,' she said for the fifth or sixth last time, and made herself rise and move away from the bed. 'Sleep well. Call me if you need anything . . . I'll be awake . . .' her voice trailed off. Already, it appeared, he was sleeping. She went out quietly and left his bedroom door ajar. If he made a sound, she would hear it.

She turned the television on low and slumped in a chair before it. She was too tired to think, too distracted to be entertained. She might as well go to bed herself, she thought.

So she turned off the television, tidied up, turned out the lights and checked the doors one last time. On her way to her own bedroom she decided to look in on Jamie, just to reassure herself that all was well.

Pushing the door open let in a swathe of light from the corridor. It fell across the bed, revealing Jamie lying uncovered, half-curled on one side, and not alone.

There was something nestled close to him, in the crook of his arm; something grey and wet-looking, a featureless lump about the size of a loaf of bread; something like a gigantic slug pressed against his pyjama-covered chest and bare neck.

Horror might have frozen her – she couldn't have imagined coping with something like that in the garden or on the kitchen floor – but fear for her son propelled her forward. As she moved, the soft grey body rippled, turning, and it looked at Mary. For a face there was only a slightly flattened area with two round, black eyes and no mouth.

In her haste and terror Mary almost fell onto the bed. She caught hold of the thing and pulled it off her son, sobbing with revulsion.

She had expected it to be as cold and slimy as it looked, perhaps even insubstantial enough that the harsh touch of her hands could destroy it. In fact, it was warm and solid and surprisingly heavy. And it smelled like Jamie. Not like Jamie now, but like Jamie as a baby: that sweet, milky scent which made her melt inside. Like Jen's baby. Like every helpless, harmless newborn. She closed her eyes, remembering.

Mary pressed her face against the soft flesh and inhaled. No skin had ever been so deliciously, silkenly smooth. Her lips moved against it. She could never have enough of touching and kissing it; she wished she was a cat and could lick her baby clean a hundred times a day.

Responding, it nuzzled back, head butting at her blindly, and she unbuttoned her blouse. Her breasts felt sore and heavy with milk, and she longed for the relief of nursing.

Somewhere nearby a child was crying, a sound that rasped at her nerves and distracted her. Someone was tugging at her clothes, at her arm, and crying, 'Mummy,' until she had, finally, to open her eyes.

A little boy with a pale, tear-stained face gazed up at her. 'Don't,' he said. 'Don't, Mummy.'

She knew who he was – he was her son. But he seemed somehow threatening, and she wrapped her arms more tightly around the creature that she held.

'Go to bed,' she said firmly.

He began to weep, loudly and helplessly.

But that irritated her more, because he wasn't helpless; she knew he wasn't helpless.

'Stop crying,' she said. 'Go to bed. You're all right.' She pushed him away from her with her hip, not daring to let go. But as she looked down she glimpsed something grey and formless lying pressed between her breasts. For just a moment she had a brief, distracting vision of a face without a mouth, always hungry, never satisfied. She thought of an open grave, and she closed her eyes.

'He needs me,' she said.

At last she felt complete. She would never be alone again.

Within the protective circle of her arms, the creature had begun to feed.

The Spirit Cabinet

Frank and Katy Matson had no sooner moved to London than they found a haunted house.

At least, Katy called it haunted. Frank did not, then, believe in ghosts, and his wife's superstitions amused him. He thought it was a cute idea, but he didn't take it seriously, when Katy dragged him away from a discussion of terms with the landlord to exclaim, 'I just saw a man – not a man, but a ghost! In the front room! This house is haunted!'

'Oh, dear, do you really think so? Well, if that's how you feel, I can just say it's not quite what we had in mind . . . '

She grabbed his arm and gave him one of her blazing, slightly near-sighted, looks. 'You will not! We'll take it!'

'But you said –'

'Yes, yes, of course! That's why! I've always wanted to live in a real haunted house, haven't you?'

Frank could not honestly say he had, but Katy's enthusiasm then, as so often, made up for his lack.

'It's perfect, just too, too perfect,' she burbled happily. 'To live in London, in an old, old Victorian house, with our very own, genuine, English ghost! Oh, wait till I write to Melissa – she'll just curl up and die with envy!'

So they rented the house which, leaving aside the question of ghosts, was in fact exactly what they wanted in terms of size, price and location. It was a short-term rental: only three months away from their own house back in Atlanta while Frank attended a company training programme, and Katy explored London.

At least, she had intended to explore London. But that first week, although the weather was mild and sunny, she scarcely budged from the house. London had many charms, but they could not compete with the lure of a real ghost. As soon as Frank had left in the morning Katy began her vigil. She wandered through the house, returning again and again to the front room where she had seen, so briefly before he vanished, the bearded man in an old-fashioned suit. But he did not reappear. As she drifted restlessly through the sparsely furnished rooms, Katy, in her long skirt and gauzy white blouse, looked rather like a ghost herself.

Then, one evening as Katy sat in the front room, an unread book in her lap, listening to the muffled, hollow sound of Frank singing in the bath, something alerted her. Something – a flickering on the edge of her vision – caught her attention. Not stopping to question, she rose and walked to the door, then turned to look back into the room.

Everything had changed. Instead of a well-lit, under-furnished space, she saw before her a shadowy room filled with heavy, dark furniture. The glow of a coal-fire in the grate showed her a small, stocky, bearded man standing very still and staring at her. She had the impression that there were other people in the room, but she found it hard to shift her attention from the man in front of her to look. She had seen him before. He was her ghost.

Katy took a step forward and put out her hand as if to touch him, but she never had the chance. As soon as she moved, everything was gone. The room was once more in her own time: normal, well-lit, familiar, and empty.

Katy closed her eyes, clenched her fists at her side, and smiled, blissfully. It was true. He was real. And he would be back.

That experience gave her the patience she needed. Now she truly believed, and instead of trying to catch her ghost, she was willing to wait for him to catch her, instead.

As she explained to Frank: 'It's no good trying to see him when he doesn't want to be seen. It's not even like he comes to me, but more like I go to him – that he calls me to his time. Well, I told you how the whole room changed! He wasn't coming into our house – he was letting me visit *his*. Oh, I can't wait – I mean, I know I've *got* to wait, but I'm so excited – until it happens again!'

She knew by the way her husband smiled at her explanation that he didn't believe in her ghost. But he didn't disbelieve, either. They had been married very happily for three years, but for all that they shared they still had separate lives. His was made up of computers and sales, vintage cars and airplanes and money. Hers was less material, more fantastic and old-fashioned, built up out of books and movies, dreams and fears and history. Frank could not have lived in Katy's world, but he enjoyed glimpses of it, just as he enjoyed the scent of her perfume and the flash of rings on her slender fingers.

Two days later, on a Saturday morning, Frank was in the kitchen frying bacon and pancakes, and Katy was wandering around in an early morning haze, trying to remember where she had put her sunglasses, and just what it was she wanted them for. As she stepped into the front room, it changed.

Katy froze. She was afraid, not of what had happened, but of what she might do. She was determined, this time, to stay longer and see more of the past, and she couldn't risk ending the miracle by doing something wrong. She moved nothing but her eyes.

Dark: heavy draperies covered the window, and a coal-fire gleamed redly in the grate. There was only one other source of illumination: an oil lamp turned very low, hardly more than glowing through milk-white glass, set on a round table at the far side of the room. There was a lot of furniture in the room, dark, heavy stuff, and people –

The man she had seen twice before was standing in the same place, near the centre of the room, in front of the fire. He was looking in her direction, and there could be no doubt that he saw her. He seemed neither surprised nor frightened by her presence. He looked at her steadily, as if keeping her there by an act of will. Katy held her breath, waiting to see what would happen.

She felt, like a command along her nerves, the impulse to go to him. But she resisted it, afraid that any physical motion would return her abruptly to her own time.

Then he beckoned, extending one, dark-suited arm, fingers curved in towards himself, and she understood that the urge she felt to walk forward was coming from him.

So, hesitantly, Katy took one step. Nothing changed. Still she could feel him willing her forward. Another step, and another. In a moment she would be close enough to touch, but now he nodded at her to stop. His eyes looked straight into hers, telling her something, but she could not read the message. Slowly and deliberately he turned his head, looking toward the window. Katy imitated him, turning her own head, and she saw four or five other people sitting around a table. She couldn't make out any details, not even if they saw her, so she took a step closer.

And found herself blinking in the sudden morning light of a cool, empty room, feeling as if she had just fallen a very great distance in a very short time.

Katy shuddered. For the first time she felt afraid.

Frank listened to her story, keeping an eye on the breakfast preparations. When she had finished he said, 'We could move.'

'Oh, no! Why should we?'

'If you're afraid,' he said gently.

'But I'm not afraid. Well, only for a minute. I guess I just wonder if it's a good idea to live in a haunted house.'

'I thought it was what you wanted,' said Frank. 'If it isn't –'

'It is. It still is, in a way. It's an amazing opportunity. I'd never forgive myself if I ran away. But it worries me a little because I don't know what's happening. I'm not just seeing a ghost – *he's* seeing *me*. I think I'm travelling back in time somehow, back to the Victorian era, or whenever it is. Which is something I've always dreamed of – you know that! – but for it to happen in this way . . . I don't have any control over it. I have to trust him, a stranger. I can only do what he wants me to do.'

'No,' said Frank, as unemphatic and practical as ever. 'That's not exactly it. You can't choose when you go back, but you can choose how to respond. You do have control. You told me that you knew when he wanted you to do something, but you didn't *have* to respond. He lets you know what he wants, and you decide whether or not to do it. He's not controlling you any more than I am when I say, "Let's go down to Windsor today." He's giving you suggestions, not overpowering your will. And you've already figured out that you can come back to our time by making the slightest physical movement of your own. So if you're worried, you know what to do: turn your back. Leave the room. You can always escape. He can't stop you from moving; he can't keep you there.'

Katy gazed at her husband, wondering how much he believed.

Was he simply humouring her? Was this a game they were playing together?

'I wish I could share it with you,' she said. 'I wish you could go there with me.'

'So you don't want to move?'

'I don't want to move. I'm not afraid any more.' She smiled. 'I can't wait to see what happens next!'

But she did have to wait. That was the point. She was waiting on the will of a ghost. This could become a ridiculous obsession, Katy told herself, but she wouldn't let it. She decided to leave the house every day when Frank did, and explore London as she had always intended.

There was so much to see, and so many ways of looking at London, but Katy had her own particular interest now. She was in search of Victorian London. Everywhere she went she wondered if her ghost might have walked down this street, seen that building. Such thoughts seemed to bring him closer. Her reading was chosen with him in mind, too: fat paperback volumes by Trollope, Dickens and Eliot were always tucked into her bag. She wondered if she would be able to learn, from furnishings and clothing, what year she had been enabled to visit, and went to the library to browse through illustrated books and old fashion magazines. One such rainy day Katy found an engraving from 1869 which made her catch her breath. There was something very familiar about it – what did it remind her of? She looked at the title: 'At the Séance'.

Then she understood. *That* was what had happened in the front room of her house back in Victorian times. They were having a séance. That explained the darkness, the people sitting in silence around a table. They must be spiritualists, and the bearded man, the man who saw her, was the medium. As for herself, she was the ghost.

She had to stop herself from laughing out loud in the library. But of course she was a ghost. Why not? Spirits had to come from *somewhere* – why not the future as well as the past? As a woman of the 1980s she was as insubstantial to a man of the 1860s as he was to her. Both were real, but not at the same time. Had any ghost ever felt itself to be a ghost? Ghosts were not the remains of dead people – the whole theological issue could be avoided – ghosts were people living elsewhen. Ghostliness was not a permanent state, not a matter of unquiet souls, but was a matter of perception, the result of passing momentarily through some time and place not your own.

Pleased with herself for figuring it out, Katy began to delve into books about spiritualism, but she found no reflection of her ideas. Certainly the spiritualists of Victorian times never imagined they might be in touch with the living, or the yet-to-be. Their faith was in a contact with the spirits of the departed: the dead could live again, speak again, through them. And as most spirit messages concerned the happy time they were having in the after-life, it seemed that the spirits themselves agreed with the prevailing view that they were dead.

If, in fact, there were any spirits at all. For as Katy read on, even allowing for the bias of modern, rational writers, the history of spiritualism appeared a mass of self-contradictory absurdities, and the most outrageous, and obvious, deceptions. Most mediums were shabby con-artists, deceiving a public eager to believe. She read about mediums who practised simple conjuring tricks, or used their feet like hands; about spirit voices produced by hidden phonographs or a confederate using a speaking-tube from another room; about ghosts made of paper or bits of clothing moved by invisible wires . . .

'But *I'm* no trick,' said Katy to Frank that evening. 'I'm real, and so is he. My medium must have had genuine psychic powers, to be able to make contact with me. Even if he didn't know what he was doing . . . do you see what that means?'

'Tell me in the cab,' said Frank. 'If we don't leave now, we're going to be late for the theatre.'

Katy couldn't even remember what play they had decided on. 'I'm sorry,' she said, feeling guilty. 'This is all I ever talk about these days . . . I know it must be boring for you.'

'I like hearing about it,' Frank said. 'I like knowing what interests you. How else can I share it? If you ever stop talking about him, I'll think the worst: that you're having an affair with that bearded geek.'

'He's *not* a geek!'

'Uh-oh,' said Frank. 'It *is* an affair.'

She laughed and denied it, but she was blushing. Because sometimes it did feel like the build-up to an affair, the way she was always thinking about him, wondering when she would see him again, trying to find out more about him, fantasizing conversations with him.

'He's not my type,' she said. 'I like tall skinny blonds, you know that. Besides, he's dead. It's more like reading a really good novel, but only a few pages at a time. Or like being a detective.'

'OK, Sherlock,' he said. 'Just don't forget your faithful Dr Watson.'

'Maybe next time it happens I could shout, "Watson, I need you!"'

'I'll come running.'

Although part of her cherished the specialness of her experience, Katy would have liked to share it with Frank. It might make the experience less special, but it would make it more real, she thought. And because she felt safer with Frank nearby, she continued to avoid spending much time in the house alone.

She made her next discovery in one of the junkier antique shops of Camden Town, where she had gone to browse among the postcards, china, jewellery and other small bits and pieces which would make nice souvenirs and gifts for friends back home. She couldn't look at anything large or expensive, but as she eased her way around the dusty chairs and ancient tables which made the tiny shop an obstacle course, she found herself noticing a particular piece of furniture. It wasn't particularly attractive, and she couldn't think at first why it had drawn her attention. It was some sort of cabinet or small wardrobe, a squarish box with two doors, standing less than four foot high. Katy moved closer, putting out her hand, and, as she touched the wood, she knew.

She had already seen it – or its ghost-double – in her own front room. Aware of it then only as a dark, unfamiliar shape between herself and the people at the table, now, as she felt it solid beneath her hand, she recognized it beyond any doubt. It had been *his*.

Without even a token protest at the price, Katy paid for it and took it home with her in a cab.

Frank was not pleased. 'Shipping stuff home is expensive, you know that. We *agreed*. And it's not even like this is some great antique – it's crummy now, and it was crummy when it was new. No matter how cheap it was, it's not worth it. The wood is bad, and just look at the workmanship – look inside at these shelves, just look at the way they –'

'It wouldn't have had shelves in it originally,' Katy said. 'That's why they don't fit right. Someone put them in later, it's obvious. I thought we could take the shelves out.'

'Take them out? Why? What did you think we could use it for? Why did you buy it?'

Katy shrugged, suddenly uneasy. She had let her enthusiasm run away with her again. 'I don't know . . . I wasn't really thinking about using it, or taking it back to Atlanta. In fact, I don't particularly want to take it home with us – we might as well leave it here. But I had to buy it, I just had to, as soon as I saw it. It belongs in this house. It was here before. I recognized it as soon as I touched it. And when I knew it belonged here – well, I just couldn't leave it sitting in that junk shop, I really couldn't. I had to bring it back here to this house.'

'A present for your ghost? Oh, all right, Katy. How can I be jealous of a ghost? As long as we don't have to worry about shipping it to America, I won't ask what you paid for it. I hope it wasn't much.' He gave her a hug of forgiveness, and brightened. 'It might be useful, anyway, while we're here. You must be tired of keeping half your clothes in a suitcase under the bed. We could put sweaters and jeans and things in here, on the shelves. Wonder what it was used for before the shelves were put in?'

'I think I know,' said Katy. The idea had come to her as she held the box steady in the cab; she remembered something from her readings on spiritualism. 'I think it was a spirit cabinet, and that my – my medium used it for the séances he held right here in this room.'

Frank arched an eyebrow. 'He kept his liquor in it?'

'Not that kind of spirit, silly.' She hugged him back, and took advantage of his restored humour to launch into an explanation. 'Mediums had things called spirit cabinets. I'm not sure exactly how they were meant to work, or the theory behind them, because the book I read implied that they were just another opportunity for faking ghosts. Somehow or other the ghost was supposed to materialize inside the cabinet, and the sitters could talk to them – but not touch them – and look at them there. Maybe some of the cabinets were like magicians' boxes, with false backs or bottoms, but I had a good look at this one before you got home, and there's nothing like that. If anyone ever got in this box it must have been in the ordinary way.'

'You think you might be able to get your ghost to materialize inside it in *our* time? Do you want to hold a séance?'

'Oh, no, nothing like that.' There was something almost shocking in the idea of that well-dressed, Victorian gentleman crouching in the cabinet, pretending to be a ghost – even if he *was* a ghost. 'I hadn't even thought about using it. It just seemed like the right thing to do when I saw it, to buy the box and bring it back here. It's a link, you know, another connection to the past.' She moved away to examine the cabinet again. She took hold of one of the shelves and tried to move it, but it gave not at all under the pressure of her fingers, no matter how she tugged. There were four shelves, each one a thick, solid plank tightly fixed in place.

'These shouldn't be here,' she muttered, almost to herself. Then she looked at Frank. 'Will you help me take the shelves out?'

'Take the shelves out? What for? I thought we were going to use it for our clothes. If we take the shelves out, it'll be totally useless, just an ugly box taking up space.'

To Katy it seemed obvious that the next step, after returning the cabinet to its home, was to restore it to its original condition, but she saw that Frank was fast losing sympathy with her ghost story. He had been so good about it all along, and he was so seldom annoyed with her, that she did not persist. She wasn't giving in – in a few days, she thought, she would approach Frank about it again, or even take the shelves out herself. Once it was done he would have to accept it. But for now she would go easy, try not to be obsessive.

'Let's leave it here for now, all right?' she said. 'I should clean it out really well before we start putting our clothes or anything in it.'

'You're right,' he said. 'Wouldn't want any ghost-moths getting in our clothes . . .' He grinned, and she smiled back, and saw him relent still more. 'Maybe it *should* be in this room,' he said. 'If that's where you think it belongs. The bedroom is awfully small and . . . . I guess it looks kind of nice in here.'

'It belongs here,' she said. 'And I know where I belong.'

'Yeah?'

'In bed with you.'

In the middle of the night – two o'clock by the glowing radio-alarm clock – Katy woke suddenly, as if someone had spoken her name. But Frank was sleeping peacefully beside her, and although she listened, straining her ears against the silence of the house and the distant, outside noise of traffic, she could hear nothing else. Yet she knew her awakening had not been by chance – she knew she *had* been called. And she knew that if she went into the front room she would find her bearded medium presiding over another (or perhaps it was always the same) séance, with all those long-dead Victorian ladies and gentlemen waiting silently, hoping for Katy's appearance.

She lay in the darkness, smiling. She wondered if, this time, she would speak to them. She turned her head on the pillow to look at Frank, and wondered if she should wake him. The compulsion to go into the front room became stronger.

It's my own compulsion, she told herself. No one else was controlling her. She could stay in bed and go back to sleep. Nothing but her own curiosity, her own desire, made her move.

She looked again at Frank, thinking of taking him with her. But Frank didn't believe, and Frank had not been called as she had been. What if his presence spoiled it?

Katy got up and reached for her robe, moving carefully so as not to disturb her husband. She was in no danger, she told herself. She knew what to do. She could return to her own place and time whenever she wanted, merely by making some motion not directed by the medium. The difficulty, really, was in letting herself be directed in order to stay in the past a little longer.

Next time, Frank, she thought. When I've figured it out more. She blew him a kiss, and walked out of the room, down the short corridor, and into another time.

As before, there was a coal-fire glowing and the lamp turned low in the stuffy, over-furnished room. Again, the stocky, bearded man stood before her and beckoned, silently drawing her into the room. When she turned her head this time, again by his direction, she immediately picked out, among all the extra furnishings her room lacked, the spirit cabinet, standing in exactly the same spot where she had put it.

The recognition gave her a small thrill of accomplishment.

Yes, she had done that, she had done her part in making this connection between past and present possible. She felt even more pleased, even more necessary, when the bearded man indicated that she should climb into the cabinet. She understood what was happening – after all, she had read about séances and spirit cabinets – and so she did not pause or object, but climbed inside quite willingly. She did not mind when he shut the doors and she was in total darkness. In a moment, she knew, he would open the doors again and display her to his audience. But although pleased and excited, she was also just a little bit uncomfortable. The cabinet was an awkward size, and she hadn't been able to get entirely settled before the doors were closed. She didn't want to spoil the séance by moving, but she was afraid one of her legs was getting a cramp.

The police thought it must have been a bomb, although none of the neighbours reported an explosion, and the rest of the room was undamaged. Only an explosion of the most tremendous force could have driven solid wooden planks, two inches thick, right through the woman's body like that.

The husband had found her, early in the morning, and the police put it down to shock when he claimed responsibility for her death, because nothing he said made any sense.

'It's my fault,' he kept repeating. 'She told me – she told me how it worked. If only I'd taken out the shelves right away, when she told me, she could have come back alive.'

The Colonization of Edwin Beal

Edwin Beal was looking forward to the end of the world.

Not just *any* end of the world, however. He had no use for the idea of nuclear war: that ending was too final by half. He didn't want all life wiped out, just most of humanity. It wasn't the destruction of the physical world that he craved, but the end of civilization as he knew it.

Driving home from work each day, Edwin customarily passed a boundary sign which declared the London Borough of Brent a Nuclear-Free Zone. It made him sneer, when it didn't make him sad. It was so pathetic, individuals imagining they could opt out of humanity's collective madness if the worst came to pass. He thought of the county councillors, and all the inhabitants of Brent, sleeping soundly in their beds, imagining that now the target would be painted somewhere else, imagining they would survive intact while London burned around them.

Sometimes, as he laboured in the mills of the large American computer firm which paid him so well for designing software, Edwin toyed with a nuclear scenario, imagining some terrorist organization bombing New York or Washington. It would have to be an indigenous American group, however, or what was left of the American military-industrial complex would take vengeance on the evil foreigners, and American vengeance would lead, inevitably, to global war. London would go if there ever were such a war; and with it, all of Britain. Edwin did not imagine that even he could survive a nuclear holocaust. And survival, for Edwin, was what it was all about.

Financial catastrophe would be better; collapse of the stock-market, of the worldwide monetary system. Everyone would head for the hills, then, but Edwin would have a head start.

At least, he hoped he would. Crawling home through the miserable London traffic on Friday afternoon (somehow it never mattered how early he left on Friday: it was as if everyone else had the same idea at the same time, and the rush hour started then), Edwin thought impatiently ahead to the narrow, rather decrepit house in Haringay which he called home, and visualized letters lying on the mat. Letters with airmail stickers and stamps from Australia or America. Some positive response to all the job applications and inquiries he had despatched *must* be forthcoming.

He had imagined it would be easy. After all, he had a skill, and he wasn't picky about *where* in North America (Australia was second choice) or with what company he got a job. But if there were jobs in America, they were not for him. No one was willing to import him, and Edwin was beginning to feel that time was running out. He was having dreams, telling him the end was near. He was terrified of leaving it too late. He had to escape, had to get off this tiny, crumbling island to survive. He had to save himself.

When he was younger, Edwin had imagined running away to Scotland or Wales and surviving there after the collapse of civilization. He had devoured science-fiction stories about new ice ages, or the death of grass, of plagues, wars and alien invasions, and had determined that when things began breaking down, from whatever cause, he would be on the road to the north, pack on his back, ready for a new life in the wilderness.

But now that he had acquired the survival skills he had once only imagined, and had spent several rough Highland holidays, Edwin no longer found Scotland satisfactory. It was too close, too small, like all of Britain. Once the cities started to go, people would head for the country, and there were bound to be too many who would have the same idea as Edwin.

No, he wanted the space and emptiness of a whole new continent to fill himself. He wanted to be a new pioneer. A whole new planet would be even better, but although he still read science fiction, Edwin had not, since his teens, seriously believed that this was a possibility open to him. Even if, say, a faster-than-light drive was invented, the resultant space programme would be too late for him – he would be too old, and probably of the wrong nationality, to be picked as a participant. He would have to make his own opportunity, on this earth.

There was a parking space directly in front of his house. This was so rare that Edwin took it as a sign and, indeed, when he opened the door he found three airmail letters. But all of them, when opened, provided only disappointment. They were formal notes thanking him for his interest and expressing the ritual regret that there were no openings for him. Edwin went on standing in the dark, rather damp little entrance-hall. He could hear voices, not in English, from next door. He didn't even want to go upstairs and log these replies and check on how many more chances he still had.

But there were other ways to get what he wanted, Edwin told himself. He had a fair bit of money saved up, and he could sell his house and go to Canada as a tourist, to vanish into the north woods when his visa expired.

It was possible, too, he thought, that in America the collapse of civilization was not so imminent as it was here. Perhaps it was only Britain that was collapsing, and if he went to America he would miss it all.

These thoughts cheered him, and Edwin set aside his mail and went down to the cellar to change into his gardening gear, planning to get in a couple of hours of work before dinner.

Outside, the routine labour of digging in and breaking up the soil left his mind free, and his thoughts slipped all too easily into a well-worn fantasy.

The smashing of windows and bottle-glass, a strong smell of petrol and licking flames. Hoarse, violent voices shouting, not in English. He'd left his escape late, but he had everything he needed in his rucksack, always ready at a moment's notice. He didn't think he would have to fight his way out of the city, but he wouldn't have minded. Nobody paid any notice to one large, strongly-built white man walking purposefully through the mad confusion of the streets; they were all too busy with their looting and raping.

A woman's scream: it was Jennifer-from-the-office. She was surrounded by dark-skinned youths pulling at her clothes. He glimpsed a breast, and her pale, terrified face; heard their coarse laughter.

He needed no weapon but his fists –

Well, maybe a broomstick would be better, snatched up, deadly in his hands as –

But there were four of them, maybe five.

The gun slipped easily into his hand; without even the memory of having drawn it, it fitted there as if –

Not a hand-gun, but something bigger. He wore it slung across his back. He wouldn't even have to shoot them because the mere sight of it –

Edwin thought of the ads in *Soldier of Fortune* magazine, and longed with a hopeless passion for America. It was so easy there to have a gun – everything would be easier in America, including, no doubt, the women.

Jennifer's pale face, adoring and grateful as she clung to him, panting.

Jennifer, tearing off her blouse (the lacy white one) to bind his wound. It was only minor, but one of her attackers had cut him with a knife, and Edwin had been forced to shoot. He wanted to explain to her that he wasn't violent, he didn't like to kill, but he'd been forced, he'd had no choice – but she stopped him talking with her delicious mouth.

In his excitement, Edwin stabbed the fork more deeply into the earth than was necessary, and then was jarred back on his heels as he struck something hard.

Frowning, he stabbed again, exploratively. It seemed much larger than any rock left in this garden – after all the years he had worked it – should be: the size of a football, at least. He could have left it, but curiosity drove him now. He wanted to bring it up and see it, so he threw the fork aside and began to dig with the shovel. The light was nearly gone by the time he brought the thing out, but even in full daylight Edwin wouldn't have known what he held.

It was not a rock. Beneath the clinging dirt, the surface of the thing was hard and shiny, rather like plastic, and a mottled brown and yellow colour. It was about the size of a soccer ball, nearly as round, but heavier. Edwin frowned at it, tapped it with a fingernail, and listened to the not-quite-hollow click. He tried to clean the dirt off as he speculated on its intended use. Was it a children's toy, or some bit of decoration? How had it come to be buried in his garden? It was seamless, he thought at first, the surface flawless beneath the soil. Then his searching fingers found a slight concavity, a small depression in the hard, slick surface of the globe. He pressed it with a fingertip, fancying that it gave slightly to his touch, and then, with shocking suddenness, it opened. His finger slipped inside, quite without his intending it, and as he jerked his hand back he let the thing fall to the ground.

Edwin stood a moment, breathing hard, trying to understand.

It was nearly dark. He decided to take the thing inside, to get a better look at it. He pushed at it with his foot, making it roll, trying to see the opening, but there was no sign of it. He was nervous about picking it up, fearful that it would open again for his fingers, but he managed to conquer his fear and carry it into the kitchen without mishap.

There he cleaned it carefully with a damp sponge and found no cracks, no indentations, no flaws whatsoever in the smooth, now shining, surface. He raised it closer to his face, squinting slightly, and suddenly he thought he saw it, a darker spot against the mottled brown.

It opened like a mouth and *something* shot out: something like a worm or a snake or a turtle-head extended itself from the opening and bit him on the nose.

Edwin screamed, and was ashamed of the noise as soon as he heard it.

Having struck, the thing retreated. Edwin was holding a hard, plastic ball without any apparent holes, flaws or openings. It might have been a dream except for the throbbing of his nose. Carefully, he set the ball down on the draining board, and went upstairs to the bathroom. He was shaking. Although his nose hardly hurt at all, he could see in the bathroom mirror that it was very red, and swelling rapidly. He stared for some time at his own reflection and prodded his nose, but no understanding came to him.

He went back downstairs and stared at the thing from a safe distance. What could it be? Some sort of tortoise? He'd never heard of anything like it, and he'd always been a fan of television nature programmes. He was certain it didn't belong in England, but even as some more exotic creature it seemed unlikely. Perhaps it belonged in the sea? It couldn't be some grossly outsized insect . . . perhaps a carnivorous plant? He would have to find out. On Monday, he would start phoning around. For a moment he was almost sorry it was a weekend, since that meant

he'd have the thing around, a mystery, for two days. If he could
have brought himself to touch it, Edwin would have put it back
in the garden. But he decided discretion was the better part, and
left it on the draining board. He was careful to close the kitchen
door, shutting it safely in, before he went up to bed that night.

By then, the lump on his nose had grown quite alarmingly
large, but it still did not hurt. Edwin decided he would visit the
doctor in the morning: it wouldn't do to be too casual about an
animal bite, particularly when it might not even be an animal
that had bit him.

Perhaps there was some infection, he thought, as he settled
rather shakily between the sheets. He certainly felt feverish, and
sank at once into strange dreams.

Jennifer-from-the-office was biting his nose. He slipped his
hand beneath her sweater only to find her lovely large soft
breasts encased in hard shell. He pressed and pressed at them
in frustration, and finally they yielded to him, they opened like
mouths and bit his hands. Jennifer was biting him all over,
and he was in an ecstasy of painful lust. Tormented beyond
endurance by her teasing, he grabbed her head and forced it to
his groin. But even as he moaned in happy anticipation, feeling
her mouth on him, Edwin was aware that something was very
wrong. Jennifer's head had no hair on it. Jennifer's head was
hard and shell-like. And Jennifer's mouth, nibbling at his cock,
was quite the wrong size.

It wasn't Jennifer and it wasn't a dream. Somehow, in his
sleep, he had come downstairs. He was awake now, lying naked
on the cold, kitchen floor, clutching the thing he'd dug up in the
garden with both hands, letting it bite him.

Edwin managed to sit up and hurl the thing away from him.
But he knew, with a horrible sick feeling, that it was much
too late. The damage, whatever it was, had been well and
truly done.

He was covered in red lumps, the smallest no worse than
mosquito bites, the largest almost the size of golf balls. There
were two of those on his hairy chest, a bizarre parody of a
woman's breasts. Swallowing his sickness, Edwin forced himself
to touch one of the swellings. It was hard, almost as if it *was*
a golf ball beneath the skin, but despite his squeamishness it
wasn't painful. He could see the one on his nose without the

aid of a mirror, and he knew he must look like a clown with a big, red ball for a nose.

'Well, at least it doesn't hurt,' he said, touching the end of his nose with a fingertip.

And then it burst beneath his finger, and then it *did* hurt.

Something came out of the lump when it burst, but Edwin couldn't see what it was for the involuntary tears of pain which filled his eyes. When he could see again, he saw a creature like a tiny terrapin, head and four rudimentary limbs protruding from a mottled brown shell. There were differences, but it was recognizably the same sort of creature as the thing he had dug up in his garden. Blood or some other liquid dripped down his face. Shakily, Edwin made his way to the kitchen sink to clean himself. But while he was doing so, one of the lumps on his chest burst.

His knees buckled with the pain, and as he went down he banged his head on the sink: almost, but unfortunately not quite hard enough to knock himself out.

Lying on the floor in a daze of pain and dread, Edwin set himself to counting the lumps on his body. They were increasing in size – he didn't need to touch them to know that – and it was obvious that when they reached some critical circumference they burst, and the creature inside was born.

He had counted twelve when one of the two on his left hand exploded, making further counting – or any sort of coherent thought – temporarily impossible. But when he had recovered, Edwin continued his grim self-exploration with as much determination as if, by knowing the worst, he could somehow change things.

There were twenty left. They were bursting at five- or six-minute intervals. Edwin decided there was no point in even trying to phone for help. A doctor – presuming he could get one to come out – could give him some pain-killers perhaps, but wouldn't be able to change what was happening. The only thing for it, Edwin thought, was to endure. He kept careful count of each emerging terrapin, for he wanted to know when it was finally over. The next two hours were the longest and most terrible of his life.

But when it was, finally, over, despite his sickening exhaustion and physical misery, Edwin felt a kind of triumph. Not merely because it was over and he had survived, but also because it had occurred to him that *this* – this creature he had dug up in his garden, these creatures that had come out of his body – was the end of the world as he had known it. These creatures were invaders from another planet, and they were going to bring about the downfall of civilization.

He looked at them, his twenty-three alien creatures crawling about on the linoleum, snapping at each other with razor-sharp teeth, and he almost smiled.

Painfully, Edwin hauled himself to his feet and went and opened the back door. Then he fetched the original shell, and bowled it out into the garden. One of the babies noticed, and scurried outside.

'Curious?' said Edwin. He held the door open and watched as two more of the creatures ventured out into the wide world. 'Go on,' said Edwin. 'Plenty of room for everyone . . . a whole new world to conquer. Go on, outside.'

Three more made their way across the threshold into the garden, their mode of progress a curious cross between a slide and a waddle. Edwin waited, speaking encouragingly, but at least half of them paid no attention, showing no interest in leaving the kitchen, and eventually he grew impatient. He fetched the broom and swept them out, sneering at them when they snapped ineffectually up at him.

'Go now, while it's still dark,' he said. 'London is sleeping. It's yours! This is your only chance. Once they wake up, they'll kill you. You're easy enough to crush when you're so small. I could smash the lot of you now, with this broom, but I won't. I'm a collaborator. Didn't expect that, did you? Didn't know you'd find somebody willing to help you colonize this planet. Now, hurry up. Go on, before I change my mind. Go find somebody else to bite.'

When they were all outside, he locked the door, from habit, and stumbled upstairs. He paused in the bathroom to clean himself up. One glimpse of himself in the mirror told him more than he wanted to know. He looked like an ambulatory corpse, covered with raw, festering wounds. He couldn't bear the thought of taking a bath, so he cleaned himself gingerly with a flannel. He had mostly stopped bleeding, but his wounds were seeping some other, colourless fluid. He hoped it was a healthy reaction, for even if it was something he should try to stop he didn't have the faintest idea how, and besides, he was nearly asleep on his feet.

Edwin Beal fell into sleep almost as he fell into bed, and he slept like the dead. Some hours later, some way into the morning, the sound of breaking glass woke him.

He opened his eyes but lay still, too tired and groggy even to try to move. Glass . . . a window . . . the sound had come from downstairs. Someone had broken a window, broken in. He told himself to get up and prepare to repel the intruder, but his body did not respond.

Edwin blinked in frustration, and came more fully awake. Conscious now, he tried to move his arm, and could not. Nor could he move either leg. Yet he could feel the muscles flexing and straining – he wasn't incapable or paralysed, but he was *bound* in some way.

With tremendous effort Edwin managed to raise his head, and he saw the fine, strong cords that bound him to the bed. Not cords at all, really, but something that looked like dried mucous. It was the stuff that had seeped out of his wounds. One strand of it, from his nose, looped across his cheek and ear, tugging his head back to the bed, so that it was only by straining to the utmost that he managed to achieve a rather lopsided view of his trussed body. His neck muscles ached. With a groan, Edwin let his head fall back onto the pillow.

He could hear them on the stairs: a clumping, slithering sound as they knocked together and some of them fell back. Stairs must be difficult for them; they were probably annoyed that he hadn't stayed put. Why should they bother to seek new worlds until they had used up the old one? Edwin wondered how much they ate, and how quickly. He wondered how long he would survive.

Lizard Lust

Under the bridge the young men would gather and wait. Maybe they were junkies; maybe criminals; maybe they only wanted a place to smoke forbidden cigarettes and tell lies about sex to their friends. Occasional glimpses showed they were just boys, really, and I was old enough to be their mother. But I wasn't their mother; I wasn't anybody's mother. Afraid I'd be prey, I tried to avoid them.

The most direct route between my home and work was by a footpath which passed under the railway bridge. Mornings, that was the way I almost invariably took, despite the people huddled in the shadows beneath the bridge. But there was nothing threatening about them; theirs were the sad, battered shapes of the homeless. They made me uneasy, but not like a gang of young men. I felt sorry for these people sleeping on cardboard under bridges or in doorways, rooting through rubbish bins, and sometimes I gave them money, knowing it could never be enough, but I didn't like it when they came into my library.

But of course it wasn't mine; the library belonged to the people, and they were people, too. They had a right to come in to escape the cold or the rain, to fall asleep in the chairs, so much more comfortable than a cardboard box on the pavement. But their indifference to the books around them offended me, as did the rank smell of them, and the personal oddness which, I knew, must be driving away other, legitimate library users, the pensioners and housewives and students who once had come in greater numbers.

I couldn't send them away, knowing they had nowhere else to go. I didn't want them, but neither did anyone else. I let them stay. I got on with my work among the books during the day, and in the evenings I went home, not usually by the footpath.

More often I took the longer journey by the main road, crossing over the bridge rather than under it. Sometimes I took the bus. Sometimes there was shopping to do, or I would meet a friend for a drink or a meal before I went back to the small flat where I lived quite happily alone.

It is not uncommon for a woman in London to live alone. I lived alone, and I worked in a library, and I loved to read. I loved my life. I can't believe it's lost forever.

A stolen pencil. Bits and pieces of paper scavenged here and there. A loose floorboard provides the hiding place. This is all that is mine. I have to steal moments in which to write, and there is nothing but this, my own words, to read. Of all the losses, all the cruelties I have suffered, that may be the one I mind the most. My books.

There are some books here, I've seen them, but –

'Women can't read,' says Gart.

I was stupid enough to want to prove I could, as if that would make any difference. There were some books in the workroom, where I'm not supposed to go, and I went and got one – I opened it at random and looked at black shapes scrawled on white. I thought at first it was another alphabet and language, something like Bengali or Gujarati, but when I looked more closely I decided it was not real writing but gibberish, like something a child scribbles, pretending to write. I spent far too long trying to make some sense of it, and I was caught. My last contact with a book: Gart hit me in the face with it.

Women can't read, says Gart, and it's true. For us, instead of books, there are picture-boxes, series of illuminated, richly-detailed unmoving images, mostly of lizards.

I was a librarian in London. Words from another world; words from a dream. They have no meaning here. London. Librarian.

Walking to work in the mornings I saw the homeless huddled beneath the bridge. Later they turned up in the library. They didn't always come, seldom more than two at a time, and I thought I'd made my peace with them.

But I didn't like it when their numbers increased. The day I saw the newcomer, I tensed with immediate dislike and worry.

He might be the one to finally, fatally shift the balance from public library to seedy waiting room. I watched him vanish amid the shelves and then emerge with a stack of books and sit down at a table to read.

Had I mistaken a normally poor, badly-dressed person for a down-and-out? I went for a closer look.

He was dirty, not simply shabby, and, the hallmark of the homeless, he wore layer upon layer of ancient clothing. A filthy knitted cap had been jammed onto his head, from which a few curls of greasy hair escaped. Beneath a summer-weight khaki raincoat was a heavy, mustard-brown wool jacket, beneath that a brown, V-necked jumper, beneath that a greyish shirt, beneath that – something about the size of a big, fat cigar bulged beneath shirt and wool, near the base of the V-neck. Just as my puzzled gaze fell on it, he looked up from his book.

His eyes were blue and bloodshot. His face was round, hairless, and young. Then he smiled, revealing stained, crooked teeth and a glimpse of wet tongue, and looked much older. My eyes returned to the bulge beneath his shirt. It moved.

He grinned as if we shared a dirty secret.

'You want to see him,' he said in a low, soft voice.

'What?' I wanted to look away but I didn't. Why? After all that has happened, I find it hard to remember my innocence and lack of fear. Surely I felt the menace rippling from him like heat. I must have known I was in danger, even if that wasn't a weapon beneath his shirt. Yet I wasn't frightened. I felt safe in my own library. Safe enough to be curious.

'He's very big,' the dirty man went on in his soft, insinuating voice. 'He's very big and fierce and it's all I can do to control him. I don't know what he might not do if he gets a sight of you, I really don't . . .'

He was crazy, I thought, but what was it that lived under his clothes? Suddenly, something brilliantly grass-green poked out above the V of the sweater, between two buttons on the shirt. It was a small, flat, triangular head with liquid black eyes. Not a snake, but something a little larger and more squat. A lizard.

As soon as I'd seen it, he shoved it back beneath the layers of cloth.

One of the children has been ill, so I've had no time to myself,

110

no hope of writing, for the past week. Maggs, she's called. My favourite. I didn't begrudge the time spent looking after her; I'm relieved she's better now, and wouldn't have objected if she'd wanted a few more days recovering at home. Maybe I should have insisted. There's more to it than recovering physically, after all, as it wasn't a normal illness. She'd been assaulted.

It happened under the bridge, of course. That's where the young, single men go with their lizards, to take them out in the shadows and stroke them, boast to each other and wait for the women to come.

They say their creatures are dangerous, fierce, violent, maddened by the sight of a woman. They give their pets the names of weapons: Blade, Pistol, Slasher, Destroyer, Womansplitter. They say a woman and a master and a lizard together is the meaning of life, but a woman with a lizard alone is dead meat.

That's what they say; this is what I know: the lizards are from two to six inches long. They have four little legs and a body a couple of inches wide, at most. They have no teeth. They have no claws. On Maggs's body, as on my own, are scratches, bruises left by boots and fists, and the marks of human teeth.

He grinned and lurched to his feet, and with the movement came the stench of him, like a blow, making me flinch. It was the rank, sour smell of unwashed flesh swaddled too long in filthy clothes, but it was the wrong smell. It was the smell not of a man, but of a dirty woman. Now I saw that although dressed like a man, she was, of course, a woman. I couldn't understand how I had been so mistaken. How had I missed the meaning of the beardless face, the voice, the way she walked? I looked at her chest and she hunched slightly, holding both hands up protectively.

'You don't want him getting excited,' she said. 'He sees you looking and he'll want to take a bite out of your pretty face. I'd try to hold him back, honest I would, but sometimes he's just too strong for me.'

She was a woman of about my own age, maybe younger, probably still in her thirties. I wondered what had gone wrong in her life. I felt the most profound sense of pity, of connection, imagining myself in her place. She obviously needed help; maybe mine?

That was how I got involved. That was why I didn't throw

her out, then and there. It was pity for her, or, rather, who I thought she might be. It wasn't the lizard; it was nothing to do with the lizard.

Maggs has picture cubes. She stares at them in a kind of trance while listening to stories on the radio, or to her records. A lot of women use them in this way. Much of what I understand I have learned from Maggs. The oldest of the children, she's no longer a child. She talks to me and isn't impatient with my boundless ignorance. We like each other. She's my only friend.

The stories she likes best on the radio, and her favourite records, are a kind of pornography, I suppose, although she thinks of them as romance. They don't work as either of those things for me, because they're about lizards. About women and lizards.

My own fantasies have nothing to do with lizards. Nor do they have anything to do with sex, or other people. All my yearnings now, both willed and unwilled daydreams, are for my lost solitude and the ordinary realities of my former life. I imagine myself cleaning my flat, dusting the books, sitting behind my desk in the rich silence of the library, dealing with routine filing and overdue notices. The things I once took for granted or found tedious are the pleasures I long for now. To be able to sit alone and read a book and fear nothing. If I could have my old life back, I'd never again wish for a man to rescue me from it; I'd never even think about getting a pet for company.

In my sweet dreams I'm back in the library, working. I look up and see someone come in, and I go over to speak to her. At that point, the dream becomes a nightmare. Why did I have to speak to her? Why did I let her show me her lizard?

'I'm afraid you can't have an animal in here . . . this is a public library, you know, and other people . . .'

'Go away,' she said, seating herself again and turning her attention to her books. 'I'll let you see him later.'

The books were human biology texts. She was looking at them upside down.

If she was mad, as she must be, it might not be safe to anger her. I decided to leave her alone. After all, she wasn't bothering anyone, and it was only a lizard, not anything dangerous.

Lizard Lust

They say that the sight of a lizard drives a woman wild with desire. Any woman, any lizard, the merest glimpse. Once she's seen a lizard, a woman can't rest content until she can put her hands on one. Until she can feel it moving against her flesh, tiny feet scampering over her skin, its coolness nestling in her warmth. She wants one for her own. But lizards belong to men; they're death to women. A woman can know a lizard only through a man's intercession. So she gives herself to a man, becomes his slave and does whatever he asks in exchange for a few precious moments at night, in the dark, when she can feel the lizard, set free, moving or resting on her bare flesh, and she can pretend, she may even believe, that it is her own. A woman will do anything, sell herself to a man she despises, just to be close to a lizard. That's what the men say.

No. The truth is, I don't know what 'the men' say, and I don't believe in 'the men'. I certainly haven't seen any. All I know is what Gart and Maggs have told me, and what I've guessed from things overheard, from the picture-boxes, from my own experience.

I feel nothing when I look at a lizard. I have never felt anything except a mild curiosity and now, increasingly, fear and revulsion, not for the harmless creature itself, but for what it represents. I am immune to whatever strange powers they possess. I am not like other women. Of course I'm not. This isn't my world. I don't belong here.

Gart smiles cynically. 'Then why did you come? Why do you stay?'

This is what it's like for me with the lizard:

I'm alone in the bedroom with Gart who turns out the light. I undress as quickly as I can, my nervousness making me clumsy. I won't be as nervous once I'm in bed, but until then I feel like prey. Anything might happen. Although he usually punishes me with the light on, sometimes he'll attack me in the dark, without warning or provocation. Once I'm actually in the bed, though naked, I feel more safe. Gart seldom hurts me in bed, never badly. There is a kind of truce in effect while we're in bed together which allows me to relax.

Sometimes we talk. I talk about my world, or ask questions about this one, and Gart responds in a way very different from his sneering, domineering daylight manner. We talk as if I'm not his captive and he's not my master.

Sometimes we make love. That's something I feel guilty about. I'm ashamed of myself for allowing it to go on and for enjoying it so much. Gart is my enemy, and nothing that has happened between us in the dark has ever altered his violent cruelty to me later. How can I love such a man?

The answer is, I don't love the man. I love the woman he is at night, the woman who comes out when the man takes off his clothes.

I am not homosexual. I have never felt any inclination in that direction. When I was younger I had a satisfying, fairly active sex life, but for various reasons (a dislike of casual sex, a determination not to get involved with married men) once I was past thirty, love affairs were few and far between. At the time Gart shambled into my library I hadn't had a boyfriend for two years. Yes, I did regret it; yes, I did feel frustrated at times, but I never thought of having an affair with another woman. My women friends were my *friends*, and one of the important things about friendship, I think, is that it isn't sexual. Gart has never been my friend.

At first when we made love I would try to pretend Gart was a man. I remembered past lovers and I fantasized, ignoring the reality as best I could. But after a short while I stopped that. I knew I didn't want to make love to the man Gart pretended all day to be, but the woman who came out in the dark was someone else. She was my lover.

Whether we talk or make love, always, at some point, Gart asks if I want to have the lizard. When I agree (I always agree: once from fear of angering him, now from the wish to please her) Gart puts the small creature into my receptive hands, or somewhere on my naked body.

I don't find it erotic or arousing at all, but the feel of a lizard on my naked flesh is, although not actively pleasant, not unpleasant, either. It's easy to tolerate; it's not something I would miss if it stopped. I think of it as something Gart wants to do, which I don't mind. Other women must feel something I don't. Is it possible the lizard exudes some sort of chemical to which they are sensitive and to which they become addicted? That seems likely; certainly it is preferable to the other thought that haunts me, that the women here are no different, physically, from me; that what they feel for the lizard is a fantasy, a cultural neurosis, a gigantic, psychological con.

It was as I was reshelving books, sometime late in the afternoon, that I noticed she was gone. I'm sure I was more relieved than disappointed. Of course I thought of the lizard. Something like that was too unusual to forget. But thinking about something, wondering about it, remembering its dazzling green and the lithe curve of its neck, is not the same as needing something, or even wanting it.

I took the footpath home from work. I didn't need to go shopping or out to dinner. The bus was slow and often crowded. Walking was more pleasant, and it was early summer, so I wouldn't be walking in the dark. I had no reason to be afraid.

'You were looking for me,' says Gart. 'You thought you might find me under the bridge – there was nowhere else, and you had to look, didn't you? You had to see my lizard again.'

After so long here I have come to doubt my own perceptions. Maybe my memory is wrong. Maybe, subconsciously, I was being drawn . . . Yet I remember no compulsion, no sense of need or even strong desire. I was just walking home, not searching, when I found her, loitering on the footpath, not quite under the bridge but not quite clear of it. When I came near she looked at me as if she'd been expecting me, and said, 'I'll let you touch him, but it'll have to be in the dark, so he can't see what you are. Otherwise, he might kill you, and I wouldn't want that.'

He says, 'You could have run away. You could have said No.'

She put her hand on my arm. The smell of her made me want to throw up. She said, 'Come with me under the bridge.'

Although it was horrible, and I felt almost a mother's agony when Maggs came home bruised and bleeding from her encounter under the bridge, I also felt a kind of relief because this surely meant she was a woman. Had she not been hurt she would have gone back to try her luck again, and eventually she might get her own lizard. That's what makes a man, according to Gart. Those who have lizards are men. Gart says she is a man. But I know that's not true.

Her body, like mine, is a woman's. It is possible to be confused about many things in the dark, but of this I am certain. Gart does not have a penis.

Is Gart an exception, a freak, or are all the men in this place like her? Can it be that that they are *all* women? That they all look like women to me doesn't mean they are. That I've only ever seen girl children doesn't mean there aren't boys somewhere, perhaps being raised separately, or in secret. They say that all children are girls, but then sometime in adolescence they begin to change. They say the lizards can tell the difference . . . or maybe the lizards make the difference. Girls become men or women depending on what happens to them during the crisis of adolescence, the drama which takes place beneath the bridge.

Gart says that men get lizards and women get babies. But if they are all female, where do the babies come from?

'A man and a woman and a lizard,' says Gart, impatiently. She thinks I'm an idiot, not because I ask questions about such basic things, but because I keep asking the same questions again and again and don't – won't – can't believe the answers. But neither does she believe in my reality, where sex is established long before birth. And I won't believe the most important human distinction can be made on the basis of keeping, or not keeping, a pet.

To these people, so like me they could pass in my world, the lizard is the source of all power, the lizard makes everything possible, even travel to other worlds.

After the mother of her children died, Gart didn't like being alone, but was afraid to go under the bridge again. She might get a new woman there, but because she was older, not as quick or as desirable as the others, it was also possible that some particularly strong or ruthless child might steal her lizard, unmanning her.

'Dagger wouldn't let me risk it,' said Gart. Her hand was inside the voluminous pullover she liked to wear at home and she was stroking the lizard nestled between her small breasts. 'Dagger didn't want to be parted from me, so when this kid came at me, and looked like hurting me, under the bridge, Dagger took us out of there, both of us went *through* – into your world, as it turned out.'

'How?'

116

'Everybody knows that lizards can travel to different dimensions, and sometimes they take their friends.'

'How? What makes it happen? What were you doing just before?'

Gart's smile became unpleasant. 'It won't do *you* any good to know. If you ever tried to steal Dagger he'd rip you to pieces. You'd be dead meat before you could even leave the house. Even if you thought to kill me first –'

'I wouldn't, I wouldn't!'

'– he'd tear you into bloody chunks and then he'd disappear. So what are you asking questions for, if you're not plotting against me?'

'I'm just curious,' I said, pleadingly. 'I just wondered what it felt like to travel from one world to another.'

'You ought to know that.' And then, even though there were children in the room with us, Gart reached over and took hold of a handful of my hair near the scalp, and tugged hard. 'Don't you remember how it felt?'

Yes. I was beaten and kicked and dragged through. It felt like dying.

Although Gart says that the children's mother died of an illness, what Maggs has told me makes me believe that Gart killed her. And if I stay here long enough I have no doubt he'll kill me, too.

'Come under the bridge and I'll let you see him.'

She tugged at my arm. I felt safe because she was a woman. So I went under the bridge with her. It seemed easier not to fight. I didn't know enough to be afraid.

'You say you're different. You pretend you don't care about my lizard. Do you think I'm stupid? Do you think I can't tell how much you want it? You'd do anything for me, just for the chance to be near him. Why did you come under the bridge with me if you didn't care?' Gart pulled me by my hair, off my chair, and flung me to the floor. 'Why did you come with me?'

'I'm sorry, I'm sorry, I'm sorry!' I didn't then, but I know now to be afraid.

Under the bridge, the woman unbuttoned her shirt and pulled

at the V of her jumper until I saw the slight swell of her breasts and, nestling between them, something green.

I leaned closer to see, and then a pain in my stomach made me double over and I couldn't breathe. I didn't understand what was happening until she hit me in the face with her fist, breaking my nose. She kicked me in the side of the head when I was down, and then, when I tried to protect my head, she kicked me in the ribs and kidneys. The pain was horrific and incomprehensible. There was no chance for me to fight back, even if I had known how. I choked on my own attempts to scream.

'Why do you stay, if not for Dagger?' he shouts, drawing his foot back for a kick. Now, I start screaming before I feel the pain, in the vain hope that it will make him stop sooner. I'm aware of the children's fear as they huddle in the corner, watching. Well, let them be afraid, let them see what he does to me, let it warn them what it is to be a woman in this world.

Maggs didn't come home after school yesterday. Then it was dark and she still hadn't come home. The wounds from the last attack had scarcely healed; it had not occurred to me that she might rush back for more punishment. I had thought her safe for just a little while longer. I dared Gart's anger to insist he go out and look for her. He claims to care about the children, but I don't think he can love Maggs as I do. She is my only friend; her existence is all that makes my life here bearable.

Gart brought her home. He found her lying in a shallow culvert not far from the bridge, badly battered but alive. One of her legs was broken in several places. We had to get the doctor in to set it. Afterwards I could hear Gart and the doctor drinking and laughing together in the parlour, man to man.

I sat at her bedside and held her hand. 'Why?' I whispered, staring down at her poor, swollen face.

'I have to. What else can I do? You know. It's why you went with father.'

'No. That's not true. He tricked me. I didn't know. I thought he was a woman. If I'd had any idea what would happen, that he would beat me up and kidnap me, I'd have run so fast in the other direction . . . It was nothing to do with the lizard; I certainly didn't want it, I didn't need it . . . things are different in my world, I've told you.'

'Then why don't you go back there?'

The way she echoed her father's cruel questions, yet innocent of malice, made me shiver, and I suddenly wondered if she had ever believed my stories of another reality, where women and men were equals, friends who treated one another kindly, where lizards had no power. I wondered if I believed it myself.

'I don't know how to go back. If I knew how, I would, I promise you, and I'd take you with me.'

'A lizard would take you back, if you had one.'

'Well, that's a useful thing to know.'

'Worth risking a beating? Wouldn't you try to get one if you knew it could give you what you want?'

'But lizards won't stay with women –'

'You don't believe *that?*' Her voice got louder in scorn. 'Do you think it was a lizard who broke my leg and punched me in the face, and – if lizards couldn't be stolen, men wouldn't be so afraid. They wouldn't have to keep beating us up, to keep *us* afraid. They'd just laugh, let us try, watch us fail and laugh again.'

The laughter of the men came to us from the other room.

'All that stuff about two sexes is ridiculous,' she went on, more quietly. Her voice was hoarse, raw from screaming. 'We're all the same, my sisters and me and all the kids at school. Some are stronger or meaner or luckier than others, and they'll find lizards, or take them. They're called men after they have lizards, not before, and it's not the lizard who decides. You and father have the same sex – or haven't you noticed, in the dark?'

'Yes, I had noticed, but I thought . . . I thought Gart must be an exception, there must be real men somewhere.'

'You thought Gart was a woman and the lizard made an exception for her? They're all exceptions.'

'But if there aren't any men, where do babies come from?'

She made a sound of weariness and pain. 'I don't know. I expect I'll find out soon. They say it's the lizards, and maybe . . .'

'Oh, Maggs, what happened?'

'I don't know,' she said again. 'It was dark . . . there were a lot of them, holding me down, and I wasn't conscious all the time. If I find out I'm pregnant . . . well, I used to be friends with a girl at school. She's a man now, she's got a lizard but no woman, and I think she'd probably set up house with me if I asked. We always liked each other.'

I tried to protest but she wouldn't listen, she knew better. Nominally I was her stepmother, and older, but she had more experience of life.

'I have to. I've tried to get my own lizard and I failed. I keep trying, and eventually they'll kill me. The smart thing is to admit I can't have my own and settle for sharing someone else's. If it's someone I like, he might not feel so threatened by me. Not all men are brutal to their women.'

'But why – oh, Maggs, why not forget the lizards, why not imagine a life without one?'

'Imagine? I know what it would be like, and it's no life. Don't you know how they treat free women? Have you ever met one? Nobody will give work to someone without a lizard – not decent work. They're always suspicious of someone like that. I could be locked up for treatment. Gart certainly wouldn't stop them, and nobody would listen to you. And then there's the single men, the ones who can't get women of their own free will . . . sooner or later one of them would decide to take me and I wouldn't be able to stop him . . . certainly not if I was pregnant. I'd rather choose the man I have to live with, thank you.'

Her hopelessness brought tears to my eyes. I wish I could save her.

We're alone in the house, Maggs and I. It doesn't matter if she sees me writing because she won't betray me. I'm going to teach her to read and write. We'll have time, while she's laid up with her broken leg, and although literacy is a skill useless in this world, we're not going to stay here forever. We're going to get out. All we need is a lizard.

They can travel, and they can take us away from here. Maggs says she knows how.

She is perceptibly better every day. Young bones do knit fast. We have grown closer, too, spending so much time together, refining our plan. It's going to work, I'm sure. Together we can get a lizard, and the lizard will get us out.

It's going to have to be Gart's, although I resisted the idea at first. Under the bridge is the traditional place, and there are so many lizards there. No one would expect two women to be working together, so we'd have the benefit of surprise.

But there are only two of us, as Maggs has pointed out, and under the bridge if there is one man there will be several. Unless we managed to incapacitate our chosen victim *very* quickly and quietly, the others would come to his aid, and we might not be able to escape in time.

Now I know what other women feel. I hesitate to ask for the lizard in bed, afraid that Gart will be suspicious, that he will react with violence. I find it harder and harder to give the lizard back. I struggle to stay awake, hoping he will fall asleep before me, wondering, if he does, if I would have the courage to take it and run.

I no longer think of sneaking out of bed and running away in the middle of the night. I no longer find it hard to think of hurting him. I no longer think of him as 'her'.

Gart gave me the most vicious beating of my life, more damaging even than the first one. He attacked me for no reason just at the time when Maggs was starting to be able to walk again. Does he suspect that we've united against him? Is that why he wants to keep me helpless?

I must get well quickly. Maggs is restless. She's not pregnant, thank heavens, but next time – there must not be a next time. I see the cultural and biological imperatives working in her, and know she can't wait forever. We must take our first chance and act together, swiftly, ruthlessly.

Gart is dead. The children are staying with friends. And Maggs and I are waiting for the night.

This will be the last time I write here, the last piece of paper I fill with words no one but me can read. I'm going home. It will, it must, be true.

I feel very odd. Dazed by it all, and hurt: the wounds he inflicted throb and flare with pain. Maggs was less battered and also she's stronger, which probably accounts for her manner: the high spirits of youth and a natural impatience with my slowness. I've been so downtrodden by Gart that I couldn't think what to do after we'd killed him. I stood there like an idiot, tears in my eyes and my gorge rising, unable to act.

Maggs scooped up the lizard and dropped it down the front of her shirt where it nestled as if she were its natural owner. Then she set about cleaning the room, eliminating all signs of struggle, and giving me the firm, clear orders I needed to help her.

Somehow I hadn't thought of all the sordid details of afterward, of cleaning the body and getting it into the bathroom to make it appear Gart died of a fall; it never would have occurred to me to arrange for the children to stay the night with school-friends. But then I had imagined we'd leave this world for mine just as soon as we got our hands on the lizard. It's not quite that simple, says Maggs. We have to be in the right place for it to work, and the right place is under a bridge. Bridges are transitional places, where crossings are possible. I should have guessed, of course, for didn't Gart take me under the bridge? I should have known. She says we'll wait until dark, when there will be fewer people around, and it will be safe.

I'm scared. I didn't think it would be like this. I had imagined triumph, and a quick getaway. Not all this waiting, this fear and pain and the need to go under the bridge again. Somehow, when Maggs says that everything is going according to plan, I am not reassured. If there is anyone else under the bridge when we go, if even one man should decide to attack me, I'm too weak to fight, he'd finish me off. Maggs tells me not to be stupid. Maggs says she'll protect me. She seems different, as if already possession of the lizard has changed her. But I can't bear to think that. She's still Maggs, my almost-stepdaughter, my ally, my only friend. I have to believe that. I have to trust her. There's nothing else to do. I must go under the bridge with her.

Skin Deep

Danny stood on the balcony, rubbing his chest absently and staring into a stranger's room, loneliness a hunger inside him. On the brown and white speckled floor he saw a black canvas espadrille. It looked tiny, more like a child's shoe than a woman's. He could see a chair, and the end of the bed. Slung on a wire hanger something white – a vest or sleeveless shirt – was drying in the still, warm air of the courtyard, blocking part of his view into the room opposite. He waited, but there was no sound from the room, and no one appeared. After a while he went back inside, pulling the glass doors to and bolting them shut.

He had been in Bordeaux four days and nothing had happened. He was alone. Left alone, he thought. He still couldn't quite believe it. Every time he entered the apartment he knew he was an intruder. Molly, who had given him the keys, had told him it belonged to Jake and Emma Lowry, friends of her parents from North Texas. Danny had believed her until he arrived and saw how it was furnished; saw the French books and records, and the suits hanging in the wardrobe. In the bedroom, in a small wooden box which held cufflinks, keys, coins and a religious medal, Danny had found a photograph of Molly. It was her passport picture; he had a copy in his billfold.

He should have gone right then, and checked into a hotel – maybe even the one across the courtyard, the one with the room he had just been staring into. But he hadn't come to France to stay in a hotel and be by himself. He wasn't entirely sure why he *had* come to France, after Molly left, but now that he was here he wanted to stay where she would be able to find him, in case she changed her mind again. It had been so sudden, so crazy, the way she had gone off to California with some other guy, leaving Danny with the plane tickets, the keys to a borrowed apartment, a French-English phrase book, and a letter which explained nothing at all. Danny had already sublet his apartment in Austin, and it was too late to register for the university's summer session anyway. He could have gone back to stay with his parents in Plano, and maybe found a job for three months, but that would have been too humiliating. They hadn't approved of his plans for the summer; they thought that Molly was leading him around by the nose – that was the phrase his father used in his mother's presence, anyway. So Danny had had to make a big deal about how much he wanted to go to Europe, how this was a chance he had to take, and a wonderful educational experience. He pointed out that he needed a language to get his degree, and that the best way to learn was by living in a foreign country where he would be forced to speak it regularly.

'But you took Spanish in high school,' his mother objected.

'That doesn't mean I can speak it. Anyway, I'm sure I'd like French better. I love all those French movies.'

'It's that girl.'

Danny shrugged his big shoulders uneasily. 'Of course I'd rather be with her,' he said. 'Maybe I wouldn't have thought of going to France without her, but it makes sense. She's really good at French, so she'll help me. It always helps to have somebody to study with, so I'm bound to learn more. But it's not just Molly. I could stay here and work construction like last year, but why should I, except for the money? I've never been anywhere. Travel is an educational experience. Everybody says so. Don't you think I should do different things, see the world, while I can?'

'We're not giving you any extra money,' said his father.

'I know that. I'm not asking you to. I've got enough. And we've got a free place to live. That's another good reason for going with Molly. We can live really cheap. Her parents have these friends who have a place in Bordeaux that they're going to let us use for free.'

Danny hadn't told his parents when Molly left him. They would be relieved, and smug, and sorry for him, and he couldn't stand that. He'd shrugged it off to his friends, saying that he'd have a lot more fun in France without a steady girlfriend tying him down, and most of them, he thought, had bought it. After all, they knew that before Molly he had gone out with a different girl practically every weekend. For Danny, there were always plenty to choose from. They didn't know, most of them, that Molly was different.

The plane ticket was already paid for, so he might as well go to France. Maybe it would be an educational experience, like he'd told his parents. And maybe Molly would change her mind again. He knew that, without her, he was going to feel lonely wherever he was. What he hadn't realized was just *how* lonely he would feel, alone in a foreign country. He missed not only Molly, but all sorts of things he had always taken for granted: the availability of uncomplicated companionship, people he could sit around with and talk about football or music; stuff on television; the old familiar places for hanging out. And it was always easy to meet girls in Texas – you just started talking to them wherever you saw them: in the supermarket, behind the counter at the Burger King, sitting on the rim of the campus fountain, their pretty faces turned up to the sun. But here, here he was frozen, unable to make a move because he did not speak their language.

Danny put on a clean shirt and went out for dinner. He was already in the habit of going to the same place every night, a cheap, comfortable, family restaurant on the Quai de la Monnaie. Molly would never have let him get away with that, but Danny liked the sense of continuity it gave him. He liked the way the fat, homely waitress beamed with pleasure when she recognized him.

For variety, Danny travelled a different route every time. He never worried about getting lost – he had a strong sense of direction, and this was a port city. Despite the ancient, weirdly twisting streets, it was never difficult to untangle the way to the waterfront. He thought of this as sightseeing, a way of getting to know this foreign place, and he didn't enjoy it much. Walking through narrow back-streets, many of them cobbled, trying to avoid the traffic and the dog turds, was a tortuous and tiring experience. He guessed the old buildings ought to be interesting, but he didn't like to draw attention to himself by stopping and staring too obviously. He knew that his clothes, his attitude, even his size, marked him out as a foreigner. He couldn't help that, but he didn't want to look like a stupid tourist, so he always walked as if he knew exactly where he was going, and was expected somewhere at a specific time.

His round-about walk took him a little longer than usual that evening, and for the first time all the tables were occupied when he arrived. Danny hovered uneasily in the doorway, but before he could do more than think about going away, the waitress had spotted him and steered him, with a rambling, incomprehensible speech, to a seat at a table with two women.

'Um, *excusez-moi*,' said Danny. He felt very large, looming between two petite, blonde females.

'You're American?'

Danny smiled broadly, relief cheering him even more than the first glass of wine always did. 'Yes! You too?' He looked at his companions now with open interest. The prettier one had to be at least thirty, but the one with glasses was probably closer to his own age.

'Good heavens, no,' said the older one. 'English. I'm Abigail, and this is Tommie.'

'Abigail. Tommie. I'm Danny. It's good to meet you.'

Tommie and Abigail looked at each other, almost smiling.

'Have you been here long?' asked Danny. 'You probably come over to France a lot from England, right?'

'Right,' said Abigail. 'Business as well as pleasure. Right now, we're on a wine-buying trip.'

'You are,' said Tommie. 'I'm just along for the ride.' She looked at Danny. 'This is my first time in Bordeaux.'

No beauty, but she was kind of cute, he thought, admiring the fit of her scoop-necked T-shirt. 'Me too,' he said. 'In fact, this is my first time to France . . . my first time to Europe . . . my first time *anywhere* outside America.'

'And what do you think of it?'

'Well. It's certainly very . . . French.'

Danny was enjoying himself more than he had in what seemed like a very long time. It was so easy, no effort at all to make Tommie giggle and respond – at first with his words, but soon simply by a look or a smile. He had to be more careful with Abigail. She wasn't so easy, and he didn't want her to feel like the odd one out. If he was to have a chance with Tommie alone, he couldn't risk getting on the wrong side of her friend.

At the end of the meal – eaten at the leisurely pace of

the French – Danny felt they were all good friends, and was confident of agreement when he suggested they move on to a sidewalk café for a brandy.

'What a very good idea,' said Tommie. 'That's my favourite part of France: sitting in cafés, drinking, watching the world go by . . . I could spend hours like that. But I'm a night-owl, Abby's not. She'll want to go back to the hotel and have an early night.'

'I would like a brandy,' said Abigail.

'Oh, well, all right; just one, then,' said Tommie.

Danny would have stopped at the first café he saw, but the women insisted they must make some token gesture to exercise after their meal, and so, avoiding the dark back streets, they wandered along the avenues for a quarter of an hour until Tommie called a halt by seating herself at a small, round metal table in front of a well-lit café calling itself '*Des Arts.*'

'We'll wait here till Hem comes by,' she said.

'I'd rather see Gertie,' said Abigail.

'You *would.*'

'Who?'

They looked at him.

'Quite right,' said Abigail. 'This isn't Paris. If any dead author came by here it would be Mauriac.'

'He's not my idea of good company. Don't offer him a drink if he *does* show up.'

Conversation had been easy in the restaurant, but now Danny felt out of his depth. He was relieved to see the waiter arriving with their drinks.

'What are y'all doing tomorrow?' Danny asked. 'I mean . . . did y'all have plans?'

'Y'all . . . I love that,' said Abigail. 'It sounds so much nicer than "you-all" – I thought that was what Southerners were supposed to say. You-all. Y'all. But what's the proper response? Should I say "we'll" – not we-all, surely – do folks in Texas say "we'll" instead of we?'

'Of course they don't,' said Tommie. 'Really, Abby, you are too silly. We is already plural. But English doesn't *have* a plural form of you, or it didn't until the Texans kindly invented one.'

'There *is* no plural form of me,' said Abigail. 'But I suppose they must teach grammar differently in Texas. I love, you love, y'all love, he, she and it love . . .'

'What I meant,' said Danny, looking at Tommie, 'was that maybe, if you didn't have any plans, we could –'

'We'll be in St Emilion tomorrow,' said Abigail. 'I will, anyway . . . Tommie may want to change her mind.'

'I'm not missing my favourite wine,' said Tommie with a vigorous shake of her head.

'So . . . you're leaving Bordeaux?'

Tommie looked at him. She reached across the table and briefly touched his hand. 'It's just a day-trip. We'll be back.'

'Maybe we could have dinner then? I mean, all three of us?'

'Maybe,' said Tommie. 'Tell me where you're staying, and I'll be in touch.'

'It's not a hotel; it's an apartment, on the Rue St-François. And there's a telephone.' He tore the order form out of the back of his *French for Travellers* book, and wrote down the address and telephone number for her. 'Tomorrow?'

'Maybe. If we're back in time. Don't wait for us, though.'

'I'm sure we'll run into each other again,' Abigail said. 'We'll be travelling a lot, but Bordeaux is our base.'

Tommie knocked back her brandy. 'We'd better go,' she said. 'This stuff is going to take effect in a few minutes, and I want to be near a bed when it does.' She smiled at Danny. 'Thanks for the drink. It was a lovely evening.'

'Yes, we've enjoyed sharing a table with you,' said Abigail. 'We must do it again sometime.'

'Wait, I –'

'No, no, don't get up. The night is young. There's no reason for *you* to turn in just because we are. Besides, we're not going in your direction. Stay and have another drink. We'll meet again.'

'*Au revoir*,' said Tommie.

'*Au revoir*,' he echoed.

He felt lonely as soon as they had gone, out of place by himself at the small table. He ordered one more brandy, and, as he swirled the heavy liquid around the bowl of the glass, dreamed of Tommie's voice on the phone; of seeing her face light with pleasure at the sight of him; of walking alone with her through the twisting streets of Bordeaux. When her face became Molly's, he decided it was time to turn in for the night.

Entering the dark bedroom, Danny saw that there was a light on in the room across the courtyard. Without stopping to think about it, Danny opened the doors and stepped onto the balcony. And, suddenly, there she was, a tall, slender figure half in shadow, half illuminated, like something from a dream. The breath caught in his throat at the sight; he thought he had never seen anything more beautiful.

She looked back at him, unsmiling. She must have seen him, a dark figure on a dark balcony. There was nothing but air between them. Danny knew he should speak, but he was struck dumb. The simplest French words had gone out of his head, and he could not speak to her in English. Not only did it seem rude, but the scope for misunderstanding seemed horrifying. If only *she* would speak first; say some word to identify herself or acknowledge him –

A blink, and she vanished. Had she ducked down, or calmly moved aside? Danny couldn't tell. He waited, hoping for her return. The light from her room went out. In the sudden, enveloping darkness, Danny's skin crawled. He stepped backwards, into the room, closed the doors, locked them, and drew the curtains across to shut out the night.

As he lay in bed, waiting for sleep, he tried to remember what the woman in the hotel room had looked like. All he could recall was an impression of great, and strange, beauty. She had been exotic, not ordinary, but he could not recall what had given him that impression. Was she Asian? Her hair, he thought, had been dark . . . but as he fell into sleep even those few, physical details were forgotten. In his dreams she and Tommie and Molly were one.

Yet the next time he saw her, he recognized her immediately.

It was late morning the next day. He'd had his coffee and croissants in a café by himself, and was already feeling bored with the day and his plan to visit the Galerie des Beaux Arts, about which Abigail had been so enthusiastic. He was wandering along the Cours Victor Hugo when he saw the woman seated alone at a sidewalk table. His heart began to race.

'*Bonjour*,' he called, approaching, smiling. '*Bonjour, Mademoiselle*.'

She looked at him with fathomless black eyes, and he could not tell if she had recognized him or was seeing him for the first time, but – '*Bonjour*,' she said.

'*Puis-je* – ?' he gestured at the table. But she gave no indication of understanding. He fumbled in his pocket for the English – French phrase book and finally found out how to ask if he could join her. '*Me permettez-vous de m'asseoir ici?*'

She shrugged, then nodded. It was not a warm invitation, but he took permission eagerly, gratefully, scraping a chair up to the little round table and gazing at her, wanting nothing else in the world but to be allowed to look at her.

Already, he was certain he could never grow tired of looking at her, or accustomed to her beauty. Of what did that beauty consist? Her eyes were so dark they could only be called black; he could see no division between pupil and iris. They were not exactly oriental eyes, but neither were they occidental. Her lips were thin rather than full, her nose rather flat. Her hair, black and shining, was short, cut sleekly against the outline of her skull. Her skin had a warm, coppery-golden glow. Danny looked at her arm lying on the cold white enamel surface of the table and he struggled against the desire to touch it, to test the warmth and smoothness he could almost feel against his tongue.

It was a relief when the waiter came and Danny could look away. He ordered two coffees.

'*Parlez-vous anglais?*' Danny asked the woman.

'*Non.*'

His heart sank, but Danny drew a deep breath and turned again to his phrase book. There was a section called 'Making Friends'. He looked at the limited selection of conversational openings, feeling frustrated before he began. He was never going to find out what he wanted to know. He wanted to know everything. He decided to start with her nationality.

'*D'où êtes-vous?*' he asked.

She said something he couldn't quite hear.

'*Pardon?*'

She repeated it: a single word, but one he didn't understand.

'*Je ne comprends pas.*'

She shrugged.

'*C'est une ville? Une ville française?*'

130

She shook her head. '*C'est mon pays.*'

Her country. '*Quelle est votre nationalité?*'

She said something, maybe the same word, Danny wasn't sure. He didn't recognize it as the name of any country he knew. He looked through the list in his phrase book, where the names of continents and countries were given in both French and English, and he offered it to her. She glanced at the page for barely a second, shrugged and looked away. Maybe she couldn't read.

He asked her name: '*Comment vous appelez-vous?*'

She turned her head and gave him a sideways look. It was, somehow, an intimate look; almost as if she had touched him. '*Je m'appelle Shesha,*' she said.

'Shesha? Shesha,' he said. And then again, tasting it. 'Shesha.'

She smiled at him, and he smiled back. He patted his chest. 'Danny,' he explained. '*Je m'appelle Danny.*'

'Danny,' she said. He had never heard his name sound foreign before. She smiled again, and this time he saw the quick movement of tongue between her lips.

Without thinking, he reached for her. It was only his hand on hers, but at the contact the expression froze on her face, and she pulled away.

'I'm sorry,' he said. 'I mean, uh, *pardon, excusez-moi,* I didn't mean anything by it, just –'

'*Au revoir,*' she said, standing and leaving him in a single, smooth, graceful motion.

'Wait – please – Shesha –' But he was clumsy and slow. She had taken him by surprise; he had to pay for the coffee before he could run after her, and then he found that she had vanished down some twisting alley and was gone.

Danny cursed himself in a low, bitter voice, using the foulest expressions he knew. Then he calmed himself, and continued on his way to the city art gallery. It wasn't the end of the world. She was shy and he had been clumsy, but he would see her again, and he could repair the damage. He would study his phrase book carefully over lunch, and work out some sort of apology that she would understand. Maybe they didn't speak the same language, but they would work out a way to communicate. He was certain he had not misunderstood her smile; it was just that his timing was a little off.

131

He went home in the late afternoon, and then, although bored, restless and hungry, waited several hours before going out to dinner, hoping for a glimpse of the woman across the courtyard, and hoping, also, that Tommie would call. But the telephone did not ring, and there was no sign of life in the hotel room. He went out, finally, had a meal by himself in the usual place, and then proceeded to the café where he had said goodbye to Abigail and Tommie and sat there sipping brandy and staring at passers-by.

He was on his third brandy when he saw the two English-women. His heart lifted, and he sat up straighter in his chair, hoping that he wasn't drunk. He wanted to call to them, but decided to wait until they were closer. They were walking towards the café and would probably see him in a minute anyway.

Abigail was talking, head down, concentrating on her words and not her surroundings. Tommie might or might not have been listening to her companion; her head was up and her eyes glanced around, her attention quick and changeable.

Then she saw him. Danny was sure of it. Their eyes met across the distance. He grinned, waiting for her answering smile.

It never came. She turned her head and said something to Abigail, touching her arm, turning her away. They crossed the street without another glance in his direction.

Danny couldn't believe it. What the hell was going on? Women didn't run away from him – they never had, until Molly. But since Molly . . . had her desertion marked him in some way? Did he seem desperate? And Tommie, that plain, plump little girl, who did she think she was? Who did she think *he* was, to treat him like a social leper?

Anger boiled up inside him, but it couldn't disguise the fact that, more than anger, he felt hurt and loneliness. Tommie and her rudeness mattered even less than the nameless, black-eyed beauty who had abandoned him earlier that day, and both of them were nothing compared to Molly. Molly, who had said that she loved him. Molly, who had left him, for reasons she couldn't explain or he understand.

He didn't want to think about Molly. He ordered another brandy.

As he was making his drunken, wavering way home, he saw

a figure waiting for him in the shadows on the corner nearest his apartment building. He recognized the slim figure instantly. He knew he had something to say to her when they met again, but he could not recall the words now. He turned his head away. He would have his meaningless, drunken revenge now by elaborately and obviously ignoring her.

But Shesha did not let him pass. She grabbed his arm with a grip a wrestler might have envied.

'*Excusez-moi*,' she said. 'Danny. *Je suis désolée . . . s'il vous plaît*, Danny . . .' There was more, which he did not understand. But out of the rush and stumble of words he understood two things. One, that she was apologizing for having run away from him earlier; and two, that French was no more her language than it was his.

'It's OK,' he said, his words cutting across the hard work of hers. He wanted to reassure her in French, too, but couldn't remember how. 'It's all right. I forgive you. Hey, don't you speak any English at all?'

She looked blank.

'OK,' he said loudly. 'OK. *Comprends*, OK?'

He stared at her until she read the meaning in his face. Her anxious expression relaxed, and she nodded. He looked down to where she still gripped his arm, painfully hard. She let go.

They looked at each other, strangely shadowed in the sodium glow of the street-lamps. He thought again how beautiful she was, although it was memory and fantasy rather than sight which told him this.

She smiled at him. Her eyes and her mouth glinted softly out of the darkness. 'Danny.'

He thought he knew what that meant, but when he moved to kiss her, she slipped out of his grasp and would not be held.

'Shesha, please. *S'il vous plaît*.'

She shook her head and stayed teasingly out of reach.

He stared at her, dizzy with drink and desire. 'Come home with me.'

'Hmmm?'

'*Chez moi*.' He suddenly remembered the words of an old song. '*Voulez-vous coucher avec moi?*'

She took a step back, but still smiled. '*Pas encore*.'

'Not yet?' That was hopeful, at least. 'When? *Quand*?'

Her shoulders rippled and she looked up, making a gesture at the sky. Danny put his head back and saw a thin slice of moon floating above the city.

'*Pas encore . . . pas ce soir*,' she said. Not yet, not tonight.

What did that mean? He tried to touch her, but she evaded him easily. 'Just one kiss,' he said pleadingly. He held up a finger, and touched it to his lips. 'Just one.'

She shook her head. '*Pas encore.*'

'When, then?' He remembered the word for tomorrow. '*Demain?*'

She hesitated. '*Demain*,' she said, and paused. Then, more firmly, '*Demain, demain.*'

'Tomorrow,' said Danny. 'Well, I probably am too drunk to be much good to you tonight, you're right. But tomorrow. I'll hold you to that, you know; I can find you.'

'*Demain, demain*', she said again. Then: '*Au revoir.*' She slipped away on the word, around the corner, and vanished into the shadows. He did not pursue her. He listened to the sound of her heels against the stone. He inhaled deeply, then wrinkled his nose at the familiar whiff of drains. His body was tingling. He looked up at the moon again. '*Demain*,' he said to the empty street, and he made his way home.

As he was undressing for bed, Danny found that Shesha's grip on his arm had left a mark, a thin, reddish weal such as might be left by the impress of a rubber band. He rubbed at it and, to his relief, it soon faded.

They were sitting in a cafe, at a round metal table, and staring into each other's eyes. Danny suddenly realized that he couldn't look away from her, no matter how he tried. She might have hypnotized him. Then she blinked, and the spell was broken, and Danny woke, heart pounding hard with fright.

There had been something wrong about the way she blinked her eyes, something not normal. And he had the feeling that it wasn't just in the dream, that it was something he had noticed about her earlier and was just now remembering, just now making sense of. That was what was so frightening about it. That it was real, and not normal. Just before he fell back to sleep, Danny understood what it was: she had closed her eyes from bottom to top.

In the morning (it's *demain*, he thought) Danny realized no definite rendezvous had been arranged with Shesha. He decided to wander around the city as usual, see a couple of churches, do some shopping, sit in cafés writing postcards home, and let her find him. She could find him if she wanted to, he thought.

But the day passed and there was no sign of her.

At five o'clock, Danny went back to his apartment, planning to have a shower and change before going out to dinner. He went out onto the balcony and looked across the courtyard. The shutters had been closed that morning, but they were open now, and he could see Shesha. She was wearing an extra-large T-shirt, pacing the floor and rubbing her bare arms as if she were cold. She moved in and out of his line of sight, apparently unaware of him. He stared, and tried to will her to look his way, but she never turned her head. Her face was as still as a mask, eyes fixed on something he couldn't imagine.

Watching her, Danny felt both fear and desire. He remembered the dream – if it had been a dream – and felt again the strength of her fingers encircling his arm. He remembered the tip of her tongue, glinting between her lips. Her beauty was a power he didn't understand. He wanted to kiss her and to hold her, to feel her tongue in his mouth and her arms and legs wrapped fiercely around him.

He didn't even pause to close the balcony door as he went out.

There were small sounds of movement from within, but they stopped as soon as he knocked. '*C'est moi*,' he said. 'It's Danny.'

He waited, listening to the silence, and then he knocked again. After a very long time she opened the door.

She looked at him without expression. He saw fine lines around her eyes, and wondered if she was older than he had thought. Maybe it was just dry skin: it looked duller today, lacking the marvellous golden glow he remembered. The T-shirt, which fell almost to her knees, was white. Big black letters across the front spelled SUCCESS.

'*Bonjour*,' he said.

She said nothing. He had the weird feeling that she didn't remember him. He kept a friendly expression on his face. '*Voulez-vous sortir avec moi?*' Do you want to go out with me?

135

She shook her head again.

Danny reminded himself that this was not her language, either. '*Para manger*,' he said, uncertain if that was right. He mimed eating and drinking. 'Food. Dinner. Yes?'

She shook her head again.

Still he didn't get mad. '*Pourquoi?*'

Shesha sighed, and made a strange, writhing motion with one hand. '*Je ne pas prête.*'

'*Prête?*' He remembered that meant 'ready'. 'Oh, you mean you're not dressed. That's OK; I'll wait. *Je restez . . . vous . . . vous . . .*' Awkwardly he mimed putting on clothes.

'*Demain*,' she said.

'*Demain* . . . dammit, it *is demain*, it's *demain* now, *aujourd'hui*, today!'

'*Demain*,' she repeated with no more expression or emphasis than before.

'*Pourquoi demain?*'

She made the motion with her hand again. What did it mean? What was she trying to mime? He thought of a fish, or a snake, or an eel swimming. '*Demain . . . je change . . . je change ma peau.*'

'Change? Change what? How? *Pourquoi no aujourd'hui?*' Frustrated by his lack of words he moved towards her, into the room, but she held up a hand like a traffic cop, stopping him. '*Pas encore. Demain.*'

He was sick of being turned away, refused and ignored for reasons which were never explained. He grabbed hold of her arm, hardly knowing whether he meant to push her aside or pull her to him, but rough with the intention of hurting, of showing her that he meant it.

She hissed. Beneath his fingers, the flesh of her arm split open, the skin bursting beneath the pressure and tearing like dessicated rubber. Something dark and wet glistened beneath the brittle, broken skin.

Danny recoiled. He was shaking. She wasn't. She cradled the injured arm to her breast and looked at him, almost smiling.

'*Demain*,' she said. '*Demain, ma peau . . .*' with her other hand she made a sweeping, slicing gesture from forehead to crotch, and then she did smile, and showed him the tip of her tongue.

'*Pardon*,' said Danny hoarsely, backing away down the hall. '*Je suis désolé . . . excusez-moi, pardon.*'

'*Au revoir*, Danny,' she said. '*A demain.*'

'No way,' Danny muttered to himself, halfway down the stairs. He was never going to see her again if he could help it. It made no difference how beautiful she was, or how lonely he was – there was something seriously *wrong* with her. Wrong mentally, he didn't doubt, as well as physically. The worst thing was that, despite his revulsion, he was still aroused.

He decided it was time to leave Bordeaux, time to give up the fantasy that Molly would come back to him. In the morning he would take a train to Paris, and after a week there maybe he would go to London. At least the people there would speak English. When he ran out of money, he would fly back to Texas. He didn't have to explain his decision to anyone.

After dinner in a new restaurant, Danny walked down to the train station to check the schedule and buy himself a one-way ticket to Paris. He felt more at ease with that settled, and stopped in a bar for one farewell cognac before going home to bed.

As soon as he stepped through the door, Danny knew something was wrong. His body, tensed to run or fight, knew even before his brain figured it out. There was a lamp glowing gently in one corner. And there she was, glowing in the light of it, standing in the bedroom doorway, naked as the day she was born.

She was impossibly beautiful. Her skin had a silvery sheen, unlike anything he'd ever seen. *She* was unlike anything he'd ever seen. He could have gone on looking at her forever.

'*Bonsoir*, Danny. *Voulez-vous coucher avec moi?*'

He did, oh, how he did. She was his dream come true. And he was terrified. Danny shook his head. He fumbled for the words that would make her leave. '*Laissez-moi tranquille*,' he said. Leave me alone.

She laughed at him. 'Danny,' she said, caressingly, and then something else which he didn't understand. She beckoned, and the movement made her arm shimmer. He saw that the skin was loose, about to fall off.

'*Dépêchez-vous*,' she said. Hurry up. She smiled at him and backed into the bedroom, naked, shimmering, desirable, terrifying.

Sweating, he took a few steps forward. It had to be a joke, a trick of some kind. That couldn't really be her skin coming off. She had wrapped herself in plastic, or painted herself with glue.

He could hear her in the bedroom, chanting in what he took to be her own language. If snakes could sing, would they sound like that?

Reaching the door, he closed his eyes and pulled it shut. It was a big, heavy door with an old-fashioned skeleton key which worked from either side. His hands shook like an old man's as he locked her out of his sight.

Out of sight, but not out of hearing. As the tumblers in the lock clicked heavily home, Danny heard her voice soar high in surprise or sorrow. He waited, sweating, for what came next. Surely she would assault the door, or plead with him in her primitive French.

But nothing happened. Silence now on the other side of the door. Danny sat heavily down on the couch. His passport, money, clothes were all in the other room with her, and that meant he was trapped. He couldn't leave. He couldn't do anything but wait for her to make the next move.

He woke with a start to find himself sitting on the couch. Wondering, he stood up and began taking off his shirt as he walked towards the bedroom. When he saw the locked door he remembered. He touched the wood.

'Shesha?'

Nothing.

Perhaps he had dreamed the whole thing? He leaned against the door, pressing his ear against it, and listened. He thought he heard a rustling noise, and the sound of irregular breathing, but those might have been the sounds he made himself. Danny felt weak and exhausted, and he remembered the fear he had felt earlier. He remembered how the skin had hung on her, and the sight of her tongue between her lips, and knew that no matter how crazy it was, he was not ready to open that door.

Finally, he stumbled back to the couch and lay down. His heart was beating so hard he was sure he would never fall asleep, but when he opened his eyes the room was light. Somehow the night had passed.

He sat up and looked around the room. Everything was

ordinary. His legs were cramped from the way he had been lying. He looked at the locked door and listened to the silence, beginning to feel ashamed of himself. If she was still in there –

I won't say anything, he told himself. I won't kiss her. I won't let her touch me. I'll just get my things together and go.

The key made a very loud noise when he turned it, and Danny winced.

'Shesha?'

She was lying on the bed. The sight of her body outlined by the window-light aroused such a mixture of emotions – relief, shame, desire – that even if he'd had words to express them he would have been too choked to speak.

It was only as he was standing over her, hand descending towards her naked shoulder to wake her gently, that he realized it was not a woman on the bed, but merely the shell of one.

An almost perfect shell. A fine line bisected her from scalp to crotch, showing where the outer casing had split open.

What had come out of it?

Danny whirled, scanning the floor. His skin crawled, but he forced himself to bend low enough to see under the bed. There was nothing there but a few dust-balls. The balcony doors were open.

Whatever she was, whatever she had been, she was gone.

He looked at what she had left behind. The skin was translucent, not transparent, and if he didn't look too closely he could almost believe it held solid flesh. It had the same dusky golden skin-tone he had admired in life. He touched it gently, but his fingertips told him nothing.

Cautiously he lifted her, gathering her into his arms, and then he couldn't help himself: he pressed his lips to hers as if he could breathe life back into the hollow shell and kiss her awake.

At the first, moist touch of his lips, hers dissolved. He cried out, and her face crumbled before the blast. At the same time the pressure of his embrace, gentle though it was, shattered the illusion of wholeness, and the woman-shell disintegrated.

Ash, skin fragments, dust, covered him and the bed, clung to his body and clothes, drifted to the floor to be carried off by the passing breeze. Soon he would have nothing left of her, not even the certain memory that she had ever existed.

Danny sat alone on the bed and told himself that he was safe.

A Birthday

Although they both lived in London, Peter Squyres did not see his mother very often. Once every few months, moved by a feeling of duty, he would phone her and a meeting would be arranged. Sometimes he took her out to dinner, and sometimes he went to her house in Holland Park. He was twenty-three, lived in a shared flat in Wood Green, had friends, hobbies, and a job in a bank. His mother, in her mid-forties, had a mysterious, busy life into which he did not enter. This seemed to suit them both.

Although they both lived in London, Peter Squyres did not see his mother very often. Once every few months, moved by a feeling of duty, he would phone her and a meeting would be arranged. Sometimes he took her out to dinner, and sometimes he went to her house in Holland Park. He was twenty-three, lived in a shared flat in Wood Green, had friends, hobbies, and a job in a bank. His mother, in her mid-forties, had a mysterious, busy life into which he did not enter. This seemed to suit them both.

One morning, unusually, she phoned him at work and invited him to come round that evening for a drink. While he hesitated, trying to think what to say, she went on, 'I know it's short notice, but I've only just remembered that it's my birthday, and I thought it would be nice . . .'

His eyes went to the calendar on the wall, and he felt guilty.

'Yes, of course,' he said. 'I'd love to. I was meaning to drop by, anyway, after work, to bring you a present.'

'Lovely,' she said. 'Shall we say sixish? Just a drink. You've probably made plans for dinner, so I won't keep you long.'

'Why don't you let me take you out to dinner?'

'No, Peter, I wasn't fishing for an invitation. Don't change your plans for me.'

'It's no problem . . .'

'Peter, don't fuss. I asked you for drinks. Just drinks,' she said. 'Sixish.'

He had to phone his girlfriend, then, and tell her about the change in plans.

'I didn't know you *had* a mother,' said Anna.

'What does that mean? Don't you believe me? It's her birthday. I really couldn't say no . . .'

'Yes, of course I believe you; don't get in a state. It doesn't matter. I understand about parents, believe me. Let's make it another night.'

'We can still have dinner tonight,' he said. 'I want to see you. How about the Malaysian place, at eight? I'll phone for a reservation, all right?'

'If you like.' He couldn't tell if she was annoyed or indifferent. She might even be smiling, pleased by his persistence. Only part of his difficulty was due to the fact that he couldn't see her expression. Peter and Anna had known each other for about three months, and had started sleeping together two weeks ago. He had thought that would make a difference, that sex would make things clear and definite between them, but it hadn't worked like that. He still didn't know what she thought, or how she felt about him, and it seemed he was always worrying, trying to please or placate her, as once, long ago, with his mother.

'I'll see you at the restaurant at eight,' he said. 'I miss you.'

On his lunch break he went out to buy a present for his mother. He bought red roses and then, at a loss, a bottle of Glenfiddich.

'Happy birthday, Liz,' he said when she opened the door. He had stopped calling her 'Mummy' when he was five.

She accepted his gifts with a gracious smile and conventional expressions of pleasure, as if he were any guest, any man she knew. There were always men in her life, but which of them were her lovers, or if one had ever meant more to her than the others, Peter never knew.

'What can I get you to drink?' she asked. 'G & T?'

'G & T, yes, please.' He sat down and watched as she fixed the drinks – his elegant, beautiful mother. Her hair was dark, without a trace of grey, cut short and sleekly styled. She wore black silk trousers and a quilted Chinese jacket. Her shirt, also silk, was white with an odd, abstract pattern in red.

As she handed him his drink he frowned, seeing dirty fingerprints on the glass.

'This glass,' he said, rising, 'it seems to be – I'll get another . . . .'

She reached out to take it from him, and then he saw that her hand was bleeding.

The whole hand was covered in blood.

'What?' she asked at his exclamation.

'Your hand,' he said, afraid to touch it, afraid of putting pressure on the wound and hurting her. 'You're bleeding.'

She looked down at her hand with a grimace of distaste, and put it behind her back. 'It's nothing,' she said. 'I didn't realize . . . I'll go wash it off.'

'Do you want me to help? Let me look . . . How did you hurt yourself?'

'It's nothing,' she said again. 'It happened earlier . . . it looks terrible, I know, but it doesn't hurt at all. It's nothing. Let me clean up . . .'

She seemed less concerned with her injury than with his reaction to it. When she had gone he stared down at the pale carpet, looking at two, small, dark red spots. Her whole hand had been covered in blood. How could that be nothing?

She came back in, holding up a clean, unblemished hand. 'See? Nothing.'

She let him look, but when he tried to touch she pulled her hand away. 'I'm all right, Peter, honestly. Why don't you get yourself another glass?'

He did as she said. But when he came back he looked at her blouse and saw that the abstract pattern had altered. There were more red splotches on the white silk now, and they were larger.

'You're bleeding,' he said, shocked. 'Liz, what *is* it? What's wrong?'

She looked down and pulled the jacket closed, and fastened it, hiding the bloodstained blouse. He saw how blood sprang out on her fingertips as she used her hands. He saw a line of blood on her neck, seeping above her collar. Horrified, he saw that her feet were bleeding, too.

'I'm going to call a doctor,' he said. 'Or hospital . . . who's your doctor?'

'Peter, sit down and don't be silly. You don't know anything about it.'

Such was the force of habit – she was his mother, after all – that Peter sat down again. 'What is it?' he asked, trying to sound calm. 'Do you know what it means?'

'I'm not hurt,' she said. 'There's nothing wrong. No cuts or scratches. The blood . . . it's just coming from my pores, like perspiration. There's no injury. I'm not in pain. I don't feel any weaker for the blood I've lost, and this has been happening all day. There's nothing a doctor could do.'

Rivulets of blood were rolling down the smooth black leather of her shoes to be soaked up by the rough weave of the carpet.

'But it's not normal,' said Peter. 'Bleeding like that – there's something wrong! How do you know a doctor couldn't –'

'Hysterical bleeding,' she said calmly. 'Have you heard of that?'

He could not imagine anyone less hysterical than his mother. Even now, when anyone would be frightened, she was utterly rational. Her silk trousers stuck to her legs, dark and wet. 'I've heard of hysterical symptoms,' he said. 'A woman who thought she was pregnant, who showed all the signs of pregnancy, even fooled the doctors, but . . . it was an imaginary pregnancy, an hysterical pregnancy, not real. Do you mean this is like that? Do you mean it's not real blood?'

'I feel very well,' she said. 'If I had lost as much blood as I appear to have lost, I can't believe I could feel this well. On the other hand, if it's not blood, what is it?' She opened her hand, and they both stared at the blood that pooled to fill her cupped palm. After a moment she looked about, finally poured the red liquid into a crystal ash-tray. 'It stains like real blood,' she said. 'I'm going to have to have these carpets done . . . I don't think I'll ever get it out of the mattress.'

'How long? How long has this been going on?'

'I suppose it must have started in the night. The early morning, really. It was the bed's being wet which woke me . . .' A flicker of emotion, then. 'It was a shock, I must admit. I have a strong stomach and the sight of blood, my own blood, has never really bothered me. I remember how much blood there was when you were born; when the midwife put you in my arms, you were simply covered in blood, every inch of you, and that didn't bother me at all – and yet, this morning, when I saw myself in so much blood . . . I had to think . . . it took me some time to realize that there was nothing wrong – nothing *else* wrong – with me, and that I felt fine.' She shrugged. Blood began to seep from her cuffs, fat drops spattering the carpet.

'Just because you feel all right – look, you *must* see a doctor.

No matter how you feel . . . you can't go on like this, just bleeding forever.'

'Yes, of course, I know that; I haven't lost my mind, Peter. And I haven't been alone, I've spoken to someone about it, to a nurse. She agrees with me. I'll see a doctor if I have to, if it doesn't stop naturally. But I'm sure it will stop . . . If it's still happening in the morning, I promise you I'll phone my doctor.'

'Morning!' Peter leaned forward, distressed, almost spilling his drink. 'You don't mean you're going to wait until tomorrow?'

'It's too late to phone anyone now.'

'But you can't go on bleeding like this all night! Doctors have answering services – there'd be someone on call. What's the nearest hospital?'

'Peter, do calm down, please. I have been taking care of myself for years. This is not an emergency. I do have some knowledge of what doctors can and cannot do, and I am not going to go and sit in some hospital casualty ward for hours when I can be comfortable here at home. If I must see a doctor, I would like it to be my own doctor, someone who at least knows me. I can wait. It's not going to get any worse in the next few hours.' She raised her glass to her lips and drank while red from her fingers rolled down the side of the glass.

'That's crazy,' said Peter. 'You don't know it's not going to get worse, you don't know anything about it. You're not a doctor, you can't know. If something should happen – anything could happen. I won't let you stay here on your own all night.'

'I've already thought of that, and I'm not going to be on my own. I've asked Jean to come round just as soon as she gets the old lady settled for the night.'

'Who?'

'Jean Emery. She's a registered nurse. She looks after the old dear next door. Has done for the last few months. We've got to be quite good friends, and she often pops in for a cup of tea or a drink and a chat. In fact –' here Liz released a small, triumphant smile, 'in fact, I've already seen her. She's seen *me*. Everything's under control. She agrees that there's no need for me to rush off to a doctor. She doesn't think there's anything a doctor could do. She's trained, Peter. She'll know if I need help, if anything starts to go wrong. She'll know what to do. She's agreed to stay the night. So you see, there's nothing for you to worry about.'

Peter drank the rest of his gin and tonic and went to pour himself another. 'I want to meet this woman before I leave you. I'd like to talk to her.'

'Well, of course. Nothing could be easier. Would you pour me another drink, too, darling?'

They had little enough to say to each other at the best of times. Now it was impossible. Her illness, or injury, made everything else sink into insignificance. Peter wished he could call a doctor and hand the problem over to someone else. Frightened and ill-at-ease, he drank too much. Liz left him after quarter of an hour to shower and change. She returned wearing a black jersey dress. It covered most of her body, but left her lower legs bare. He couldn't stop staring at them. When the first bright drops of blood appeared he felt guilty, as if the pressure of his gaze had done it. Every few minutes she wiped her hands on a dark cloth which she then tucked into the chair cushions, out of sight.

'Your face isn't bleeding,' he said.

'No, not yet. But my scalp has started.'

He shuddered, finished what was in his glass, and looked at his watch. Nearly eight o'clock. He thought of Anna, waiting in the restaurant. He was about to ask if he could use the telephone when the doorbell chimed.

Jean Emery wore a crisp uniform and cap, and the very sight of her made him feel better. She was probably his mother's age, but her black hair was well-sprinkled with grey, and instead of Liz's elegance she had a kind of solidity, and an air of practical efficiency which Peter instinctively trusted. He looked from her clear, hazel eyes to her humorous mouth and liked her still more. He reminded himself that he was drunk. With a belligerence he didn't feel he demanded, 'You know what's happening to my mother?'

'You must be Peter,' said the nurse calmly. 'I'm glad to meet you at last; Liz has told me so much about you.'

'But what about her? Is she going to be all right?'

The women exchanged glances.

'He's worried about me,' said Liz.

'You didn't explain . . . ?'

Liz wrinkled her nose ever so slightly, pursing her lips in distaste, and Peter, staring at her, was assailed by a memory more than fourteen years old. She'd had that same expression when he asked her where babies came from, and she had given him a vague and unsatisfactory answer.

Jean gave a sigh that was half a laugh. 'How about a cup of tea, Peter? I could certainly use one.'

'I'm drinking gin,' he said.

'Perhaps you've had enough gin for now, eh?' She had a smile that stopped his anger. He nodded obediently.

'I'll put the kettle on,' said Liz, and left them alone.

'Sit down, Peter, do. I've been run off my feet today.' Jean settled herself on the couch.

'Look, I'm sorry if I seem a bit abrupt, but I'm very worried about my . . . about Liz. She won't let me call a doctor.'

'There's no need for a doctor.'

'But she's bleeding!'

Jean nodded. 'Yes, and I can see that's very worrying for you. Will you believe me when I tell you there's nothing to worry about? It's a change, and of course there are some risks; understandably, you're nervous. But you needn't be frightened. There is nothing wrong. Your mother is going to be fine.'

'But what's . . . what's happening?'

For just a moment Jean's steady gaze seemed to flicker, and Peter intuited reluctance to speak about female secrets to a man. 'She's my *mother*,' he said fiercely.

'Yes, of course, of course. That's why . . . Your mother is a very special woman, I don't know if you appreciate that, Peter.'

He nodded impatiently. 'Just tell me what's wrong.'

'Nothing is wrong. That's what I want you to understand. This is a normal . . . Have you heard of what they call the "change of life"?'

Peter frowned. 'Yes, of course. It means when women . . . when women can't . . . when women stop . . . at a certain age . . . ' He felt hot and uncomfortable.

'Yes, I think you understand. You needn't spell it out.'

'But I thought that was when women *stopped* bleeding!' he blurted.

Jean smiled. 'You weren't wrong. But people aren't all exactly alike. It takes different women in different ways, the change of life.'

Liz came back into the room then, bearing a tray. 'Here we are,' she said.

Peter looked at his watch. He was sure he was blushing. He had blundered in where he was not wanted, and he knew he wouldn't be able to question Jean further. Maybe it would be all right; she was, after all, a nurse, and Liz seemed comfortable with her. Nagging away at him was the awareness that even if he left now he would be almost an hour late to meet Anna.

'I can't stay,' he said. 'I'm supposed to meet someone for dinner.'

'Of course, I didn't mean to delay you,' Liz said. 'Run along. Really, Peter, you needn't worry about me.'

He looked at the blood pooling at her feet, and then he looked at Jean. 'Are you *sure* . . . ?'

'Quite sure,' said Jean.

'And you'll stay with her?'

'I will.'

'And call a doctor if there's anything . . .'

'Oh, Peter –'

'You have my word. Now run along. Come back in the morning, and see how different everything will be then.'

'I will,' said Peter. 'I will be back in the morning. But if anything happens tonight, if there's anything you're worried about, or anything you need, please ring me. It doesn't matter what time it is. All right?'

The nurse nodded. 'All right.'

He was afraid that Anna would not be there, but she was in the Malaysian restaurant, eating. She looked up from her satay, unperturbed, as he rushed in.

'I went ahead and ordered, I didn't think you'd mind. You can start eating some of mine and then just order whatever else you like.'

'I'm sorry I'm late, but –'

'Oh, that's all right. I know how parents can be.'

'It's not that – there was something wrong – I mean, something really odd, very peculiar – she was bleeding, and it wouldn't stop.' He knocked the chair over on his first attempt to sit down. 'Sorry. Anyway, I tried to get her to phone a doctor, but she wouldn't, and of course I couldn't just leave –'

'Peter, have you been drinking?'

'A couple of gins. Well, maybe three or four. It was a shock. I mean, well, if you'd seen her, the blood just coming out.' He made flowing motions with his hands.

'Blood? What are you talking about? Your mother?'

'Yes, that's it. All day, she said. Just coming out of her pores. All over her body. I'd never heard of such a thing and it spooked me, I don't mind telling you. But then Jean came in – she's the nurse – and she wasn't bothered a bit. Explained it to me, calmed me down. Change of life, she said. Well, of course I'd heard of that, but I had no idea it could be like that, that kind of bleeding.' He gestured at his shirt. 'Her clothes were soaked in blood, absolutely soaked. She said her scalp had started bleeding, too, but I couldn't see it: her hair looked OK to me. I guess the only part of her that wasn't bleeding was her face. Really strange. Made me feel quite ill. But she said it didn't hurt a bit, and Jean said it was really pretty normal.'

'Normal?' said Anna.

The look on her face stopped him. He nodded, but uncertainly.

'Peter. Do you know what you're saying? Are you telling me that your mother was soaked in blood? That she was bleeding all over? That's not normal. There's no way that could be normal. She was like that when you left her?'

'She was with a nurse.'

'A nurse who says it's normal.'

Peter felt suddenly like a balloon that has lost all its air. He no longer knew what had happened, what was true. Jean said one thing, Anna another. Who could he believe? 'What shall I do?'

'I think we'd better go back there, to your mother's house, and see.' She caught the waiter's eye and summoned him with a nod of her head. 'The bill, please.'

'You're coming with me?'

'Yes. It will be better. Then one of us can stay with her and the other go for help, if need be.' Then she gave him a more personal look, and reached across the table to touch his hand. 'Of course I'm going with you. If you want me.'

'Oh, yes,' he said. 'Yes, please.' He smiled in relief. Anna cared, and he wasn't alone.

They took a cab to Holland Park. On the way, Anna mentioned that her flatmate's mother was a doctor, and she spoke of her own first-aid training. Peter was grateful for her level-headed practicality, but mostly he was simply grateful for her presence, glad to have her hand to hold. Now, he thought, everything would be all right.

But when they rang the bell to his mother's house, there was no reply. Peter was quick to panic. 'She said she'd stay – she promised!'

'Maybe they've both gone – maybe she took her to hospital after all. Do you have a key?'

'Oh . . . yes, of course I do.'

The front room was empty. The blood on the carpet looked even more horrible now it had dried. Peter put his arm around Anna and walked with her through to the back of the house.

The bedroom was like an abattoir. Jean was there, her once-fresh uniform a bloody mess. There was no sign of Liz. But lying on the bed was a tiny baby, all red, as if covered in a glistening second skin of blood.

'You're just in time,' said Jean.

The baby opened its mouth and began to squall.

'Hush, hush, Lizzie,' said Jean. 'Hush, now, Peter's home.' She lifted the baby and held it out towards Peter. 'Congratulations,' she said. 'You have a lovely daughter.'

A Mother's Heart: A True Bear Story

'Father Bear, Father Bear,' called the young man softly, crouching in the wood, not moving.

'Father Bear,' called the young man softly, crouching beneath the thick soft sky from which the round moon, like his wife's face, looked out, pitiless in sleep.

'Father Bear,' he said again, a little more loudly as the doubt crept in, and he moved his head, trying to see where the old bear slept. There was a sound like many insect wings as the bear moved on its bed of leaves.

'Father Bear,' said the young man again. 'Father Bear, you must help me. My wife does not love me. My children do not respect me. I need that promotion. Help me, and I'll be good to you.'

He waited, scarcely breathing, for the reply.

A soft growly sound came out of the darkness, and he did not think it was unfriendly. He saw what might have been the gleam of an eye, and then it vanished, and he heard the crunching flutter of the dry leaves as the old bear settled back into sleep.

The children had built a log shelter for it. They were the first to find it, of course. It was in the woods behind their house.

The house was built on a ravine, and the backyard went sloping down into wilderness. The front of the house looked out onto a very ordinary street, but the two children found in the back quite another world.

On the day the children met the bear they came in for lunch unable to think of anything else. They ate their sandwiches and whispered to each other. Their mother was curious about the secret and annoyed that they did not confide in her. She chastised them sharply for whispering at the table.

Without strain, the children switched into a private language.

The mother listened so intently that she cut her finger slicing the meat for sandwiches, but she couldn't guess what they were talking about. When, as they were leaving, they asked if they might take along an extra sandwich, or a piece of fruit, she said they might not.

'If you're still hungry you can come back inside later, or wait until dinner,' is what she said to their outraged faces, but she said to herself, 'Give them food to feed all the children in the neighbourhood? Certainly not.'

The children's mother had nothing to do. The house was clean. Her children would not play with her. It was too early to start dinner. She stood by the kitchen window, one hand touching the sun-warmed glass, and stared down the brief expanse of lawn into the tangly wood. The children were only flashes of colour, patches of red and blue cloth, of blonde hair between the trees as they darted about like bright flies. She could not tell what they were doing, nor if they were alone or with friends. If she went down there they would stop their game. She reflected upon how annoying children were; how greatly they enjoyed confounding and confusing their elders.

She put the children to bed early that evening; fetched them from their play before the last light had faded from the sky.

'I wish you weren't our mother!' cried the little girl, her face screwed into childish rage.

'Everyone else is still out playing,' said the little boy, as reasonably, thought the woman, as his father.

'You've been staying up entirely too late,' she said. 'Don't think you can get away with it all the time.'

The little boy closed his eyes; the little girl stared at the ceiling.

'Would you like a story?' the mother asked, solicitous now.

They would not speak to her.

'Any book you like,' said the mother. 'What were you doing down in those woods, anyway? What was so important out there that you missed your favourite show?' But they were sulking now. They wouldn't tell her.

'All right,' she said, cheerful because she, after all, was the grown-up. 'Be like clams, then. Sleep tight.'

She closed their door softly behind her and went swiftly to the back of the house, out, and down into the woods. The ground was springy from the last rain, and her heels sank into the earth.

In one deep part of the wood, in a circlet of trees, she found the half-completed log house. The children had built it of fallen logs and branches they had found in the woods, and of rocks from the dry, flat bottom of the ravine. They had worked very hard on it, and their mother suddenly wanted to kick it down. But instead she became a proud mother again and went back up to the house with a half-smile on her face for the cleverness of her babies.

The father learned about the bear by not caring about the bear. The children spoke around him as he sat in his den reading his paper; they spoke as if their father did not quite exist – was a troublesome spirit given to bestowing favours and as frequently to rescinding them. They spoke and he heard, and later, when he needed something like the bear, he believed.

That night when he needed the bear was the culmination of many nights. He and his wife had been to a party and he had discovered his wife dallying with another man. He had not taken it well. He had been, he was told, very uncool. He was stoned, although he didn't think he was, and later that night as he lay beside his sleeping wife, fragments came together in the way in which they are said to do for madmen and geniuses, and he suddenly saw the picture and saw it whole and clear.

That was the night he supplicated the bear, and at the time it did not seem at all an odd thing for him to be doing.

The following day the young man brought his offerings down to the bear: a fine large honeycomb and several bags of nuts, all from the finest health-food store. Carrying these packages down into the woods in the light of late afternoon did seem an abnormal thing to do, but he had made a promise the night before, and he wouldn't shirk it now.

He found the shelter and noticed that the roof had been made by draping an old tarpaulin across the logs. He recognized the tarp as one that had lain in the back of the garage for a long time unused.

He left the honeycomb and the piles of nuts beside the rock that seemed to guard the entrance. He saw other offerings beside the rock: two cookies, a small bunch of onion-flowers, and a piece of paper covered with crayoned hearts and his children's names. He smiled at that, and wondered what they had asked of the bear. His offering looked very fine indeed beside these childish ones.

His wife was standing at the kitchen window, brooding; and she saw him go down into the woods with his sacrifices. She could not tell what he was carrying, but because she was in a morbid frame of mind, it seemed to her that each of those bundles might contain parts of a dismembered body.

'He has murdered someone,' she thought idly. 'Murdered someone at the office who stood in the way of his promotion, and now he is bringing the man home in parts, to bury him in our woods.'

Her husband a murderer – how neatly everything could be solved by that! She decided that perhaps she would send the children with shovels and a tale of buried treasure into the woods to dig. When the body was discovered, her husband would be arrested, everyone would pity her, and she'd have a no-questions divorce.

She had been feeling sorry for herself all day, regretting her marriage. The light, she thought, was a long time coming, but finally she saw her husband for what he was: a man interested in nothing but money. And only the other night she had met his antithesis – the most wonderful man . . .

After dinner the woman went down into the woods. She saw the offerings outside the shelter, looked at them, and thought. Then she went back to the house and sipped her sherry. When she put the children to bed she asked them point-blank what lived in the little house in the woods.

The little girl answered, wearing that look of coy expectancy children assume when repeating a remark they know to be cute: 'A bear. Isn't that right?' She turned to her brother for confirmation and he, equally aware of his audience, nodded vigorously. The woman was left with a feeling of unrest, trying to decide if they were fantasizing, or . . . telling the truth?

She sipped her sherry for the rest of the evening and brooded and finally decided that her own precious children would not lie to their very own mother, and her husband *had* left a large honeycomb in the woods, ergo, there was a bear living in the woods. Now, what was she to do with that?

Later that night, when the moon was at its brightest and she was at her highest she left a low-voiced quarrel with her husband and ran out into the yard. She stopped at the edge of the wood, afraid to enter, and called out in a voice pitched to the bear and any other gods of the forest, called out her wretchedness, her unhappiness, the unfairness of it all. There was a man, she said, a man who understood her and who would give her what she wanted. She asked for a way to leave her husband, to go with this man and be happy.

Her husband looked at her in fright, she thought, when she came on her dew-wet feet back into the house.

'What did you ask him for?'

'Go to sleep,' she said contemptuously.

He grabbed her by the arm. 'How did you know about it? What did you ask for?'

She lifted her chin at him. 'You'll just have to wait and find out, won't you?'

'You won't get anything,' he cried out, forgetting the sleeping children. 'I know you, and you could never humble yourself enough to ask properly. You would demand, you're always demanding, and you must –'

'How would you know what to do? How would you know if crawling on your knees is better than standing –' Then she stopped and laughed. In their bedroom the children had gotten into one bed together, made a cave beneath the blankets, and told each other stories about the bear. The woman changed her tone.

'You're really crazy,' she said. 'You actually think there is some mythical creature out there that grants your prayers.' She knocked her head with a knuckle. 'You have gone right over the edge. And if you think I'm going to stay with you any longer,' she said, feeling herself stronger by the minute, as if someone were helping her, letting her know what to say, 'you're even crazier. I've got good reason to leave – and they won't let you keep the children, either, after I tell them about this bear of yours.'

They were shouting at each other for much of the rest of the night, but the children eventually fell asleep in spite of it as did, finally, their parents.

The furs were in the back of the cedar closet, as the bear had told them. The children found the furry, warm bearskins back beneath a pile of dresses and coats that their mother had been · meaning for years to send to the Salvation Army. The children took the skins into the playroom, closed the door, and romped around on the floor, growling and pretending to be bears. The play made them hot and tired; and because they had slept little the night before, they lay down together, with the furs wrapped around them, and pretended they were asleep. After a while they were asleep, and that was when the change took place.

The young man had to get up in the morning and go to work because he didn't want to lose his job even if he did lose his wife. She waited, pretending sleep until he had gone, and then she was on her feet and once again filled with the righteous indignation of the night before. She ran about, muttering to herself, packing the things she would need most. The rest could be sent for later. Finally she went to get her children. She had heard them playing in the playroom earlier, but now it was ominously silent.

She thought at first they were two shaggy dogs. They raised their heads, peered at her with their weak eyes and snuffled when she cried out. She decided that they *must* be dogs, however much they might look like bears. She looked about for something with which to chase them out, and caught up the children's play broom.

They ran from her, hastily and clumsily, their great claws scrabbling and clicking against the wood floors. A lamp was overturned and a vase of flowers knocked off an end-table, but at last she saw them outside, running for the trees.

She never saw her children again.

The young woman did eventually run away with her wonderful new man, but was never happy. He, it turned out, was a used-car salesman with all the faults of her husband and few of his virtues. Too, he was as obsessed with money as her husband, but he did not have quite so much of it.

The young man was given his promotion, but later lost his job to a computer.

But the children, at least, lived happily ever after. For it is the prayers of her children that a mother's heart heeds, and the bear, of course, was a she-bear, and had been searching for her cubs for a great many years.

The Other Room

It was sometime past midnight when Charles Logue mounted the front steps of the house he still thought of as his grandfather's.

His grandfather had been dead thirty-five years: Charles had never known him. The house, unlived in, had been his own property for ten years. Still, Charles thought of it, when he thought of it, as his grandfather's house.

The house had been built solidly of wood in the days when families required a lot of room. The front porch was long and deep, and there had once been a screened veranda above it. Grandly pillared and gabled, it was an imposing, old-fashioned house in a once-gracious neighbourhood now gone to commerce. It had been stripped, gutted and subdivided to hold small businesses in the early '60s.

Charles Logue stood on the porch, remembering evenings spent reading comic books on the splintering wooden steps in the last light of the day, until his mother or grandmother scolded him for ruining his eyes and sent him running across the street to join in a game of kickball or fox-and-hounds. He remembered the sound of cicadas, the sudden flare of fireflies in the deep shadows under the oak trees, the smell of freshly-cut grass and baking cookies.

The keys jangled together – an adult sound – as Logue found the correct one and unlocked the front door. He entered uncertainly, trying to recall the present floorplan. The old one was still clear in his mind, and he knew he would have to superimpose new walls and spaces over the rooms of his memory.

There was a health-food store and a lawyer's office on the first floor; upstairs, he knew, was a record store and something called 'Woman/Space'. It might have been much worse – next door was a beauty parlour/fortune-telling operation, and a few houses down was a gift shop Logue had heard was a cover for more illicit business.

Something – broken glass? – ground and slipped beneath his feet as he walked slowly into the high-ceilinged hall, gazing at the health-food store's display window. Bands of white light from the street revealed dim shapes, boxes of tea, bags of nuts and bottles of vitamin tablets. But Logue didn't see the present display, nor the ghost of the parlour once in that space. He was caught up in his misery again, thinking the thing he could not forget, the central fact of his existence for the past year:

His daughter was dying.

There had been room and time for hope, once. There had been an operation that was supposed to save her. But it hadn't. It hadn't helped at all. There was nothing any of them could do but watch her, every day, draw a little closer to death.

Already she had gone so far that it was hard for the living to talk to her, hard to pretend or to say anything that had meaning, impossible to comprehend her experience.

There was the barrier of physical pain, and the agony of observing, without being able to lighten or share, her suffering; there was the fuzzy, sense-numbing wall of drugs around her; but highest and sternest of all the barriers was Death, which she approached steadily, leaving her family and friends helpless in the distance.

He sat for hours beside her bed, holding her bony little hand until his arm was numb, trying to pull her back by sheer force of will. He tried to pray. He would have made any bargain with god, devil or doctor, but everyone told him there was nothing, now, that anyone could do. Nothing he could do but hope for a miracle or wait for the end.

Beyond tears, beyond hope, standing in the heart of the old house, Charles Logue pressed his hands to his face and shuddered.

Charles Logue first came to the house when he was eight years old, at the end of a long journey, late at night. The reason – although his parents did not tell him – was that the old man was dying. It was a uniting of the family, a last chance for togetherness and forgiveness at the end.

Under ordinary circumstances Charles' mother would have

noticed he was 'coming down with something'. But in her own excitement and worry about her father, she was impatient with the boy's whining and fidgeting, and saw them as signs only of childish restlessness with a long car trip. To keep him entertained, she told him stories about her childhood in the house they were now going to, including the information that the house contained a secret room, accessible through a hidden door.

'I won't tell you where it is,' she said mysteriously. 'I'm not sure anyone in the house remembers it nowadays. I discovered it myself when I was a girl. You can have fun looking for it, and using it as a hideout.'

The prospect cheered Charles almost to the point of forgetting his discomfort, and he passed much of the trip in fantasies about finding the room and putting it to good use.

It was very late indeed by the time they reached the house, and Charles was bundled off to bed in a room filled with the lurking shapes of strange furniture. He wasn't made to take a bath, or even to brush his teeth, and he was put to bed – the grown-ups talking all the while over his head, oblivious to him – in his underwear, then left alone.

He lay quietly for a few moments, hearing the voices and footsteps move away from him and down the stairs. He gazed at the rectangle of light which was the doorway, blinking his eyes, which, like the rest of him, felt sore and hot.

Irritably, he kicked the covers off. The rasp of the sheet against his bare arms and legs annoyed him, and the air was so close he could hardly draw a satisfying breath. He got up and padded softly to the door.

The upstairs hall, he saw, was long and narrow, lit by a chandelier which hung above the landing at the turn of the stairs. It hurt his eyes to look at it – it seemed all fiery, faceted crystal, shooting light in all directions – so he turned his face away from the stairs to the winding hall to the left. It made a sudden turning after a few feet, and he could not see past the projecting corner.

As he stepped out into the hall, Charles suddenly wished he had not left his bed, however uncomfortable it was. His body ached, his throat hurt too much to swallow, and now, after having been so hot, he was shivering uncontrollably.

He called for his mother in a plaintive voice. But there was no reply. No one came. Charles realized that he could hear no one in the house, which surely meant that, wherever his parents had gone, they could not hear him, either. He could call until he had no voice left, and no one would come. Helplessly, because he felt so very sick, Charles began to cry.

But not for long: he was a brave, sensible boy and knew crying wouldn't bring his mother if she couldn't hear him. He would have to go look for her.

He turned to the stairs again and stopped short. They seemed to be moving, like the steps on an escalator he had once been afraid of in a department store. They crept back and forth between shadow and light. They taunted him with hidden teeth: step on me and I'll suck you under and chew off your legs.

Charles moaned softly, closing his eyes against the dizzying back-and-forth motion. He dared not go near those treacherous stairs. He leaned against the door-frame, calling for his mother in a hopeless whisper. Tears seeped from his eyes and rolled down his face.

Gradually, through his pain, Charles became aware of voices. Soft voices, muffled by a wall, but they were somewhere nearby, upstairs. He stopped sobbing and held his breath to listen, to be sure. It might not be his mother, but that didn't matter – any grown-up would do. Someone to take him back to bed, make him comfortable, and climb safely, carelessly down the stairs to fetch his mother back to him.

He turned and began to make his way down the hall, away from the stairs and the light. His legs were weak, so he leaned against the wall for support. He could feel the voices through the wall, a slight vibration, but when he paused to listen he could not make out any words. But the voices went on rising and falling, a comforting, natural sound. Behind this wall he would find a room with people sitting and talking together.

Yet when he finally came to a room, the door gaped on black emptiness. Charles stared, disbelieving, into the silent darkness. Where were they, those people he had heard through the wall? Had he missed a previous door?

Shoulders slumping, head reeling with dizziness, Charles turned back and pressed his ear against the wall. Yes, the voices were still there. They were clearer now: he heard a woman say his name.

Excited now, he hurried, certain he had only missed the first door in his weariness. But he came back to the room he had started from without finding, in the long, empty stretch of corridor, any entrance to a room where people sat together and talked about him.

There had to be a door, Charles knew. He did not see how he could have missed it, open or closed.

Unless it was a hidden door.

He remembered then, with another surge of excitement, that his mother had told him this house had a secret room, behind a hidden door. That must be it!

He retraced his steps, leaning against the wall now less from weakness than from the hope of finding some difference in the surface, some bump or indentation or crack which would indicate the hidden door.

And at last he found it, just as he had imagined.

There was nothing more than a light depression, a smooth dip in the wood about the size of a grown man's thumb. Charles put his own thumb in the spot and pressed. There was a clear, distant click, and then a long, straight crack appeared in the wall, expanding as the door swung open.

The room was surprisingly large for a hidden room, Charles thought as he entered it. It was long and furnished like a waiting room or hallway with wooden chairs and dark oil paintings in heavy gilded frames. The floor was a dark, polished wood, and a rug patterned in maroon and brown made an aisle down the centre of it. Covering the far wall – or perhaps hiding a doorway – was a straight, heavy curtain.

Charles gazed around at this unexpected room and, suddenly, felt frightened.

'Charles.'

A whisper in the empty room.

'Who's there?'

Behind him he could hear the smooth, latching sound of a door falling shut. The faint echoes of his high, frightened voice hung in the air. The heavy curtain ahead of him moved slightly, although the air was perfectly still.

He could not go back, Charles told himself. He must be brave.

He had come here to find someone, and he would. He had heard their voices. His mother knew about the secret room, perhaps she was waiting for him on the other side of that curtain.

Bravely, he walked the length of the room, and took hold of one corner of the stiff, heavy fabric. As he raised it, he felt a gentle waft of scented air against his face. Breathing it in made his heart beat a little faster, but he didn't know why. It was a sweet, slightly musky smell, strange to him, but exciting.

The newly-revealed room was enormous, with an immensely high, airy ceiling that made Charles think of churches. The room was filled with a pale, blue-white light that seemed to have no particular source but simply was, like the air. The walls and floor were made of a highly polished white stone which had within it flecks which caught the light in a silver gleam.

There were people in this room, and the sight of them terrified Charles.

He had been looking for people – had heard their voices and come expecting to find someone, but he was not prepared for what he had found. These people were certainly not his relatives – they did not look like any people Charles had ever seen before.

Most startling was their colour. They were white: bone, chalk, dead white. They looked as if, instead of flesh, they were made of porcelain.

They were unnaturally thin and tall, with elongated necks and arms. When they moved – as now, they moved towards him – they undulated.

Charles didn't dare run – he felt too weak to escape them, and the idea of being caught by them was far more horrible than merely confronting them. So he held his ground, braced himself, and prayed they would not touch him with their dead-white hands.

'Dear boy.'

It was a woman's voice, gentle as music. He looked up into a narrow, elegant face. It wasn't human, but there was something beautiful about it all the same. Charles stared at her, his fascination winning over his terror. Her face seemed to glow with a faint light, and her long, narrow eyes glittered like blue ice.

'Come with me, dear boy, and rest yourself. I'll make you comfortable.'

161

Before he could think to pull away, she had rested her pale hand on his head, and immediately Charles felt soothed and cooled. He was no longer feverish or sore, and his initial terror of these strange people had been lulled. They looked strange, but they seemed so kind . . .

'Let the boy alone!'

It was a loud, coarse shout, completely out of place in this ethereal room. Charles was vaguely irritated by it. As he turned in the direction of the sound, he saw a large, angry man bearing down upon him. The man, like his voice, was equally an intruder here. He was an ordinary man, old and fleshy. His face reminded Charles of an old hound-dog, and he wore a red-and-white striped robe which was garish in this place of muted colours.

Charles shrank away from the stranger, against the woman who had offered to comfort him.

With surprising strength, a bony, freckled hand pulled Charles from his refuge. 'Get out of here, boy!'

Then the ugly old face swooped in close. 'Who are you, boy? You look familiar, somehow.'

Charles craned his neck to see how the white people were taking this intrusion. There were perhaps a dozen of them gathered around, all standing quietly, with no readable expression on their thin, still faces. He turned back to the old man. 'My name is Charles Logue, sir.'

'Charles. Logue. My name is Charles, too.' His voice quickened with eagerness. 'Logue . . . are you Elaine's boy?'

'Yes, sir.'

'But what are you doing *here*?'

'We came to see my grandfather.'

'Bless you, son, I'm your grandfather. I mean how did you come *here*?'

'Through the secret door. My mother told me there was one. I heard voices through the wall, and looked until I found it. They said my name.'

'*My* name,' the old man said softly. 'You shouldn't be here, boy. It's no place for you. You go on back now, and find your mother.'

'You come with me,' Charles said.

The old man closed his eyes and shook his head quickly. 'Go on, now.'

Charles looked up. The lady who had offered him comfort was smiling at him. He had a glimpse of small, pointed teeth, like a cat's.

'Please,' whispered Charles to his grandfather.

The old man straightened to his full height. 'Let the boy go,' he said. 'You have no business with him.'

The encircling crowd did not move or speak. The old man bent down and spoke softly to Charles: 'We'll walk toward the curtain. The first chance you get, you must run for it, without looking back and without waiting for me, understand?'

Charles nodded and put his hand trustingly into his grandfather's. They began to walk, slowly, and the white people gave slightly before them. But they moved at a snail's pace – Charles realized that his grandfather did not want to touch, even to brush against, these people, and, not understanding why, he grew more frightened.

Finally they came near the curtain. The white people did not seem anxious to be close to it, and moved away, making a gap in the circle through which Charles saw he could escape.

His grandfather gave him a push, then, and Charles ran as he had been told to, without pausing or looking back. As he slipped behind the heavy curtain, he heard a woman's voice right at his ear, as if she ran at his side, saying,

'You'll come back. When you understand, you'll come back to me.'

Now a grown man, standing in the house he owned, Charles Logue was afraid to go upstairs. He didn't know which he feared more: finding the room, or not finding it.

Thirty-five years before, when he had recovered from his long illness, young Charles had begun to search again for the hidden door. The adults had told him that his grandfather was dead and buried in the ground – and what a pity they'd never met – but Charles knew better. He knew where his grandfather was, and he meant to find him, to save him, somehow, from the strange people who kept him prisoner.

But no matter how many times he walked the length of the hall, no matter where he pressed or knocked or scratched, he could not find the door again. His efforts were noticed, the object of amused speculation by the adults, and finally his mother had taken pity on him and told him that the secret room was downstairs. She had even showed him what she called the secret room – a stuffy little cave beneath the stairs, accessible through a door at the back of a closet.

It made no difference: Charles knew what he had seen. He refused to believe it had been only a dream, and, for the rest of the summer that he stayed in the house, Charles continued to look in vain for the door, the room, his grandfather.

Would it be any different this time, Charles wondered. Could it? Leaving aside the question of dream or reality, why should he succeed now when he had failed so many times as a child? Was it enough that he was an adult now and fully aware of what he proposed to do? That he was willing to sacrifice himself to save his daughter? He would try to leave the room with his daughter, but if a life was called for, he would give up his. All he asked was the chance.

He pressed his hand to his forehead, checking his fever like a key or a weapon. Would it be enough to get him in? But his hands were cold, and he could not tell if his face burned or not.

Coming down with this virus, three nights before, tossing restlessly in his bed, Charles had had a dream. In the dream he had gone again to that hidden room and there had seen his daughter, surrounded by those thin, white people. The look of mute terror on her face as she sought to find a familiar human being in that place had torn his heart, and he had woken crying and calling her name.

He knew she was there – he had heard her speak to them. He had seen the blue shadows of that room in her eyes. He'd heard her initial fear turn to a weak fascination as, in a drugged half-sleep, she begged them to touch her with their cool, white hands and take away her pain.

I come with pure heart and clear intentions, thought Charles, only half ironically. His mouth was dry. Please, let me save her.

He began to mount the stairs. The bannister was new and ugly, but the steps beneath his feet seemed to be the same ones he had climbed as a boy, so old that a shallow depression was worn in the centre of each broad step by years of footsteps.

He heard voices above his head. Dimly, through a wall, he heard them.

Charles froze, holding himself perfectly still and silent, and listened intently. The murmur of voices came again, a distant, familiar rhythm.

He let out his breath in a sigh and continued to climb. He had been right to come here, after all. They had let him hear them; they would let him find the door again.

But the upper hall was not empty, as it should have been. He was not alone. There were others here, dark figures moving swiftly toward him, harsh human voices; he scarcely had time to realize that something was wrong and he was in danger before the sudden, intense pain took him into a suffocating blackness.

When he came to, he was standing in the antechamber with the dark oil paintings on the walls and the wooden chairs lined up beneath them. So he must have found the door, although he did not remember how or when.

His head ached abominably, and his shirt was wet – with blood, it seemed. He didn't stop to reflect on it, but hurried toward the tapestry hanging at the end of the room.

As he lifted one corner of the heavy curtain that rich, strange, musky scent came to him again for the first time in years. He breathed it in, feeling pleasure and nostalgia so sharply that he wanted to weep. He still did not know what the smell was, but it was beautiful.

The other room was just as he remembered it. His eyes went to his daughter at once, picking her out easily amid the strange, pale people. She sat on the floor beside a chair, and the person in that chair encircled her loosely with a bone-white arm.

Charles called out her name, and she turned her face towards him. The helpless, drowning look she gave him nearly broke his heart. She was almost past saving; she would have to be pulled away. But he would; he would do it, he would make her leave, thought Charles, and, hunched against the pain growing in his side, he began to walk towards her.

'You've come back at last. I've been waiting.'

It was the woman who had spoken to him during his first visit. She had not changed at all. She was still beautiful in the non-human way of stone or statue or insect with her dead-white, faintly glowing skin, her frozen eyes, her oddly elongated limbs. The sight of her made him shiver with something much more profound than cold or fear.

Before he could think to avoid her, she touched his side and then his head with the white branch of her hand.

'Let me make you comfortable,' she said.

The pain vanished instantly. Despite himself, Charles felt weakly, slavishly grateful to her. He had not realized how badly he was hurting until the pain had gone.

'Come and sit with me and let us talk together,' she said. 'It's what we've both been waiting for since you were just a boy.'

Charles could not imagine why he had ever wanted to run from her. She was so beautiful, and her touch was so soothing. Her voice was music that he wanted to listen to forever.

He knew now why he had come here, why he had dreamed of coming back and searched for the hidden door for so many years. His daughter – sad little thing – had never been more than incidental in his decision.

He put his large, rough fingers into her smooth hand and let her lead him away.

Dead Television

Personally, I blame Thomas Alva Edison. I know most people hold Marcus Vandergaard responsible, but Marcus, though he could never admit it, was only the dead inventor's tool. Yes, of course I'm prejudiced – I can't deny that I loved Marcus – but I'm also *right*.

Check this, from Edison's 1920 diary: 'If what we call personality exists after death, and that personality is anxious to communicate with those of us who are still in the flesh on this earth, there are two or three kinds of apparatus which should make communication very easy. I am engaged in the construction of one such apparatus now, and I hope to be able to finish it before very many months pass.'

Marcus always liked being compared to Edison. He, too, was a brilliant, eccentric maverick with a wide-ranging, startlingly creative intelligence and a talent for making money. He was too easily bored and too quirky to make a good team-worker, and he couldn't limit himself enough to be a specialist. He liked to follow his ideas wherever they took him, and to go there by himself.

But unlike Edison, Marcus had no mystical leanings. He was a solid, sceptical materialist, and I'm sure he had no sympathy with Edison's weird theory about memory consisting of subparticles which travelled through space and lodged, in swarms, in human brains, creating intelligence. After death, Edison thought, the swarm might disperse, or stay together until they found a new host for the original personality. I'm certain Marcus never believed in reincarnation, nor in the survival of the personality after death – until, of course, we all *had* to believe it. So why should his genius lead him in that direction?

I am no scientist. But I have my own talent – I might even say genius, if that didn't sound immodest. But others have called me genius, and surely not *all* the critical acclaim can be put down to the novelty value of a serious composer and orchestral conductor who is also a fairly attractive young woman. The work survives. At least, I hope it will. Anyway, having my own talent, I understand what drove Marcus. Even without understanding what he did, I know how the work can take over, demanding expression. Maybe, for Marcus, dead television began as a joke, or as something else entirely. Maybe it was unintentional. I once sat down to write a song for my niece's birthday; three weeks later it was a chamber opera.

I used to think I was most myself when I was composing, which may seem odd because there is also the sense at those times of being *taken over* by inspiration, of being inhabited by some other force, greater than oneself. It can't be forced or willed, that divine gift, that possession. I miss it, sometimes, but I won't let it happen again. The possible results are too terrifying.

Composing isn't just a matter of inspiration, of course. There's the work that follows. The construction. The fooling around. The hard slog. The mistakes. The testing and discarding, the reluctant compromises, the agony, frustration, dreariness, boredom and depression of writing music, leading to the ultimate, always qualified and partial, satisfaction. And I miss the work just as much as I miss the divine gift. Neither means anything alone – they have to go together. It was Edison (again!) who composed the formula my high-school music teacher used to write on the blackboard: 'Genius is one per cent inspiration, and ninety-nine per cent perspiration.'

What I'm saying is, that one per cent in Marcus Vandergaard may have been Edison, swarming around the cosmos for years as a disincarnate entity, desperate for a chance to make himself real again.

Everybody remembers where they were when it first happened, and I am no exception. I was the second person in the world to have the experience. Naturally, I didn't understand what it meant at the time.

I'd just come back from a two-week tour with the orchestra. The air in the house was stale and dusty and it felt deserted, but when I saw all the cups and coffee mugs – every single one in the house – piled unwashed in the sink, and the empty McDonald's and Kentucky Fried wrappers spilling out of the bin, I suspected I'd find Marcus out back in his workshop. As I passed through the living room again I noticed that the TV was missing, but because the VCR and CD were still in place I suspected Marcus rather than a burglar.

I was right. He was in his workshop, watching television.

'Hello, darling,' I said. 'Working hard?'

He gave me a brief, distracted glance. 'Isn't it amazing?'

I stood beside him and looked at the screen. On it was an actor dressed in a 1920s-style, three-piece, cream-coloured suit, lecturing vigorously about the uselessness of the public school system. The actor looked like the elderly Thomas Edison but the picture – in colour – was obviously not a film. It was either live television or good quality tape, and the reception was clear and vivid, much better than I'd ever seen on that particular set. 'You fixed the picture?' I guessed.

Marcus was too absorbed to reply. To be polite, and because I had missed him, I went on watching for a few minutes more in silence. But it was a remarkably boring production. The actor just went on and on in a crotchety, opinionated sort of way about teachers, the school system, and kids today. It was probably an accurate representation of Edison, I thought, but who cared? And there was nothing else, no setting, just a black backcloth behind him. Finally I got tired of waiting for Marcus to explain what was so interesting about it.

'Are you picking this up on the dish, or is it local?'

'It's Edison.'

'I can see that, but what's the play? Who's doing it?'

Finally he looked at me. 'Oh, you're back. Aren't you early?'

'No, it's been two weeks.'

'Oh. Well, I'm glad you're back.' He didn't ask about the tour, which was usual, or kiss me, which wasn't. His attention was still on the screen, and that struck me as strange. This was a man who never watched television: his boredom threshold was too low, his other interests too demanding. It had to be something technical that interested him – was the reception really that remarkable?

'Can't you switch it to something better?' I asked.

'There's only the one channel. I suppose somebody else might come through later, but Edison is just who I was hoping to see. It couldn't be better.'

'What do you mean? Marcus, what *is* this?'

'It's Thomas Alva Edison. Out of the flesh. I've invented dead television.'

If *I* had ever thought of trying to construct an 'apparatus' for communicating with the dead it would surely have been a telephone, not television. A telephone implies reciprocity, two-way communication, individuals taking turns talking and listening. With television, the message travels one way only, and the viewer is forced into the role of passive receiver. You don't *have* to listen; you can turn it off, or switch to something else, but talking back to your television set is a futile exercise. So many of the modern dead – including Edison – have been preserved on film and tape that it can't have been the desire simply to see and hear his heroes that led Marcus to convert our television set for their use. He acted on Edison's inspiration, but he had his own reasons and his own methods.

Television and not telephone because he didn't want to talk to the dead – Marcus found it enough of a chore talking to the living. Once I began living with him it became my responsibility to maintain the few non-professional relationships in his life. He seldom answered the phone, or even listened to the messages that piled up on the answering machine tape, which meant – since he never made phone calls unless they involved some absolutely vital transfer of information – that whenever I was away from home I was effectively cut off from him.

I'm sure it was psychologically easier for him to construct a receiver which might never receive than attempt to initiate a conversation with the dead. It seems impossible now, but Marcus didn't believe in existence after death. He offered the dead a channel like some cable-TV magnate giving one free to a minority group as a tax write-off – but never expected them actually to use it.

Marcus himself never knew why he did it – the idea simply took him over, as others had done before – but it was certainly no reflection of his personal belief. Quite the contrary. And it was his very lack of belief which allowed him to succeed; which made his success so deadly.

The dead have always had their channels to the living. Psychics, mediums, 'channellers', priests, shamans, all the different names for the possessed believers. Because in the past, belief was a necessary component. If you didn't believe in them, the dead wouldn't speak to you – they couldn't. What Marcus did, by his very lack of belief, was to remove belief as a necessary factor. He gave them technology, which works whether you believe in it or not. Once they had converted from spiritual to electronic power, there was no stopping them.

For a genius, Marcus could be awfully stupid. It never occurred to him that what he was doing might be undesirable, even dangerous.

To be fair to him, even if he had thought of it, why should it have seemed a bad thing? It is hard to believe now, but there was a time not long ago when people thought communication with the dead was too good rather than too bad to be true.

At first, the dead appeared only on sets which Marcus specially converted, and at first they were all scientists. Thomas Edison would talk for hours, without stumble or pause, but when he faltered he would flicker and vanish from the screen, replaced immediately by some other chatty spirit. I recall Alexander Graham Bell, Michael Faraday, Albert Einstein, Rosalind Franklin, Enrico Fermi and Marie Curie, but there were plenty more who were unrecognizable, and many who did not speak English.

News of 'the Vandergaard effect', or dead television, spread rapidly, of course. Even when reporters sneered and punned, newsreaders twitched ironic eyebrows, or frankly disbelieved, they still reported 'the news', and taped the dead speakers off the small screen of our television set, allowing satellite technology to transmit the information, with sound and pictures, all across the world. A lot of people didn't believe it, of course: they called it hoax, or mass hysteria. But belief was no longer the issue, as I have said. It didn't make any difference whether or not you believed the dead could speak as long as you saw them posturing or heard their weirdly uninflected voices on the evening news.

Within a matter of weeks the dead were appearing on television sets throughout the world; on ordinary television sets unconverted by Marcus. And it wasn't only dead scientists who could come back. Information was the key now, not belief, and anyone who knew the dead could appear on television might turn on the set and discover their late great-grandmother on screen reciting her recipe for sweet potato pie, or see Marilyn

Monroe pouting sadly and whispering breathily. For the most part, the apparitions were relatives or ancestors or famous dead people with whom the viewers felt some affinity. For example, artists appeared to artists and art-lovers; dead presidents, kings and queens appeared to historians, chief executive officers and habitual readers of popular biography; and dead film stars were absolutely everywhere. If natives deep in the Brazilian jungle weren't haunted by the dead it was only because they hadn't heard the news yet because they didn't have the technology.

I mention Brazil because I'm pretty sure that's where Marcus went when he disappeared. I imagine him in the middle of whatever few acres are left of the Brazilian rainforest, beyond the reach of the information network which his obsessive tinkering took away from us, the living, and delivered into the power of the dead. Is there such a place left in the world? If so, I think it won't be safe for very long.

Poor Marcus. He was as much a victim as the rest of us. He didn't know what he was unleashing. How could he know that the dead would prove not passive consumers, content with their one channel, but even more greedy and expansionist than the living.

There are so many of them, you see. And they all have something to say, and they all want to say it – to everybody.

They may be dead, but they're not stupid. Once they had the use of technology they used it in a big way, until there was nothing left for the rest of us.

Not just one channel, but all channels. Not just television, but radio. And then they managed to tap into telephone lines. At first they broke in on conversations, a babble of unknown, distorted voices erupting into any pause. Then they learned direct dialling, and all over the world telephones began ringing, unceasingly. Nobody else could get through; only the dead had the time and the numbers to overload every line.

My first phone call was from Ethel Smyth. I thought this was unlucky, because, although I was bound to feel a certain sympathy for her as one of the very few women who ever managed to make her name as a composer, I have never thought much of her music, and I knew from my reading that she had been notoriously deaf and egotistical and a non-stop talker, even in life. As in life, so in death: I couldn't get a word

172

in edgewise, and when, finally, in desperation, I hung up, she rang back immediately and went ranting on about the general lack of appreciation for her music.

The next caller was Erik Satie, which thrilled me. But although I do speak French, and had always imagined we would have a lot to say to each other, it was soon obvious that he couldn't hear a word I said. It was like listening to someone talking in his sleep. Whatever I said made no difference, and what he said only occasionally made sense.

I soon realized that, for the dead, the telephone was no different from television or radio. It was a one-way system, a means for transmission, not reception, and maybe that was the way they wanted it. After so many years of listening to our broadcasts and our lives, unable to participate, they had finally found a way to interrupt, to erupt back into the living world, and a little would never be enough.

At first, they came at us through the electronic media – remote, distorted, unreal, irritating but ignorable. They couldn't stand being ignored: they insisted upon being heard, and sought other ways of imposing their voices on us. Once the first barrier was breached, how quickly they all crumbled!

New films, tapes, recordings of any kind could not be made without the faces and voices of the dead appearing, overwhelming and replacing those of the living. Their words burst through and conquered ours in new books, magazines and newspapers as computers and electronic typesetters responded to their impulses. As for old-fashioned means of communication, like pen and paper – well, the dead, too, had their old-fashioned instruments: people.

Some count it an honour to be possessed, to let another soul speak through them, to live in reflected glory. If they have nothing original to contribute themselves they might welcome the chance to make it possible for Rembrandt or Picasso to paint another picture, for Colette or Dickens to write another novel, for Beethoven to compose another symphony.

But the dead are insatiable. There can never be enough willing victims. And so, as belief was no longer necessary, willingness was no longer a requirement.

We are all in danger of being taken over by the dead. It's not just an audience they want, but hosts.

I'm having dead people's dreams now – Kafka and Strindberg, at a guess. Or am I over-reacting and imagining things? It's difficult to know where influence stops and possession begins.

I've had to give up composing. I no longer know where the music in my head comes from, I can't trust any inspiration as my own. I hardly know who I am anymore, but I know I want to do my own work, or nothing. I won't let the dead compose their music through me.

Is it horribly selfish, even precious, of me to worry about something like that in this time of crisis and destruction, when civilization has broken down around us? Even if I dared try to compose, I don't have the leisure: all my time is spent on just getting by, on survival. Even if I did manage to write something new, who, besides myself, would care? Who would even know? How could I transmit it? Would it ever be performed?

In the long, dark hours I think a lot about Marcus – at least I know those memories are my own – and I wonder what he's doing now. How is life in his distant jungle? Is he still tinkering, still managing to invent things in a stone-age culture?

As soon as he disappeared, the rumours began that Marcus was dead, but I know that can't be true. If he were dead I would have heard from him by now. And not just me. If he were dead he'd be everywhere, seen and heard by millions. After all, there could hardly be a more famous dead person in the world today than Marcus Vandergaard. Fame is what immortality is all about.

Edison explained his concept of personality as memories, and it appears that the dead have a chance of survival only if they are remembered by the living. I wonder what happened to the anonymous legions of dead who never did anything when they were alive, not even produce a descendant to remember them and give them another shot at life – did their subparticles disperse? Were they absorbed by their more powerful companions? Did they simply wink out of existence, or linger to combine with other subparticles until they gradually reached critical mass and could be reborn as a wholly new personality?

Maybe that's what I am, someone wholly original, able, therefore, to bring more new creations into the world . . . if only I had the chance.

It's so unfair. I've lost everything that made life worth living . . . everything, indeed, that made me myself. The mere struggle for existence isn't life. What is life without the chance to create?

Maybe it is time to go over to the other side. Not to give up, but to desert the living and join the winners. Dead, I might have a better chance of survival.

My name is still known. I have some small measure of fame as a musician; more, the notoriety of being the woman who lived with Marcus Vandergaard.

The living have no time or space for music anymore. As time passes, I'll be forgotten. If no one remembers me, I won't be able to come back. The dead have shown us the importance of fame. Memory is the only immortality there is. I'm not going to miss my chance. If I can't live this life, I'll have another.

I'm looking forward to talking to Marcus. There is so much I want to say to him.

Bits and Pieces

On the morning after Ralph left her Fay found a foot in her bed.

It was Ralph's foot, but how could he have left it behind? What did it mean? She sat on the edge of the bed holding it in her hand, examining it. It was a long, pale, narrow, rather elegant foot. At the top, where you would expect it to grow into an ankle the foot ended in a slight, skin-covered concavity. There was no sign of blood or severed flesh or bone or scar tissue, nor were there any corns or bunions, over-long nails or dirt. Ralph was a man who looked after his feet.

Lying there in her hand it felt as alive as a motionless foot ever feels; impossible as it seemed, she believed it was real. Ralph wasn't a practical joker, and yet – a foot wasn't something you left behind without noticing. She wondered how he was managing to get around on just one foot. Was it a message? Some obscure consolation for her feeling that, losing him, she had lost a piece of herself?

He had made it clear he no longer wanted to be involved with her. His goodbye had sounded final. But maybe he would get in touch when he realized she still had something of his. Although she knew she ought to be trying to forget him, she felt oddly grateful for this unexpected gift. She wrapped the foot in a silk scarf and put it in the dresser's bottom drawer, to keep for him.

Two days later, tidying the bedroom, she found his other foot under the bed. She had to check the drawer to make sure it wasn't the same one, gone wandering. But it was still there, one right foot, and she was holding the left one. She wrapped the two of them together in the white silk scarf and put them away.

Time passed and Ralph did not get in touch. Fay knew from friends that he was still around, and as she never heard any suggestion that he was now crippled, she began to wonder if the feet had been some sort of hallucination. She kept meaning to look in the bottom drawer, but somehow she kept forgetting.

The relationship with Ralph, while it lasted, had been a serious, deeply meaningful one for them both, she thought; she knew from the start there was no hope of that with Freddy. Fay was a responsible person who believed the act of sex should be accompanied by love and a certain degree of commitment; she detested the very idea of 'casual sex' – but she'd been six months without a man in her bed, and Freddy was irresistible.

He was warm and cuddly and friendly, the perfect teddy bear. Within minutes of meeting him she was thinking about sleeping with him – although it was the comfort and cosiness of bed he brought to mind rather than passion. As passive as a teddy bear, he would let himself be pursued. She met him with friends in a pub, and he offered to walk her home. Outside her door he hugged her. There was no kissing or groping; he just wrapped her in a warm, friendly embrace, where she clung to him longer and tighter than friendship required.

'Mmmm,' he said, appreciatively, smiling down at her, his eyes button-bright, 'I could do this all night.'

'What a good idea,' she said.

After they had made love she decided he was less a teddy bear than a cat. Like a cat in the sensual way he moved and rubbed his body against hers and responded to her touch: she could almost hear him purr. Other cat-like qualities, apparent after she had known him a little longer, were less appealing. Like a cat he was self-centred, basically lazy, and although she continued to enjoy him in bed, she did wish sometimes he would pay more attention to *her* pleasure instead of assuming that his was enough for them both. He seemed to expect her to be pleased no matter what time he turned up for dinner, even if he fell asleep in front of the fire immediately after. And, like many cats, he had more than one home.

Finding out about his other home – hearing that other woman's tear-clogged voice down the phone – decided her to end it. It wasn't – or so she told him – that she wanted to have him all to herself. But she wouldn't be responsible for another woman's sorrow.

He understood her feelings. He was wrong, and she was right. He was remorseful, apologetic, and quite incapable of changing. But he would miss her very much. He gave her a friendly hug before they parted, but once they started hugging it was hard to stop, and they tumbled into bed again.

That had to be the last time. She knew she could be firmer with him on the phone than in person, so she told him he was not to visit unless she first invited him. Sadly, he agreed.

And that was that. Going back into the bedroom she saw the duvet rucked up as if there was someone still in the bed. It made her shiver. If she hadn't just seen him out the door, and closed it behind him she might have thought . . . Determined to put an end to such mournful nonsense she flung the duvet aside, and there he was.

Well, part of him.

Lying on the bed was a headless, neckless, armless, legless, torso. Or at least the back side of one. As with Ralph's feet there was nothing unpleasant about it, no blood or gaping wounds. If you could ignore the sheer impossibility of it, there was nothing wrong with Freddy's back at all. It looked just like the body she had been embracing a few minutes before, and felt . . .

Tentatively, she reached out and touched it. It was warm and smooth, with the firm, elastic give of live flesh. She could not resist stroking it the way she knew he liked, teasing with her nails to make the skin prickle into goose-bumps, running her fingers all the way from the top of the spine to the base, and over the curve of the buttocks where the body ended.

She drew her hand back, shocked. What *was* this? It seemed so much like Freddy, but how could it be when she had seen him, minutes before, walking out the door, fully equipped with all his body parts? Was it possible that there was nothing, now, but air filling out his jumper and jeans?

She sat down, took hold of the torso where the shoulders ended in smooth, fleshy hollows, and heaved it over. The chest was as she remembered, babyishly pink nipples peeking out of a scumble of ginger hair, but below the flat stomach only more flatness. His genitals were missing, as utterly and completely gone as if they had never been thought of. Her stomach twisted with shock and horror although, a moment later, she had to ask herself why that particular lack should matter so much more than the absence of his head – which she had accepted remarkably calmly. After all, this wasn't the real Freddy, only some sort of partial memory of his body inexplicably made flesh.

She went over to the dresser and crouched before the bottom drawer. Yes, they were still there. They didn't appear to have decayed or faded or changed in any way. Letting the silk scarf fall away she gazed at the naked feet and realized that she felt differently about Ralph. She had been unhappy when he left, but she had also been, without admitting it even to herself, furiously angry with him. And the anger had passed. The bitterness was gone, and she felt only affection now as she caressed his feet and remembered the good times. Eventually, with a sigh that mingled fondness and regret, she wrapped them up and put them away. Then she returned to her current problem: what to do with the part Freddy had left behind.

For a moment she thought of leaving it in the bed. He'd always been *so* nice to sleep with . . . But no. She had to finish what she had begun; she couldn't continue sleeping with part of Freddy all the time when all of Freddy part of the time had not been enough for her. She would never be able to get on with her life, she would never dare bring anyone new home with her.

It would have to go in the wardrobe. The only other option was the hall closet which was cold and smelled slightly of damp. So, wrapping it in her best silken dressing gown, securing it with a tie around the waist, she stored Freddy's torso in the wardrobe behind her clothes.

Freddy phoned the next week. He didn't mention missing anything but her, and she almost told him about finding his torso in her bed. But how could she? If she told him, he'd insist on coming over to see it, and if he came over she'd be back to having an affair with him. That wasn't what she was after, was it? She hesitated, and then asked if he was still living with Matilda.

'Oh, more or less,' he said. 'Yes.'

So she didn't tell him. She tried to forget him, and hoped to meet someone else, someone who would occupy the man-sized empty space in her life.

Meanwhile, Freddy continued to phone her once a week – friendly calls, because he wanted to stay friends. After a while she realized, from comments he let drop, that he was seeing another woman; that once again he had two homes. As always, she resisted the temptation she felt to invite him over, but she felt wretchedly lonely that evening.

For the first time since she had stored it away, she took out his body. Trembling a little, ashamed of herself, she took it to bed. She so wanted someone to hold. The body felt just like Freddy, warm and solid and smooth in the same way; it even smelled like him, although now with a faint overlay of her own perfume from her clothes. She held it for a while, but the lack of arms and head was too peculiar. She found that if she lay with her back against his and tucked her legs up so she couldn't feel his missing legs, it was almost like being in bed with Freddy.

She slept well that night, better than she had for weeks. 'My teddy bear,' she murmured as she packed him away again in the morning. It was like having a secret weapon. The comfort of a warm body in bed with her at night relaxed her, and made her more self-confident. She no longer felt any need to invite Freddy over, and when he called it was easy to talk to him without getting more involved, as if they'd always been just friends. And now that she wasn't looking, there seemed to be more men around.

One of them, Paul, who worked for the same company in a different department, asked her out. Lately she had kept running into him, and he seemed to have a lot of business which took him to her part of the building, but it didn't register on her that this was no coincidence until he asked if she was doing anything that Saturday night. After that, his interest in her seemed so obvious that she couldn't imagine why she hadn't noticed earlier.

The most likely reason she hadn't noticed was that she didn't care. She felt instinctively that he wasn't her type; they had little in common. But his unexpected interest flattered her, and made him seem more attractive, and so she agreed to go out with him.

It was a mistake, she thought, uneasily, when Saturday night came around and Paul took her to a very expensive restaurant. He was not unintelligent, certainly not bad-looking, but there was something a little too glossy and humourless about him. He was interested in money, and cars, and computers – and her. He dressed well, and he knew the right things to say, but she imagined he had learned them out of a book. He was awfully single-minded, and seemed intent on seduction, which made her nervous, and she spent too much of the evening trying to think of some way of getting out of inviting him in for coffee when he took her home. It was no good; when the time came, he invited himself in.

She knew it wasn't fair to make comparisons, but Paul was the complete opposite of Freddy. Where Freddy sat back and waited calmly to be stroked, Paul kept edging closer, trying to crawl into her lap. And his hands were everywhere. From the very start of the evening he had stood and walked too close to her, and she didn't like the way he had of touching her, as if casually making a point, staking a physical claim to her.

For the next hour she fended him off. It was a wordless battle which neither of them would admit to. When he left, she lacked the energy to refuse a return match, the following weekend.

They went to the theatre, and afterwards to his place – he said he wanted to show her his computer. She expected another battle, but he was a perfect gentleman. Feeling safer, she agreed to a third date, and then drank too much; the drink loosened her inhibitions, she was too tired to resist his persistent pressure, and finally took him into her bed.

The sex was not entirely a success – for her, anyway – but it would doubtless get better as they got to know each other, she thought, and she was just allowing herself a few modest fantasies about the future, concentrating on the things she thought she liked about him, when he said he had to go.

The man who had been hotly all over her was suddenly distant and cool, almost rude in his haste to leave. She tried to find excuses for him, but when he had gone, and she discovered his hands were still in her bed, she knew he did not mean to return.

The hands were nestling beneath a pillow like a couple of soft-shelled crabs. She shuddered at the sight of them; shouted and threw her shoes at them. The left hand twitched when struck, but otherwise they didn't move.

How dare he leave his hands! She didn't *want* anything to remember him by! She certainly hadn't been in love with him.

Fay looked around for something else to throw, and then felt ashamed of herself. Paul was a creep, but it wasn't fair to take it out on his hands. They hadn't hurt her; they had done their best to give her pleasure – they might have succeeded if she'd liked their owner more.

But she didn't like their owner – she had to admit she wasn't really sorry he wouldn't be back – so why was she stuck with his hands? She could hardly give them back. She could already guess how he would avoid her at work, and she wasn't about to add to his inflated ego by pursuing him. But it didn't seem possible to throw them out, either.

She found a shoe box to put them in – she didn't bother about wrapping them – and then put the box away out of sight on the

181

highest shelf of the kitchen cupboard, among the cracked plates, odd saucers and empty jars which she'd kept because they might someday be useful.

The hands made her think a little differently about what had happened. She had been in love with Ralph and also, for all her attempts to rationalize her feelings, with Freddy – she hadn't wanted either of them to go. It made a kind of sense for her to fantasize that they'd left bits of themselves behind, but that didn't apply to her feelings for Paul. She absolutely refused to believe that her subconscious was responsible for the hands in the kitchen cupboard.

So if not her subconscious, then what? Was it the bed? She stood in the bedroom and looked at it, trying to perceive some sorcery in the brand-name mattress or the pine frame. She had bought the bed for Ralph, really; he had complained so about the futon she had when they met, declaring that it was not only too short, but also bad for his back. He had told her that pine beds were good and also cheap, and although she didn't agree with his assessment of the price, she had bought one. It was the most expensive thing she owned. Was it also haunted?

She could test it; invite friends to stay . . . Would any man who made love in this bed leave a part of himself behind, or only those who made love to her? Only for the last time? But how did it know? How could it, before she herself knew a relationship was over? What if she lured Paul back – would some other body part appear when he left? Or would the hands disappear?

Once she had thought of this, she knew she had to find out. She tried to forget the idea but could not. Days passed, and Paul did not get in touch – he avoided her at work, as she had guessed he would – and she told herself to let him go. Good riddance. To pursue him would be humiliating. It wasn't even as if she were in love with him, after all.

She told herself not to be a fool, but chance and business kept taking her to his part of the building. When forced to acknowledge her his voice was polite and he did not stand too close; he spoke as if they'd never met outside working hours; as if he'd never really noticed her as a woman. She saw him, an hour later, leaning confidentially over one of the newer secretaries, his hand touching her hip.

She felt a stab of jealous frustration. No wonder she couldn't attract his attention; he had already moved on to fresh prey.

Another week went by, but she would not accept defeat. She phoned him up and invited him to dinner. He said his weekends were awfully busy just now. She suggested a week night. He hesitated – surprised by her persistence? Contemptuous? Flattered? – and then said he was involved with someone, actually. Despising herself, Fay said lightly that of course she understood. She said that in fact she herself was involved in a long-standing relationship, but her fellow had been abroad for the past few months, and she got bored and lonely in the evenings. She'd enjoyed herself so much with Paul that she had hoped they'd be able to get together again sometime; that was all.

That changed the temperature. He said he was afraid he couldn't manage dinner, but if she liked, he could drop by later one evening – maybe tomorrow, around ten?

He was on her as soon as he was through the door. She tried to fend him off with offers of drink, but he didn't seem to hear. His hands were everywhere, grabbing, fondling, probing, as undeniably real as they'd ever been.

'Wait, wait,' she said, laughing but not amused. 'Can't we . . . talk?'

He paused, holding her around the waist, and looked down at her. He was bigger than she remembered. 'We could have talked on the phone.'

'I know, but . . .'

'Is there something we need to talk about?'

'Well, no, nothing specific, but . . .'

'Did you invite me over here to talk? Did I misunderstand?'

'No.'

'All right.' His mouth came down, wet and devouring, on hers, and she gave in.

But not on the couch, she thought, a few minutes later. 'Bed,' she gasped, breaking away. 'In the bedroom.'

'Good idea.'

But it no longer seemed like a good idea to her. As she watched him strip off his clothes she thought this was probably the worst idea she'd ever had. She didn't want him in her bed again; she didn't want sex with him. How could she have thought, for even a minute, that she could have sex for such a cold-blooded, ulterior motive?

'I thought you were in a hurry,' he said. 'Get your clothes off.' Naked, he reached for her.

She backed away. 'I'm sorry, I shouldn't have called you, I'm sorry –'

'Don't apologize. It's very sexy when a woman knows what she wants and asks for it.' He'd unbuttoned her blouse and unhooked her bra earlier, and now tried to remove them. She tried to stop him, and he pinioned her wrists.

'This is a mistake, I don't want this, you have to go.'

'Like hell.'

'I'm sorry, Paul, but I mean it.'

He smiled humourlessly. 'You mean you want me to force you.'

'No!'

He pushed her down on the bed, got her skirt off despite her struggles, then ripped her tights.

'Stop it!'

'I wouldn't have thought you liked this sort of thing,' he mused.

'I don't, I'm telling the truth, I don't want to have sex, I want you to leave.' Her voice wobbled all over the place. 'Look, I'm sorry, I'm really sorry, but I can't, not now.' Tears leaked out of her eyes. 'Please. You don't understand. This isn't a game.' She was completely naked now and he was naked on top of her.

'This *is* a game,' he said calmly. 'And I do understand. You've been chasing me for weeks. I know what you want. A minute ago, you were begging me to take you to bed. Now you're embarrassed. You want me to force you. I don't want to force you, but if I have to, I will.'

'No.'

'It's up to you,' he said. 'You can give, or I can take. That simple.'

She had never thought rape could be that simple. She bit one of the arms that held her down. He slapped her hard.

'I told you,' he said. 'You can give, or I can take. It's that simple. It's your choice.'

Frightened by his strength, seeing no choice at all, she gave in.

Afterwards, she was not surprised when she discovered what he had left in her bed. What else should it be? It was just what she deserved.

It was ugly, yet there was something oddly appealing in the sight of it nestling in a fold of the duvet; she was reminded of her teenage passion for collecting bean-bag creatures. She used to line them up across her bed. This could have been one of them: maybe a squashy elephant's head with a fat nose. She went on staring at it for a long time, lying on her side on the bed, emotionally numbed and physically exhausted, unable either to get up or to go to sleep. She told herself she should get rid of it, that she could take her aggressions out on it, cut it up, at least throw it, and the pair of hands, out with the rest of her unwanted garbage. But it was hard to connect this bean-bag creature with Paul and what he had done to her. She realized she had scarcely more than glimpsed his genitals; no wonder she couldn't believe this floppy creature could have had anything to do with her rape. The longer she looked at it, the less she could believe it was that horrible man's. It, too, had been abused by him. And it wasn't his now, it was hers. OK, Paul had been the catalyst, somehow, but this set of genitalia had been born from the bed and her own desire; it was an entirely new thing.

Eventually she fell asleep, still gazing at it. When she opened her eyes in the morning it was like seeing an old friend. She wouldn't get rid of it. She put it in a pillowcase and stashed the parcel among the scarves, shawls and sweaters on the shelf at the top of the wardrobe.

She decided to put the past behind her. She didn't think about Paul or Ralph or even Freddy. Although most nights she slept with Freddy's body, that was a decision made on the same basis, and with no more emotion, as whether she slept with the duvet or the electric blanket. Freddy's body wasn't Freddy's anymore; it was hers.

The only men in her life now were friends. She wasn't looking for romance, and she seldom thought about sex. If she wanted male companionship there was Christopher, a platonic friend from school, or Marcus, her next-door neighbour, or Freddy. They still talked on the phone frequently, and very occasionally met in town for a drink or a meal, but she had never invited him over since their break-up, so it was a shock one evening to answer the door and discover him standing outside.

He looked sheepish. 'I'm sorry,' he said. 'I know I should have called first, but I couldn't find a working phone, and . . . I hope you don't mind. I need somebody to talk to. Matilda's thrown me out.'

And not only Matilda, but also the latest other woman. He poured out his woes, and she made dinner, and they drank wine and talked for hours.

'Do you have somewhere to stay?' she asked at last.

'I could go to my sister's. I stay there a lot anyway. She's got a spare room – I've even got my own key. But –' He gave her his old look, desirous but undemanding. 'Actually, Fay, I was hoping I could stay with you tonight.'

She discovered he was still irresistible.

Her last thought before she fell asleep was how strange it was to sleep with someone who had arms and legs.

In the morning she woke enough to feel him kiss her, but she didn't realize it was a kiss goodbye, for she could still feel his legs entwined with her own.

But the rest of him was gone, and probably for good this time, she discovered when she woke up completely. For a man with such a smooth-skinned body he had extremely hairy legs, she thought, sitting on the bed and staring at the unattached limbs. And for a woman who had just been used and left again, she felt awfully cheerful.

She got Ralph's feet out of the drawer – thinking how much thinner and more elegant they were than Freddy's – and, giggling to herself, pressed the right foot to the bottom of the right leg, just to see how it looked.

It looked as if it was growing there and always had been. When she tried to pull it away, it wouldn't come. She couldn't even see a join. Anyone else might have thought it was perfectly natural; it probably only looked odd to her because she knew it wasn't. When she did the same thing with the left foot and left leg, the same thing happened.

So then, feeling daring, she took Freddy's torso out of the wardrobe and laid it down on the bed just above the legs. She pushed the legs up close, so they looked as if they were growing out of the torso – and then they were. She sat it up, finding that it was as flexible and responsive as a real, live person, not at all a dead weight, and she sat on the edge of the bed beside it and looked down at its empty lap.

'Don't go away; I have just the thing for Sir,' she said.

The genitals were really the wrong size and skin-tone for Freddy's long, pale body, but they nestled gratefully into his crotch, obviously happy in their new home.

The body was happy, too. There was new life in it – not Freddy's, not Paul's, not Ralph's, but a new being created out of their old parts. She wasn't imagining it. Not propped up, it was sitting beside her, holding itself up, alert and waiting. When she leaned closer she could feel a heart beating within the chest, sending the blood coursing through a network of veins and arteries. She reached out to stroke the little elephant-head slumbering between the legs, and as she touched it, it stirred and sat up.

She was sexually excited, too, and, at the same time, horrified. There had to be something wrong with her to want to have sex with this incomplete collection of body parts. All right, it wasn't dead, so at least what she felt wasn't necrophilia, but what was it? A man without arms was merely disabled, but was a man without a head a man at all? Whatever had happened to her belief in the importance of relationships? They couldn't even communicate, except by touch, and then only at her initiative. All he could do was respond to her will. She thought of Paul's hands, how she had been groped, forced, slapped and held down by them, and was just as glad they remained unattached, safely removed to the kitchen cupboard. Safe sex, she thought, and giggled. In response to the vibration, the body listed a little in her direction.

She got off the bed and moved away, then stood and watched it swaying indecisively. She felt a little sorry for it, being so utterly dependent on her, and that cooled her ardour. It wasn't right, she couldn't use it as a kind of live sex-aid – not as it was. She was going to have to find it a head, or forget about it.

She wrapped the body in a sheet to keep the dust off and stored it under the bed. She couldn't sleep with it anymore. In its headless state it was too disturbing. 'Don't worry,' she said, although it couldn't hear her. 'This isn't forever.'

She started her head-hunt. She knew it might take some time, but she was going to be careful; she didn't want another bad experience. It wouldn't be worth it. Something good had come out of the Paul experience, but heads – or faces, anyway – were so much harder to depersonalize. If it looked like Freddy or Paul in the face, she knew she would respond to it as Freddy or Paul, and what was the point of that? She wanted to find someone new, someone she didn't know, but also someone she liked; someone she could find attractive, go to bed with, and be parted from without the traumas of love or hate. She hoped it wasn't an impossible paradox.

She asked friends for introductions, she signed up for classes, joined clubs, went to parties, talked to men in supermarkets and on buses, answered personal ads. And then Marcus dropped by one evening, and asked if she wanted to go to a movie with him.

They had seen a lot of movies and shared a fair number of pizzas over the past two years, but although she liked him, she knew very little about him. She didn't even know for sure that he was heterosexual. She occasionally saw him with other women, but the relationships seemed to be platonic. Because he was younger than she was, delicate-looking and with a penchant for what she thought of as 'arty' clothes, because he didn't talk about sex and had never touched her, the idea of having sex with him had never crossed her mind. Now, seeing his clean-shaven, rather pretty face as if for the first time, it did.

'What a good idea,' she said.

After the movie, after the pizza and a lot of wine, after he'd said he probably should be going, Fay put her hand on his leg and suggested he stay. He seemed keen enough – if surprised – but after she got him into bed he quickly lost his erection and nothing either of them did made any difference.

'It's not your fault,' he said anxiously. It had not occurred to her that it could be. 'Oh, God, this is awful,' he went on. 'If you only knew how I've dreamed of this . . . only I never thought, never dared to hope, that you could want me too, and now . . . you're so wonderful, and kind, and beautiful, and you deserve so much, and you must think I'm completely useless.'

'I think it's probably the wine,' she said. 'We both had too much to drink. Maybe you should go on home . . . I think we'd both sleep better in our own beds, alone.'

'Oh, God, you don't hate me, do you? You will give me another chance, won't you, Fay? Please?'

'Don't worry about it. Yes, Marcus, yes, of course I will. Now, goodnight.'

She found nothing in her bed afterwards; she hadn't expected to. But neither did she expect the flowers that arrived the next day, and the day after that.

He took her out to dinner on Friday night – not pizza this time – and afterwards, in her house, in her bed, they did what they had come together to do. She fell asleep, supremely satisfied, in his arms. In the morning he was eager to make love again, and Fay might have been interested – he had proved himself to be a very tender and skilful lover – but she was too impatient. She had only wanted him for one thing, and the sooner he left her, the sooner she would get it.

'I think you'd better go, Marcus. Let's not drag this out,' she said.

'What do you mean?'

'I mean this was a mistake, we shouldn't have made love, we're really just friends who had too much to drink, so . . .'

He looked pale, even against the pale linen. 'But I love you.'

There was a time when such a statement, in such circum- stances, would have made her happy, but the Fay who had loved, and expected to be loved in return, by the men she took to bed, seemed like another person now.

'But I don't love you.'

'Then why did you –'

'Look, I don't want to argue. I don't want to say something that might hurt you. I want us to be friends, that's all, the way we used to be.' She got up, since he still hadn't moved, and put on her robe.

'Are you saying you never want to see me again?'

She looked down at him. He really did have a nice face, and the pain that was on it now – that she had put there – made her look away hastily in shame. 'Of course I do. You've been a good neighbour and a good friend. I hope we can go on being that. Only . . .' She tried to remember what someone had said to her once, was it Ralph? 'Only I can't be what you want me to be. I still care about you, of course. But I don't love you in that way. So we'd better part. You'll see it's for the best, in time. You'll find someone else.'

'You mean you will.'

Startled, she looked back at him. Wasn't that what she had said to Ralph? She couldn't think how to answer him. But Marcus was out of bed, getting dressed, and didn't seem to expect an answer.

'I'll go,' he said. 'Because you ask me to. But I meant what I said. I love you. You know where I live. If you want me . . . if you change your mind . . .'

'Yes, of course. Goodbye, Marcus, I'm sorry.'

She walked him to the door, saw him out, and locked the door behind him. Now! She scurried back to the bedroom, but halted in the doorway as she had a sudden, nasty thought. What if it hadn't worked? What if, instead of a pretty face, she found, say, another pair of feet in her bed?

Then I'll do it again, she decided, and again and again until I get my man.

She stepped forward, grasped the edge of the duvet, and threw it aside with a conjurer's flourish.

There was nothing on the bare expanse of pale blue sheet; nothing but a few stray pubic hairs.

She picked up the pillows, each in turn, and shook them. She shook out the duvet, unfastening the cover to make sure there was nothing inside. She peered beneath the bed and poked around the sheet-wrapped body, even pulled the bed away from the wall, in case something had caught behind the headboard. Finally she crawled across the bed on her belly, nose to the sheet, examining every inch.

Nothing. He had left nothing.

But why? How?

They left parts because they weren't willing to give all. The bed preserved bits and pieces of men who wanted only pieces of her time, pieces of her body, for which they could pay only with pieces of their own.

Marcus wanted more than that. He wanted, and offered, everything. But she had refused him, so now she had nothing.

No, not nothing. She crouched down and pulled the sheet-wrapped form from beneath the bed, unwrapped it and reassured herself that the headless, armless body was still warm, still alive, still male, still hers. She felt the comforting stir of sexual desire in her own body as she aroused it in his, and she vowed she would not be defeated.

It would take thought and careful planning, but surely she could make one more lover leave her?

She spent the morning making preparations, and at about lunch-time she phoned Marcus and asked him to come over that evening.

'Did you really mean it when you said you loved me?'

'Yes.'

'Because I want to ask you to do something for me, and I don't think you will.'

'Fay, anything, what is it?'

'I'll have to tell you in person.'

'I'll come over now.'

She fell into his arms when he came in, and kissed him passionately. She felt his body respond, and when she looked at his face she saw the hurt had gone and a wondering joy replaced it.

'Let's go in the bedroom,' she said. 'I'm going to tell you everything; I'm going to tell you the truth about what I want, and you won't like it, I know.'

'How can you know? How can you possibly know?' He stroked her back, smiling at her.

'Because it's not normal. It's a sexual thing.'

'Try me.'

They were in the bedroom now. She drew a deep breath. 'Can I tie you to the bed?'

'Well.' He laughed a little. 'I've never done that before, but I don't see anything wrong with it. If it makes you happy.'

'Can I do it?'

'Yes, why not.'

'Now, I mean.' Shielding the bedside cabinet with her body, she pulled out the ropes she had put there earlier. 'Lie down.'

He did as she said. 'You don't want me to undress first?'

She shook her head, busily tying him to the bedposts.

'And what do I do now?' He strained upwards against the ropes, demonstrating how little he was capable of doing.

'Now you give me your head.'

'What?'

'Other men have given me other parts; I want your head.'

It was obvious he didn't know what she meant. She tried to remember how she had planned to explain; what, exactly, she wanted him to do. Should she show him the body under the bed? Would he understand then?

'Your head,' she said again, and then she remembered the words. 'It's simple. You can give it to me, or I can take it. It's your choice.'

He still stared at her as if it wasn't simple at all. She got the knife out of the bedside cabinet, and held it so he could see. 'You give, or I take. It's your choice.'

Memories of the Body

As she plunged the long-bladed butcher's knife into her husband's chest, Cerise realized she had wanted to kill him for years.

She had always kept her anger hidden, not only from others, but from herself as well. She deplored violence, and believed hers was a peaceful nature. She had tried to understand her husband's changing moods and needs, and when he left her she had wept, and gone on loving. Now, however, her long-denied anger was as real as the knife in her hand, and she hated him.

Murder was wonderful. Patrick let out a little moan when she stabbed him, and she echoed his sound as she sometimes did in bed, to encourage him.

She pulled the knife out and gazed at his thin, naked body, loved for so long. She wanted to cut it to pieces, to stab him in a hundred places. She bared her teeth and swung at him.

He tried to stop her, grabbing hold of the blade. He cried out. Blood stained his pale hands.

'Stupid!' she said. With a hard, impatient turn of her wrist she freed the knife from his grasp and severed two of his fingers.

'What'll I cut off next?' she asked. She was breathing hard and her body tingled, as aroused as she had ever been by love-making. 'Why don't you try to get away? Turn around, I'll stab you in the back.'

He stared down at his ruined hand and took one stumbling step backwards. She went after him, cutting him twice, opening his stomach.

'I bet you never thought I could do this. You thought you could get away with anything. You thought I was weak, I bet. Thought I'd kill myself sooner than hurt you. Stand still, damn you.'

With the next stab, the knife sank deep into his abdomen, buried to the hilt, slipping in her grasp.

'Cerise . . .' Blood bubbled on his lips as he spoke. There was blood everywhere, and a terrible, sweet smell. In sudden silence, Patrick fell to his knees, then toppled forward, onto the knife, and lay still.

She felt a surge of disappointment. She wasn't ready for it to be over. She crouched down and tried to lift him, but the body was a dead weight. 'Pat?' she said. Her smile lost its shape, and she began to pant, the smell of death so thick she could hardly breathe. She gagged, and then vomited, and then wept.

Later, she stared through a blur of tears at the little bald spot on the back of his head. She wished she could apologize to him. The hate was all gone now. She hadn't always hated him. 'Oh, Pat,' she said softly. 'I loved you. I really, really did.'

Cerise continued to crouch beside the body while the clock above the bed clicked away the seconds, still dazed with discovery, astonished by her own emotions.

The murder had been Hewitt's idea – she had agreed to it under pressure, only to please him. He would go on feeling threatened by her ex-husband forever, it seemed, unless she would agree to kill him. But even when she went down to that fancy kitchenware shop in the new mall and picked out the scariest-looking knife she could find she wasn't really planning on using it. She was sure that when it came right down to it she would chicken out. Self-defence would be hard enough, but to strike first, to kill in cold blood . . . And to kill someone she had loved! She wasn't an aggressive person. She didn't even like competitive sports, and she hated arguments. That was how she'd agreed to this, in fact. To stop the arguments she and Hewitt were having about love. She had told herself she was only doing it for Hewitt, but from the moment she had seen Patrick again, Hewitt had been nowhere in her thoughts.

Cerise rose on shaky legs and went into the bathroom to wash off the blood, glancing at the button beside the light-switch. If she pushed it, a member of the Timber Oaks staff would be with her within seconds. She decided she wanted to be clean, dressed and made-up, back in control before anyone saw her.

She was sure that was how Hewitt would have done it when he murdered his wife.

Still naked, Cerise leaned through the doorway to look at the clock. Without her lenses, she had to squint to make out the time. It was almost four, much later in the afternoon than she had imagined. They had told her she could stay the night if she wanted, or even for a couple of days. But Hewitt was expecting her for dinner. He obviously didn't think murder should take very long. She wondered how Hewitt had killed his wife, and imagined that he had despatched her with great efficiency. He'd probably walked in, said her name, shot her with one of his guns, fired again to make sure, and then drove back to the office to finalize a couple of deals. Hewitt had offered to show her a videotape of the murder, but Cerise, disliking violence, had refused.

Cerise tried to estimate how long it would take her to drive back to town, and thought about rush-hour traffic. She would be late, but she really had to wash her hair. There might be blood in it, or something else. She wished she wasn't having dinner with Hewitt tonight. He was going to take one look at her and know that she'd had sex with Patrick before she killed him.

The sex hadn't been part of the deal. Not that anything had been said, but she knew Hewitt's attitude. The murder might have been for Hewitt, but there was no way she could pretend the sex had been.

She turned the shower on hard and stepped under it, wishing she could wash away her guilt as easily as the blood.

I shouldn't have had sex with him, she thought. Then said aloud, 'It.' It, not him. That wasn't Patrick's body lying on the bedroom floor; it never had been Patrick. She had to remind herself now of what she had willingly – wilfully – forgotten during the past few hours. It was only a machine she'd murdered, a sophisticated facsimile of Patrick; not a person, only a fax.

On her senior trip in high school Cerise had met a fax of the President. So far as she knew, that was the only one, until the Patrick-fax, but from Hewitt she knew that more and more of the rich and powerful were having facsimiles made to act as decoys, and to be held in reserve against the day when medical science made possible, and age or illness made desirable, a full-body transplant. Hewitt didn't have his own – yet. He said he was waiting until they'd been perfected. He said they were still only machines, not much better than animated dolls. He was particularly contemptuous of people who had sex with faxes. He claimed to find it an inexplicable perversion.

But it wasn't like that. It wasn't the make-believe that Cerise had imagined – neither the murder nor the sex. From the moment she saw him, when his eyes met hers and he smiled with delighted recognition, she could not believe it wasn't her own Patrick, brought to this place by some trick or miracle. And when he kissed her – oh, she could never resist him when he kissed her like that. So they had made love. For hours. And it was wonderful – more like her best fantasies than anything she'd ever had with her husband in reality. Everything was perfect. And then . . .

Then the inevitable, fatal quarrel. She couldn't remember how it had started, or even what it had been about. It had been everything they'd ever disagreed about, the worst fight they'd ever had. None of her attempts to placate him had worked. All the old weapons had come out, and all the old hurts, and then Cerise had stopped backing down. When tears choked her throat and the words would not come, instead of giving in and crying she went for the knife. She had shut him up forever. She had killed him.

Cerise turned off the shower and leaned against the wall, almost too weak to go on standing.

I really killed him, she thought. I really did it.

She just made it across the room to press the button before she slid down the wall and passed out on the wet tiles.

Cerise spent the night at Timber Oaks after all – the night, and the following day. Someone phoned Hewitt to postpone her dinner date. They took care of everything; that was part of the deal.

Not all of its services were strictly legal – nevertheless, Timber Oaks was a registered clinic, with trained psychiatrists on staff. They recognized the guilt and anguish Cerise was suffering, and they knew how to deal with it. Their main effort, at first, was to get her to accept that there had been no real murder. There was no victim. No one had been hurt. She had simply acted out her aggressions on a machine programmed for that very purpose.

Shown the body of the fax, shown the software, shown how it worked and was neither living nor dead, Cerise could not lose the feeling that she had done wrong, and that someone had been hurt. 'Maybe it's true that nobody is dead, but I didn't know that – I really meant to kill him when I stabbed him; I really wanted him to die.'

'That was the Patrick in your head,' said the psychiatrist. 'The real Patrick is still alive; it's only *your* Patrick who is dead. You killed the Patrick in your head; you programmed the fax from your memories, and then you killed what you had created. You murdered an illusion. Do you really think that's the same as killing a person? You know the faxes don't feel anything – they don't think – it's all programming, not life.'

'I know,' said Cerise. 'Of course it's not the same as if I really killed Patrick – I know that. But I *could* have killed Patrick, I would have if he'd been there. That's what's so scary. I never thought I'd be able to kill. Not only am I able to, but I could glory in it – I'd never felt like that before! What's to stop me from doing it again?'

'The same things that have always stopped you. We all have unacceptable emotions inside us . . . we learn ways of dealing with them. Yours aren't out of control – they never were. Don't forget, you knew that wasn't really Patrick. Even as you thought you were killing him, a part of you knew perfectly well it was only a fax, and that you had permission to act out your aggressions on it. You're still in touch with reality; I very much doubt you would ever confuse what happened here at Timber Oaks with what happens outside.'

Cerise listened, and argued, and gradually let herself be convinced. It was time to leave this place, go home, see Hewitt, and try to come to terms with what she had learned about herself. She tucked the videotape they gave her – hard proof of what she'd done – away in her bag, wondering if she would ever be able to watch it.

The next evening, as she gazed at Hewitt across a table in one of the city's most expensive restaurants, Cerise saw for the first time how much he was like Patrick, and was surprised that she had never noticed before.

Both were rather thin, pale-skinned men with fair, wispy hair. Hewitt didn't appear to be going bald, but Cerise remembered a patch of hair with a slightly different texture than the rest, and she suspected a transplant. Both men had charming smiles, disarmingly innocent faces, and self-righteous natures. If Hewitt was better-tempered than Patrick, Cerise now thought that was only because he had enough money to smooth his way, and Patrick, although not poor, was always struggling.

The waiter filled their glasses with champagne and went away.

'Well,' said Hewitt, raising his glass in a toast to her. 'Was it a success?'

'That depends on how you define success.'

'How do you feel about your ex-husband now?'

She had woken that morning feeling a great weight gone. There was a burden she no longer had to bear. An old wound had finally healed. 'I feel . . . relieved,' she said. 'Accepting. It's over. As if he died a long time ago. He doesn't matter anymore.'

Hewitt smiled. 'You still think the murder was only for my benefit?'

'Maybe I feel better about Patrick but worse about myself,' Cerise said. 'I'm not sure it was worth it if the only way I could get free of Patrick was to murder him.'

'We all have violent impulses,' said Hewitt. 'Isn't it better to face up to them and get them out in the open instead of repressing them and pretending they aren't there?'

'Yes, yes, I talked to the shrink, too.' Cerise looked away from Hewitt's eyes – the same colour as Patrick's – at the bubbles in her champagne. 'It was so real,' she said. 'That's what makes it so hard. I really didn't know it was going to be like that.'

'If it wasn't real, there wouldn't be much point,' Hewitt said. 'You have to believe in it, or it isn't any good. I didn't just want you to kill some doll . . . I wanted you to get rid of your husband, once and for all . . . the image that you were still carrying around inside you. That's what I was jealous of – not the real man.'

'You don't have to be jealous any more,' said Cerise wearily.

'I know. And I'm grateful. I know it couldn't have been easy for you. This isn't a thank-you present,' he said, putting a small black velvet box on the table. 'It's because I love you.'

She knew what it was, and she wished she didn't. She didn't move to pick it up. She looked at him.

'I want you to marry me,' he said.

'Oh, Hew,' she said, shaking her head. 'I wish you wouldn't. I – it's too soon.'

'Am I being insensitive? Do you need time to mourn your husband?' His voice was still gentle, but there was a brittle edge to the words.

'Well, maybe I do,' she said, although she'd already realized that her mourning for Patrick was, finally, over. 'I just think I need some more time, to be sure.'

'You've been divorced for more than a year, and you've known me for nearly six months. How long does it take? I know how I feel about you.'

Just then the waiter arrived with their appetizers. Hewitt frowned down at his plate. 'What is this? Frozen? Or fresh?'

'I'm sure it's fresh, sir.'

'That's what the menu said, but I doubt it. Just a minute.' Hewitt took a small taste and shook his head. 'That's not fresh. Take it back.'

'Of course. I'm sorry you didn't like it, sir.'

'I don't like second best,' said Hewitt. 'Frozen is second best. I only eat the real thing.'

Cerise looked down at her own plate, not seeing what was on it, knowing that she would be making the worst mistake of her life if she married Hewitt Price.

After the waiter had gone Hewitt looked at her and shrugged. 'I'm not going to push,' he said. 'I'm willing to wait. If you need time, take your time. Keep the ring.'

'No, I can't. It wouldn't be right.'

'I'm not going to take it back to the store,' he said. 'And I'm not going to want to give it to anybody else.'

She shook her head.

He gave her a look that said she was being unreasonable, but put the little box back in his pocket.

Gradually, somehow, the evening got back on keel. Marriage wasn't mentioned again. They talked about a planned skiing trip, and mutual friends, and a book Hewitt was reading. She felt that he had forgiven her, and although she had wanted to be alone, at the end of the evening, when he assumed she was coming home with him, she couldn't say no. She was a little tense when they made love, but she didn't think he noticed –

he was drunk, and fell asleep quickly. Despite her dissatisfaction and misgivings, so did she.

It was late morning when she woke, the big house was quiet around her, and Hewitt was gone. He had left her a note, suggesting a place to meet for dinner, the key to one of the cars, and a Gold American Express card in her name 'in case you want to do some shopping'.

She closed her eyes, feeling a tug of purely material desire.

'I will not marry you for your money,' she said aloud, but the conviction she had felt the previous evening was lacking. She went into the bathroom to take a shower, and tried to remember what it was like making love with Hewitt. Instead, she kept remembering how it had been with Patrick before she killed him. She was aroused, and thought of looking at her tape, to remember it better. How could she have been so happy one moment, so violently angry the next? Just as well as the sex, she remembered what it had been like to kill. If she married Hewitt, would she some day be wanting to murder him? It seemed all too likely. But she doubted whether Hewitt would be willing to buy her a Hewitt-fax. Far more likely that he would order his own Cerise-fax, and kill her. She wondered what he was like as a murderer.

Cerise emerged from the shower, dried off and then wrapped herself in a huge, soft towel, although she knew she was alone, and the house was warm. The video library was downstairs, but she didn't think he would keep such a personal tape with all the others.

She was right. She found it – the Timber Oaks logo on the back marked it out at once – among the small selection of pornography Hewitt kept on the shelf behind the bedroom video system.

She felt like a spy, fearful of being caught as she slid the cassette into the player. It didn't help at all to remind herself that Hewitt had once offered to show it to her. He wasn't with her now, and she had different reasons for wanting to see it. Wiping sweaty hands on the towel, blinking eyes that suddenly felt too dry, she sank onto the bed, staring at the screen.

She recognized the bland good taste of a Timber Oaks bedroom at once. A pretty young woman with red-gold hair, wearing a dark blue silk kimono, was standing beside the bed, looking apprehensive, when the door opened and Hewitt came in.

'You wanted to see me?' said Hewitt. He was wearing a salmon-coloured suit – the height of fashion three years ago – and holding a square black leather case in one hand.

'Oh, darlin', I've missed you so,' said the woman, whom Cerise guessed to be a fax of Hewitt's ex-wife, Penny. Her voice was soft and slightly husky with a distinctive East Texas twang.

'Missed me, or missed my money?'

'Oh, Hewitt, how can you even ask? I've missed you. Let me show you how I've missed you.' As she spoke, she opened her kimono and shrugged out of it. It dropped with a silken whisper to the floor.

Cerise tucked her towel more firmly closed. She wondered if Hewitt thought her breasts were too small.

Hewitt put his case down on a chair. Now, thought Cerise. Now the gun, or the knife, would come out, now he would kill her. But he left the case where it was, went to the naked woman, and began to kiss her breasts and neck while she sighed and seemed to melt against him. After about a minute he lifted her in his arms and carried her to the bed.

She put up a small show of resistance. 'Let me . . . you get undressed, too,' she said.

'No hurry,' he said. 'Plenty of time.' He pushed her back, and knelt before her, between her legs.

Shocked, Cerise managed to lurch off the bed and across to the video, to punch the fast-forward button. So Hewitt had his dark secret, too – sex with a fax! She felt too embarrassed to watch. But even at top speed the sex seemed to go on and on: every time she stopped it, there was some new pornographic position to be flinched away from.

When she saw the gun, she returned the tape to normal speed.

The gun, a small, snub-nosed, silver pistol, was in Hewitt's right hand, carefully pointed away from the woman, who was watching him apprehensively. They were both naked, sitting on the bed.

'You said you'd do anything for me,' said Hewitt. 'How can I believe you?'

'I would – I would do anything for you. Almost. But you can't ask me to kill myself!'

'Can't I?'

'You wouldn't if you loved me. People don't. Oh, Hew, I'd die happily if it would save your life, but I'm not going to kill myself. Ask me something else to prove I love you.'

'All right,' he said. He gazed at her steadily. 'It's a real sacrifice I'm going to ask you for, Penny.'

She nodded eagerly.

'Would you give up other men for me?'

'Of course!'

'Would you give up your beauty?'

Something flickered in her eyes. 'You wouldn't love me if I was ugly.'

'Is that what you think? You're wrong. Maybe I fell in love with the way you looked, but now I love you . . . I'll love you no matter what, as long as you're alive. That's my problem. That, and not being able to believe you really love me. I need proof, Penny.'

Penny closed her eyes and said, 'All right.' Then she opened them. 'What do you want me to do?'

'I want you to scar yourself. I want you to mark your face to prove you're mine.' He leaned away from her, towards the bedside table. He came back with a razor-blade held delicately between thumb and forefinger of the hand without the gun. 'Use this. Just one little cut. On your face.' With the pistol, he traced a line on his own cheek. 'Show me you mean it.'

Penny straightened up, and took the blade from him with her right hand. Staring straight ahead at nothing, as if into a mirror, she raised her hand to her right cheekbone, placed the cutting edge of the razor there, and then drew it down in a curving sweep to the corner of her mouth. It was the delicate, assured gesture of a woman applying make-up. When she took her hand away red blossomed in tiny dots, which formed a crescent and then began to run. Within seconds half of her face was awash with blood, dripping onto her neck and shoulders.

'Again,' said Hewitt. 'The other side.'

Obediently she lifted her hand, then stopped and hurled the blade away from her. 'It hurts,' she said plaintively. 'It stings.

Is there some spray or something in the bathroom to make it stop hurting?'

'Go and get the razor. You're not finished.'

She frowned. 'Oh, yes I am. That's enough.'

'It's not enough,' he said. 'It'll never be enough.'

'It'll have to be,' she said. 'I'm through.'

'Oh, yes,' he said. 'You're through.'

He raised his hand and squeezed the trigger. Penny's face exploded.

Cerise choked on a scream and backed away, her towel falling off and making her feel even more vulnerable. As she scrambled to find her clothes she heard two more gunshots from the television, and then the sound of Hewitt weeping.

Hypocrite, she thought. Murderer. Murderer!

Hewitt hadn't destroyed a fax; he had killed his wife. She recalled his stubborn determination to have only the best, never to settle for something which wasn't 'real' and knew that Hewitt wouldn't have been content with a make-believe murder. He was rich enough to buy whatever he wanted – apparently even his wife's death.

Cerise wondered if Timber Oaks was behind it. Had they helped him replace the real woman with a fax? Or had he pulled a switch and fooled them, too? Although she had never met Hewitt's ex-wife, Cerise knew some of Hewitt's friends were still in touch with her. After her own experience at Timber Oaks, she did not doubt that a fax could deceive even Penny's most intimate friends.

She dressed as quickly as she could. The feeling of possessing dangerous knowledge made her too nervous to linger any longer in Hewitt's house than she absolutely must. She took one of Hewitt's cars because her own was on the other side of town, and drove to a nearby service station to use the telephone.

There was a listing for a Penny K. Price, and Cerise dialled the number without stopping to think what she would say.

'Could I speak to Penny, please?'

'This is she.'

The back of her neck prickled at those familiar East Texas vowels. 'I'm . . . uh, my name is Cerise Duval, and I wondered . . . I wondered if I could come visit you.'

A brief silence, while Cerise cursed herself for rushing into this without some plausible lie, and then the voice said, 'You're Hewitt's girlfriend.'

'That's right.'

'Is Hewitt with you?'

'No. I'm by myself. I wondered if I could just drive over now . . . if you're not too busy.'

'I'm not busy. You want to see me?'

Cerise bit her lip. 'Yes.'

'Oh, well, why not. Come on over.' She gave directions to her house.

At Timber Oaks, Cerise had been shown the easiest way to tell a fax from a human being. There was a slot in the back of the neck – covered by a flap of fax-flesh – for the insertion of software, and there were sockets (also covered by fax-flesh) at the base of the spine and just under the heart. Unless Penny wore a bikini to receive visitors, Cerise wouldn't have the opportunity to check for power points, but it shouldn't be too hard to find the software slot.

The Penny who opened the door to her looked exactly like the woman on the tape. It had been more than three years since her murder, but she hadn't aged a single day. 'Cerise?'

'Yes. I hope you don't mind my coming over like this?'

Penny shook her head. 'That's fine. I wasn't doing anything special . . . Would you like some coffee? Or a diet soda?'

'Coffee would be nice, if it isn't any trouble.'

'No trouble at all. I was just about to put some on for myself.' They both had fallen into the rituals of politeness, and Cerise wondered how they would ever get out. She followed the other woman into a large, light kitchen and hovered in the doorway, watching Penny take coffee pot and filters from a cupboard. She's not real, she told herself. Why wait? It was never going to be any less embarrassing, any more possible. Penny's back was to her. Now. Cerise moved swiftly across the floor, reaching for the back of Penny's neck.

Penny yelped, and dropped the box of paper filters, but she didn't pull away. Instead, after the first seconds of tensed surprise she relaxed and stood still, even inclining her head slightly to make it easier for Cerise.

There was nothing beneath her hair but warm, soft flesh, and no matter how Cerise prodded and pulled at it, that flesh did not give way, or part, or pull up. In a swelter of embarrassment, she withdrew.

'I'm sorry, I hope I didn't hurt you, I just . . .' There was no way she was going to be able to think of an acceptable explanation.

Not turning around, not looking at her, Penny said, 'There isn't a software slot because there isn't any software. Just my brain.'

'I'm sorry,' Cerise said again, helplessly. 'You must think I'm horrible. The thing is, I saw a tape . . .'

Penny turned around. She didn't look angry or surprised. 'And you thought that Hewitt had murdered me and replaced me with a fax. The perfect crime.'

'Look, I know about Timber Oaks,' Cerise said. 'I went there to murder my husband – a fax of him, I mean, of course. But I know Hewitt – and I just didn't believe he would have been satisfied with a make-believe murder.'

Penny nodded. 'You're right. You do know Hewitt. Do you still want that coffee?'

'Oh, yes, please.' She watched Penny pick up the filters and, with a quick sideways glance, go to the sink to fill a kettle. 'Don't worry, I'm not going to grab you and try to find your sockets.'

'If you'll just wait till we've had our coffee I'll take my clothes off and show them to you.'

'Look, I'm sorry, I really am. It was stupid of me.'

'It wasn't stupid,' Penny said, stopping and looking directly at her. 'And I wasn't joking.'

'What do you mean?'

'I've still got my brain, so I'm still me, right?' said Penny. 'That's what Hewitt said. That's what I tell myself. But this . . .' She gave herself a thump, flat-handed, on the breastbone. 'Hewitt bought this for me. It's not the body I was born with. It's a fax. But I'm not. Supposedly.'

'Your whole body,' said Cerise slowly. 'Your whole body's a replacement?'

Penny nodded.

'I've heard about the others they did that to . . . there's one man they've kept alive for five or six years now, isn't there?'

'"Kept alive,"' Penny repeated with a particular emphasis.

'Well, that's how they say it, that's how they talk about it on the news, you know.'

'Like they had him in a machine. Like this was an iron lung.' Again, Penny patted her breastbone. 'Still, he was dying. I wasn't. I was the first young, healthy subject, so far as I know. There are more than the ones you hear about on the news. Rich old men who don't want to die. But they have to be convinced they're dying, first – they don't want to make the switch too soon, in case it goes wrong, in case it doesn't work, or in case it's not really what they've been told. It case it isn't really like life.'

'Is it like life?'

'Oh, yes, it's like life.' Penny extended her arm. 'Here. Feel. Can you tell any difference?'

A little reluctantly, Cerise did as she was asked. Warm, human flesh. But she knew that already, more intimately. She shook her head. 'I mean for you. Is it the same for you? Is it really just like life?'

'It's like life,' said Penny. 'It's like life.' She was shaking her head as she spoke. 'Hewitt explained it to me. You don't feel things with your body, you know. The feeling is in your head. You touch my hand, but I don't feel it with my hand. The nerves in my hand send a message to my brain, and my brain decides what it feels like, and what I feel about it. It's all in the brain. If I was in a coma, the things that were done to my body wouldn't register. They wouldn't matter. I wouldn't feel them unless my brain knew about them. So this body works just like my old body. It all works perfectly well, and in some ways it's better. It's in better shape.'

Cerise watched Penny pour boiling water, and the fragrance of fresh coffee rose gently between them.

'Why did you do it?' Cerise asked.

Penny sighed. 'I did it for Hewitt.' She looked down, then directly at Cerise. 'And maybe for the money. Partly that, but mostly it was for him. Hewitt thinks he bought me. He thought I married him for his money . . . well, of course the money was part of it. If he'd been some broke college kid, the marriage probably wouldn't have happened. But everybody thought he was such a great catch, and I really wanted to get away from home, and get married, and I thought it would be so great to be his wife, to be Mrs Hewitt Price. It was OK for a while and then . . . then it wasn't. I don't know what happened. It was like I couldn't believe in it anymore; I was just going through the motions. Everything looked OK on the surface; Hewitt thought everything was fine. But there wasn't anything underneath. Maybe I stopped loving him – or maybe I just grew up and realized I never had loved him, and a beautiful house full of expensive things couldn't make up for that. That was when I told Hewitt I wanted out.' She poured the coffee into blue mugs and put them on the kitchen table. They both sat. Cerise put her hands around the mug, holding the warmth, and waited for Penny to go on.

'Hewitt just went crazy. He was sure there was somebody else. There wasn't. I guess it's a good thing there wasn't, because I think Hewitt would have killed him, really killed him. He always had this thing about other men – I don't know why, since I'm sure I never gave him any cause to be jealous.

'I felt horribly guilty, of course. After all, it wasn't Hewitt's fault I wasn't happy. He gave me everything. He didn't drink, he never hit me . . . but I wanted out. I couldn't go on like I was, just to make Hewitt happy. Hewitt seemed to think I should, and I guess I thought he was right – I had made a promise, after all, when we married; and he'd kept *his* promise. So I was in the wrong, and I owed Hewitt something. We both believed that. He'd fulfilled his part of the bargain, and I hadn't. I owed him something. So . . . I gave him what he wanted. I gave him my body.'

Cerise blew on her coffee, thinking of Hewitt's jealousy. She remembered how he had questioned her about her marriage, and how he had wanted her to kill Patrick. She had been shocked at first, but he was persuasive, and he wanted it so much. It was something she was doing for him, not for herself, and so she had let him talk her into it. Cerise no longer believed in such altruism. People couldn't talk you into things you really didn't want to do. She said to Penny, 'How much did he pay you?'

Penny smiled ruefully. 'A lot. He made it worth my while. If I left him, he let me know I'd have nothing: no money, no job, nobody to take care of me. Just my freedom, whatever that meant. But if I let him kill me, he'd make sure I was comfortable. A nice place to live, a steady income, a car . . .

and this perfect body. This body won't get sick or fat or old. At the time, that seemed really important. I'd always been terrified of getting old and falling apart physically, afraid of being ugly, and having nobody love me. And the money . . . I'd never had to support myself, you see. I never had a job; I didn't even finish college. He was offering me the perfect way out, I thought. I could buy my future with my body. That was the same thing I did when I got married. I guess I should have realized that. I guess I only got what I deserved.'

'What's that?'

'This pretty surface. It's like my marriage. All the parts are there, but they don't add up. There's something missing. I don't know what, and I don't know how to change it. I could get out of my marriage. I don't know how to get out of *this*.'

'Wait a minute – I thought you said it was just like life?'

'That's it,' said Penny. '*Like* life. Not life itself. It looks perfect from the outside, but it's not.'

'Didn't you just tell me –'

'Everything works,' Penny said. 'All the nerves and senses. But they're not mine. I'm the only one who knows that I'm not living anymore. That I can't live. I can only remember.' She gestured at her coffee, still untouched on the table before her. 'I know what coffee tastes like. I drink it, and I think I'm tasting that cup, but really I'm remembering coffee I've had in the past. If you dumped salt in it without me seeing, I wouldn't know it, I wouldn't taste any difference.'

'That sounds like something wrong with your sense of taste,' Cerise said.

'No, you don't understand; that's a bad example. It's hard to explain. But life is change . . . and I can't change anymore; I can't have new experiences. I don't have a future, just a past. It's all fake, memories of life, recycled to make me think I'm still living. I had a boyfriend for a while, but then I realized that I was responding to him, to everything he did or said, as being *like* Hewitt, or *like* Mark, or like Johnny or somebody else I used to know. I could never know *him*.'

'But you've never met *me* before. How about that? Do I remind you of someone you already know? And what about this conversation?'

'Oh, I can see you,' said Penny, sounding very tired. 'You

don't understand. I can hear you, touch you . . . the information still comes in. It's like watching television . . . but watching television isn't life. It can tell you about life, but it also gets in the way. Ever since the transplant, there's always something between me and life. This body. It works for me, but it isn't me. I thought I was trapped before. I didn't know what it meant to be trapped.'

Cerise couldn't understand what Penny was talking about. She was reminded of Hewitt's claims to supersensitivity, the way he would take two things she thought were basically the same and call one superior and the other worthless.

'What do you do all day?' Cerise asked. 'How do you live?'

'There's the money from Hewitt, so I – oh, you mean how do I spend my time? Well, two days a week I have my volunteer work at the hospital. I see people socially, go to parties . . . There's the bridge club. I go shopping. I like to read, and I watch a lot of television. Except that I'm living by myself, it's not that much different from how I spent my time when I was married to Hewitt.'

'Maybe that's what's wrong. Maybe it wasn't Hewitt who trapped you, but a whole way of life. You left him, but you didn't change anything else. You need to change your life, do something totally different, to make you feel alive again. Move to another city, travel, find a new lover, get yourself a job . . .' She shrugged, impatient because it seemed so obvious.

But Penny was shaking her head, rejecting what Cerise said even before she finished. 'You don't understand,' she said again. 'I can't change my life. It's too late for that. I can't make myself feel alive because I'm *not* alive.'

'Then Hewitt might as well have killed you,' Cerise said. 'He might as well have done what I thought he did and killed you and put a fax here in your place . . . a fax would probably do a better job of it than you; a fax would probably think it was happy!'

'He might as well have killed me,' Penny agreed, apparently deaf to the other woman's irritation. 'He took my life away . . . he might as well have killed my brain, too. Sometimes I wonder if I *can* die now, or if I'll just go on living in this body forever . . . sometimes I think he took my death away from me as well as my life. I died, and I didn't even get to experience it! My own death

. . . Hewitt sent me a tape – the same tape you saw – of him killing me. At first I thought it was horrible, I thought it was horribly cruel of him to show me what he'd done. But now I'm glad I can see it. I'm glad I know. It's the only evidence I have. I watch it a lot. I look at myself again and again . . . I watch myself die, and I try to imagine what it was like. I try to *feel* it.' She gave Cerise a wistful smile. 'It's the only death I have.'

Cerise felt the hairs prickle on the back of her neck. My brain is telling my body to do that because of what Penny is telling me, she thought. She wondered if Penny was crazy. She sounded like a hypochondriac, inventing problems where there were none. And yet . . . what could it be like to lose your whole body, every part of it except the brain, and not die, to go on living in an altered, artificial form? It was impossible to imagine, so maybe it was impossible to explain. Whatever it was, whether it was Penny's madness or Hewitt's crime, Cerise realized she'd had enough of it.

'I'm sorry,' she said. 'I really am sorry you're not happy. But I have to go now. Thank you for the coffee.'

'You're welcome,' Penny said. 'I'll show you out . . . it was very nice meeting you . . . I'm so glad you decided to call. Please do come again.'

Her ordinary, unthinking politeness struck Cerise as surreal, but it took a positive effort to stop herself from joining in with the expected response.

Filling in the gap left by the other woman's silence Penny went on, 'Any time . . . it would be so nice to see you again. And why don't you bring Hewitt next time?'

Cerise stopped by the door and turned to give Penny a hard look. 'You don't mean that. Do you?'

'Why, of course.'

'You actually want to see Hewitt again? After what he did to you? Why?'

'He won't see me,' Penny said. 'As far as he's concerned, I'm dead. He killed me, and he paid me for the privilege. I've tried to call him . . . His lawyer told me if I make any more attempts to contact him he'll stop my monthly payments. But I thought maybe if you said something to him . . . you could tell him that you phoned me; I didn't get in touch with you; he couldn't blame me.'

'I just don't understand why you want to see him.'

'I don't either. I probably shouldn't be saying this to you, of all people, but I'd go back to him if he'd have me. I think about him all the time. Sometimes he seems like the only thing in the world, the only real thing, the only one I care about. If we could get back together, I think maybe we could work things out, maybe it would be all right; he could make it all right.'

Cerise felt sick. There was no doubting Penny's sincerity. 'But he's the one who killed you – I mean, did this to you, made you like this.'

Penny nodded. 'That's why. He destroyed me, so he's the one who can save me. It makes sense, don't you see?'

'No. No it doesn't. You can't go back. You're not the same person who married Hewitt. You've got to stop living in the past. You're *not* dead, unless you decide to be. Stop remembering – do something new; *live.*'

'If I stop remembering, I will die,' Penny said. 'Remembering is all I have. But I can't expect you to understand that. You've still got your life. You've got Hewitt.'

'You didn't have to let him kill you,' Cerise said.

They looked at each other as if across a great divide. Cerise felt she didn't breathe again until she was outside the house, alone on the quiet, suburban street. Then, the sense of freedom she felt was intoxicating.

She took the videotape they had given her at Timber Oaks out of her bag, threw it to the ground and stamped on it until the plastic broke, then pulled the tape free of its protective casing. No one would ever watch this tape; she would not be able to send it to Patrick now. She wished her own memories could be destroyed as easily, but at least she knew they belonged to the past, like Hewitt. She could cope with the past because she still had a future. She put the keys in the ignition, closed the car door, and walked away from it.